'Poetic and melancholic, *Fiftee* short life feels like a stolen mom

'Haunting. Beautiful.'—Jennie *cious Things*

'Wild and captivating, this takes us right to the heart of the Brontës' story of creativity, sisterhood, and survival.'—Samantha Ellis, author of *How To Be a Heroine*

'This vivid, intimate imagining of the lives of the Brontë sisters transports us to the haunted, wild, exuberant heart of history's most extraordinary literary family.'—Meg Rosoff, author of *Friends Like These*

'A staggering achievement that breathes new life into the familiar Brontë story. By turns meticulous, arresting, and lyrical, Karen Powell is a rare talent.'—Adam Farrer, author of *Cold Fish Soup*

'Emily and her siblings have long been the fascination of many. Powell dares to take us deeper, capturing not only the voice of Emily Brontë, but also her mindset, her essence. A bold, ambitious novel.'—Sophie Parkes, author of *Out of Human Sight*

'A haunting work. Karen Powell is a fantastic writer, particularly in her depictions of the natural world where she echoes and expands on Emily's own genius.'—Bridget Walsh, author of *The Tumbling Girl*

'An immersive novel vividly capturing both the wildness of the North Yorkshire moors and the wildness at the heart of its inimitable protagonist.'—Tawseef Khan, author of *Muslim, Actually*

'Interweaving meticulous research and exacting imagination, Powell has brought Emily Brontë's thoughts and quirks, attitudes and gestures, sibling affection and rivalry alive on the page.'—Kit Fan, author of *Diamond Hill*

'Finely wrought... One of the delights of the novel is the vividness of the relationship between Emily, Charlotte, Anne and Branwell... Karen beautifully captures the changeability of the moors, their remoteness, their threat, but also their power to inspire. I loved this book, every word of it.'—Nicola Edwards, author of *This Thing of Darkness*

FIFTEEN WILD DECEMBERS

ALSO BY

KAREN POWELL

The River Within

Karen Powell

FIFTEEN WILD DECEMBERS

Europa
editions

Europa Editions
8 Blackstock Mews
London N4 2BT
www.europaeditions.co.uk

A catalogue record for this title is available from the British Library
ISBN 978-1-78770-481-7

Powell, Karen
Fifteen Wild Decembers

Cover design and illustration by Ginevra Rapisardi

Prepress by Grafica Punto Print – Rome

Printed and bound in Great Britain by Clays Ltd, Elcograf S.p.A.

CONTENTS

Cold in the earth—and fifteen wild Decembers,
From those brown hills, have melted into spring:
Faithful, indeed, is the spirit that remembers
After such years of change and suffering!
—EMILY BRONTË

He comes with western winds, with evening's wandering airs,
With that clear dusk of heaven that brings the thickest stars.
Winds take a pensive tone, and stars a tender fire,
And visions rise, and change, that kill me with desire.
—EMILY BRONTË

FIFTEEN WILD
DECEMBERS

PROLOGUE
1842

February dawn. Fog hung over the river and the earth was a cold stone, turning in the heavens. Beyond the wharf where we were moored, the city had been swallowed up. The fog dampened my eyelashes, tasted sour on my tongue.

A shout came from somewhere further down the deck followed by a flurry of activity below on the quayside, and then our little packet steamer was moving. As it eased its way out towards the centre of the river, the dank arches of a bridge loomed out of the mist. Water birds slid past the ship's hull, eyeing us coldly. Muffled shouts came from the warehouses that elbowed one another for space along the riverbank, the thud of goods being loaded on boats. As the river widened, the voices of the dockworkers caught in the fog and took on a mournful quality, like the solitary cries of seabirds on the wing. Papa wanted to look out for the Royal Observatory at Greenwich, so he and I moved to the other side of the ship, but the fog sat more heavily on the south bank of the river, blotted out all but the muddy shoreline. Papa's fingers were white from the cold now—he'd left his gloves behind at the hotel—so I sent him inside to join the others and moved to the foredeck again, glad of a moment to myself. The river grew broader still, began to swirl about us in thick brown eddies which wrapped themselves around the ship, sinewy ropes of water wanting to carry us off course. I thought of wily Odysseus trying to navigate between Scylla and Charybdis; how thrilling it must be to steer one's own vessel.

When the ship finally nosed out of the estuary, I saw that the North Sea was not the cool blue ocean of my imagination, teeming with strange life, but a grey creatureless expanse that stretched across the horizon. Grimy clouds stacked up in the distance, made it hard to tell where the sea left off and the heavens began. A stinging wind got up and the waves started to heave and then slap across the ship's bow. Spray flew high into the air, then fell on the deck in bubbling arcs, as if flung from an enormous paintbrush. A young crew member, no more than a boy, gestured to me, wanting me to go inside or else move to a more sheltered spot at the stern of the boat. I was the only passenger left on deck. The boat began to change course now, waves crashing in protest against its side.

'The North Foreland!' the boy shouted. The sea boiled and swelled beneath us, the ship's bow rearing as it pushed on through the water. To the right of us, in the direction the boy had pointed, the fog had drawn itself up for a moment. I saw a chalky headland rising above the water, waves lacing the shoreline below. 'Farewell, England,' the boy said, then gave the headland a cheeky salute. I turned my back on him and made my way towards the shelter of a lifeboat. As I skirted the flare of its rotund, wooden belly, the orange-painted planks blistered by the elements, I saw Charlotte and Mary Taylor outside the door of the main cabin. Mary had her hand on my sister's back, but Charlotte, bent almost double over the ship's railing, paid no attention to Mary's over-firm ministrations. I was pleased to see that she was being violently sick.

The plan was sound, I reminded myself, steadying myself against the lifeboat as the ship lurched, even if Charlotte would never admit to her true motive. I thought of the journey we'd made from Leeds to London several days ago, the train cutting through mile after mile of field and forest. Farm buildings were strewn across the horizon and church spires stitched the sky. Seeing the swell of a city in the distance, I had glanced across at my sister, small as a child still, feet only just reaching the floor of the carriage, and wondered how she'd managed to engineer such a trip almost entirely for her own ends. We were travelling in the opposite direction to home, to everything I held dear, simply because Charlotte needed to cure the restlessness in her bones. A wave slammed into the side of the ship now, turning the horizon. I gripped the lifeboat until we'd settled into its wake. In that moment of calm, my fingers moved to a certain spot on the sleeve of my new grey travelling dress. Beneath the fabric, I could feel the dip in my arm, the scar like a knotted, fleshy emblem, reminding me that I could withstand all manner of pain.

Later, when Charlotte had finally stopped being sick, I went in search of some tea to help settle her stomach, motioned to a crew member in the galley who seemed to be in charge of the enormous urn. By then, I'd grown accustomed to the ship's rolling motion, and found myself anticipating the waves before they came. I went back out on deck and there was nothing to see but walls of iron-grey water, lurching horizons that banked up before us and then lashed down onto the foredeck, wanting to devour our little ship. We survived though, one wave after another, minute by minute.

'Not so long now,' called a man nearby. He glanced at his pocket-watch and then ahead of us, not expecting a reply. I'd watched him half-carry his fashionably dressed wife to the rail, her pretty young face sallow, all propriety gone as she retched into the sea below. Someone held open the door for them now as he steadied her back towards the cabin. Inside, I saw passengers lying in sorry heaps, misery wiping out their individuality. I caught the smell of vomit as a crew member attempted to clear up the mess a small boy had just made on the floor. A woman nursed a child who could not be comforted and was crying itself to exhaustion. Her husband's face was pale and set and he appeared to be concentrating very hard. Any moment now, he too would fly out of the door towards the rail. And there, in the far corner of the cabin was my own party: Papa studying the French phrases he'd carefully copied into his notebook, Charlotte slumped against Mary in an exhausted sleep. As the door closed again, I turned my back on all of them and planted my feet squarely on the deck, having no wish for land.

PART 1

CHAPTER 1
1824

C harlotte was crouched beside my bed in her nightgown,
shaking me out of sleep.

'Tell Papa you want to go home,' she hissed, fingers
digging into my arm. 'All of us. Before he leaves tomorrow.'

'What?' I sat up, blinking in the darkness. It seemed only minutes ago that I'd watched a mistress moving down the dormitory,
extinguishing rushlights and calling for silence. Quite sure that
I wouldn't be able to sleep, I'd fallen almost immediately into a
deep, dream-filled slumber. Now it was taking me a moment to
resurface.

'Hush!' said Charlotte, scrabbling closer on her bare feet
like a little monkey. 'We have to get out of here.'

'But I've only just arrived,' I said.

Only that morning, I'd said goodbye to Branwell who didn't
need to go to school because Papa was teaching him at home, to
Tom kitten and Snowflake and to the chickens in the yard and
the blackbirds and house sparrows. Aunt had come to the door
to see us off, Anne clutching at her skirts and crying a little because she was too young to come with me. I kissed them both,
then held on to Papa's hand as we set off for the walk to Keighley,
from where we were to join the Leeds to Kendal coach. I did my
best not to get distracted by a little brown nuthatch searching
for grubs on the trunk of an oak, to keep up as Papa's long legs
cut through the purple moor grass. At midday our coach had
stopped at an inn, where dinner was followed by an unexpected

wait because of some problem with the change of horses. After that I fell asleep in my corner of the carriage, and when I woke, my limbs were stiff and Papa was dozing, with his chin dropped and his scarf pulled up high to save his chest from the cold. The houses along the roadside looked different now, low to the ground and built from butter-coloured stone. Deep-set windows squinted at me and leaves lay in drifts at the roadside instead of being whipped away by the east wind. I saw neat fields and copses, mild-faced sheep on a hillside. Then the land began to hunch and fall away again, as if something was simmering beneath the surface. Lone trees dotted the fields, branches like black skeletons. I slept a little more. When I woke, the landscape had changed again. Rocks pushed through the earth's pelt, fell in slate-like layers down steep hillsides. We crossed a stream dashing over stones. Dark water, white foam. I saw a snow-topped mountain in the distance, one side steep, the other falling away more gently.

'Ingleborough,' said the elderly lady who had been sitting opposite me since we left the inn. I'd noticed her earlier smiling at my questions. She pointed at the horizon. The mountain was immense, a grey god dwarfing the fields beneath, scree sliding like rubble down its slopes. When I screwed up my eyes, I could see rocky outcrops and sheer, shadowy crags. Beneath the mountain's highest point, two horizontal ridges cut through the thin veil of snow. Sunlight and shadows flickered across the lower slopes, clouds rolled over the summit. A whole world in motion! I wanted the coach to set me down right there so that I could feel the earth spinning beneath my feet.

It was dusk by the time we arrived at Cowan Bridge. As Papa lifted me down from the coach, I heard wind rushing through trees, sensed land rising somewhere in the distance. A doorway opened in a stone wall by the roadside and a servant ushered us inside. We followed her past a row of cottages edging a courtyard. I saw squares of dark earth, the remains of summer blooms, trimmed neatly back. Ahead of us, windows glowed at ground level. There was a low hum of noise. The servant led us along a dimly lit corridor to a small room with mahogany furniture and a bright fire.

Governess, wrote the headmistress in the final column of the school register. I'd already watched her enter my name, age, and today's date in the previous columns. Her hand was firm and neat, the letters looping steadily across the page, but I liked the way the ink shone wetly, looking like it might spill over in any direction. I cared only for what was immediate or magical, but I knew what a governess was and felt a kind of pride that the word was now connected to me by that column in the register. I'd come to school to learn how to earn a living, imagined the work of a governess to be irksome but insignificant, like helping the village children at Sunday School, that my real life would be unaffected. Miss Evans blotted her work and there, in the rows above this new entry, I found my sisters: *Maria Brontë, age 10, Elizabeth Brontë, age 9, Charlotte Brontë, age* 8, the ink already slightly faded, the entries dated earlier in the year.

'Charlotte is finding her feet now,' said Miss Evans, blotting the page again though it didn't need it, and then serving tea from the tray that a maid had brought in. The headmistress's hair was arranged plainly on either side of a precise parting. It looked so soft that I would have liked to reach out and touch it, the curtains too, the thick purple velvet held back with tasselled swags. I sat upright on a stool by the fire, trying to stay awake, not to drop the cup she'd passed to me, which was translucent in the firelight, its gold rim shining. A design of mint-green foliage twined from the base of the cup and curled around a handle so delicate I feared it would snap beneath my fingers. 'And Elizabeth is a sensible girl. Very good with the younger ones.' Next to Elizabeth's name in the register, I'd seen the word *Housekeeper* instead of governess. Miss Evans leaned towards

Papa as if she wished to tell him a secret. 'Maria's abilities are exceptional though, Reverend Brontë, well beyond her years.'

Papa's eyes sparkled in the dim light. He'd always taught us that pride was a sin, so must try to hide it now. 'My dear, late wife must take the credit for that.'

Miss Evans nodded as though she'd known Mamma herself. 'Her French is coming on at an extraordinary rate for a girl of ten.' Her eyes were very dark, I noticed, almost black, and when she blinked, she held her eyelids shut for longer than other people, so that she appeared to be thinking deliberate and clever thoughts. 'We do all we can to encourage her.' A sudden smile broke the surface as she turned to me. 'Now Emily, you look exhausted. A quick hello to your sisters and then to bed.'

It was the first time I'd slept in a dormitory, in a bed of my own. I'd expected to share with Charlotte, as I did at home, but she was paired with a girl of her own age, in a bed halfway down the long room, and Maria and Elizabeth were even further away, at the far end of the dormitory. Through the high window opposite me, I could see the pearly moon, a scattering of bright stars. I pulled the thin blanket around me and thought of the mountain I'd seen from the coach that morning. It too would be surrounded by darkness, but it would not be afraid.

'Hush!' said Charlotte again, placing her fingers on my lips now. She glanced down the room at the sleeping humps in each bed. 'This is a terrible place, Emily! Papa won't make us stay, not when he knows how we're suffering.'

'We are?'

'The cook is disgustingly dirty and mean and half-starves us. And the big girls steal what little food we do have, and Miss Andrews does nothing to stop them.'

'Who is Miss Andrews?' I asked, wondering in my sleepy state if I'd got the headmistress's name wrong; thinking too of the Madeira cake I'd eaten in her study earlier in the evening, which was almost as good as the one Nancy Garrs made at home.

'The cruellest woman in the world.' Charlotte's small breath was hot against my ear. 'She hates Maria most of all because she is so clever. And Reverend Carus Wilson, who is the governor, is a tyrant who detests children and says we are all going to hell. We're only allowed to write home once a quarter, so I haven't been able to tell Papa how awful everything is till now.'

As always, I had plenty of questions, but my eyelids were heavy. It was an enormous effort to keep them open. To cheer her up I said, 'He won't be cross for long,'

She shook her head impatiently. 'Nobody takes any notice of me. *You* have to speak to him, before he leaves tomorrow.' There was the sound of footsteps somewhere nearby. I saw the flicker of a lamp moving in the corridor outside. 'It's life or death!' said Charlotte, digging her fingers into my arm. 'I mean it.'

After breakfast—a thin porridge which, despite Charlotte's warning, no-one tried to steal from me—a bell rang. I followed everyone to the schoolroom and then stood and watched as girls of all ages hurried to fetch books and slates from a set of shelves to one side of the schoolroom. Without instruction or discussion, they found their seats and then bent their heads over their work, each of them appearing to know exactly what to do. They reminded me of the ants in the garden at home, emerging from their dusty nests on summer mornings with a sense of purpose. I liked to sit on the steps and watch as they moved the rubble of their lives from one spot to another, all part of some mysterious scheme.

'You'll join the youngest class with Margaret Cookson and Jane Sykes,' said the teacher who'd rung the bell. She was younger than the headmistress, had a coronet of fair hair pinned around her head. I followed her to a table near a stove at the very back of the room, where two girls of my age or thereabouts were already sitting, their slates ready. The girl called Jane Sykes had a thick plait of hair that was even redder than Branwell's and out-of-control freckles, splodging across her face and right up to her hairline, while Margaret had circles under her eyes and a thin rodentish look about her. The teacher instructed them to begin their numbers while she tested me on my reading. I'd finished the first story—a version of Jonah and the whale so simple I thought it written for infants—before my classmates had reached the end of their line of numbers. I noticed then that Charlotte's class was a little in front of ours, ten or so heads bent over shared books. Towards the front of the schoolroom, I could see Maria standing with her hands behind her back, reciting something. She looked tall and serious in her long brown pinafore, her hair glowing in the wintery light. For the next lesson we learned a short poem, and then our teacher drew a map of England and told us about King Alfred and his kingdom. At the bell, I followed Margaret and Jane to a cloakroom where we put on our shawls.

'Pretty little pet,' said an almost grown-up girl, smiling down at me and ruffling my curls as I passed.

Outside, the wind had got up and a cold sleet was driving down at a slant between buildings. The older girls were clumped beneath a covered walkway on the other side of the garden, close to the road that Papa and I had travelled along yesterday. I could see Charlotte there, talking to a girl of her own age, Elizabeth too, bending down to tie the bonnet of another child. Free from confinement, I was filled with a sudden and wild excitement. I ran up and down the garden with my classmates and then we chased each other around the flower beds, lifting our chins and howling at the sleet, then whirling each other around in a mad dance. We poked out our tongues to catch the flakes, stamped our feet against the cold earth and then it was time to go inside again.

Just before midday, my sisters and I were called to the head-mistress's study. There was no cheery fire today, just a lamp to lift the gloom. We clung to Papa and he placed his hand on each of our heads in turn.

'Be sure to take care of your little sister,' he told Charlotte. She signalled to me, seemed about to open her mouth to speak for herself instead when a storm of tears overcame her. I was just trying to decide what she wanted me to say, how to do so with the headmistress right here in the room, when Papa turned to Miss Evans. 'Do give my regards to Reverend Carus Wilson, and also to Miss Andrews. I'm sorry to have missed them.'

I tried to catch Charlotte's eye, but she was clinging to Elizabeth now. Could this be the same Miss Andrews who was the cruellest woman in the world? The same child-hating tyrant Reverend Carus Wilson? Yet here was Papa, the wisest and best of men, sending greetings to them. And Maria, who knew more than any of us and was almost as clever as Papa, not looking in the least surprised by his words. A memory then, from last summer: Papa and Aunt arguing about a book that Charlotte was reading, a collection of stories she'd brought home from the library in Keighley. Aunt had thought any kind of reading a good thing, that a bit of sentiment did no harm, but Papa said the book was sensational rubbish and *pernicious* which I knew must be a bad thing. *She has enough imagination as it is*, he'd said, then threw the book out into the hallway in one of his fits of temper. Starving, friendless Charlotte, who'd finished every bit of her porridge at breakfast this morning and then spent all of recreation talking to one of her classmates. *Life or death*, she'd said. I heard the clatter of hooves on the road outside. Papa reached for his overnight bag. Charlotte sobbed uncontrollably yet still managed to squirm from Elizabeth's arms to deliver a vicious pinch to my arm.

'Remind Anne to feed the birds,' I said.

A t dinner time, I looked up to see a girl of about twelve, with a box face and sparse fair hair, standing over me. 'Spare me a little piece won't you, new girl?' Her hand was already moving towards me. 'Brontë, isn't it?' I shielded my bowl, which contained a ladleful of thin stew and a slice of bread with a scrape of butter. Maria and Elizabeth were sitting with girls of their own age towards the middle of the room. Charlotte was at the next table, but with her back to me. At the head of my own table, sat my teacher. I tried to catch her eye, but she stared straight ahead, her mouth moving, eyes unseeing. 'You can't need that whole slice to yourself.' The girl's eyes were set deep in her square face, giving her a sly look. 'I can be your friend if you like.'

'I've friends of my own,' I said, thinking of Jane and Margaret and our games at recreation. 'And I don't like the look of you.' I picked up my slice of bread, crammed the whole thing into my mouth, then gulped it down.

'How I hate Sundays!' Charlotte looked up at me as she fastened her pattens. Every week we had to walk the two miles from Cowan Bridge to the church at Tunstall to hear the Reverend Carus Wilson preach. The Reverend was very holy but in a miserable way, his sermons designed to make everyone join him in his misery. After the first Sunday, I made sure to listen out for any matter I might be asked to repeat by one of the teachers later and took no notice of the rest. When I recommended this to

Charlotte, she was shocked. She was terrified of the Reverend, worried that I might get into trouble.

'If Papa doesn't believe we're evil then neither do I,' I told her. 'He is just as holy as the Reverend.'

'But why would he make us stay here?' She gave me a look. 'If he didn't believe it just a little?'

'He does not,' I said. I was glad she was speaking to me again.

Everything was cold about Sundays at Cowan Bridge: the walk to and from the church across the open fields, the draughty pews, the outlook for sinful children. Even the big girls—who passed the time by imitating the Reverend's solemn speech and doleful look whenever our teachers were out of earshot—dreaded the walk. Our clothes weren't quite warm enough for the winter weather and none of us had boots to keep our feet properly dry. Poor Charlotte had developed chilblains and was in agony for the whole of the day. My own feet were as wet and cold as anyone else's by the end of the walk, yet I longed for that one day of the week when we weren't confined to the courtyard and the garden for our short periods of recreation. We walked in crocodile—Jane and I holding hands and our teacher following with Margaret—so there was no chance to run free or to catch up with my sisters ahead, and yet how joyful it was to be out in the world again, the landscape opening before me like an enormous map, the black branches of an immense ash tree clutching at the horizon. The fields were edged with hawthorn, bare of leaves yet still throwing thorny sprays up to the blue December sky. The haw berries were flat crimson like the dead blood of the year, but the rosehips were a sign of hope, little lamps shining from the hedgerows. A fat robin watched from a fence post, its eye bright with curiosity, and in a thicket of oak, the glossy leaves of the holly gleamed like a secret. When the frost was hard, we slipped and slid across the frozen brown ruts left by the plough and the whole world glittered crazily, buzzards crying overhead. Sometimes the mist hung low, and we walked in silence across the fields, listening to the dripping of the trees, the muffled sound of horse hooves from the lane. Ahead of me, girls rising out of the mist like wraiths, then disappearing.

Two days before Christmas, we woke to a lacy crust of snow over the fields. I thought of Christmases at home, the band playing carols outside the Black Bull, the mantelpiece in the dining room crowned with holly and ivy, the smell of roasting goose. How we longed for the first taste of that rich, dark meat. On St. Stephen's Day, Papa would say fetch your cloaks and we'd climb up onto the moors, follow the bare paths through the winter heather with the wind crying in our ears. Then during the last week of December, snow fell in earnest, and again in the early days of January. The blankets on our beds seemed thinner than ever and the water in the pitchers on the nightstands turned to ice, had to be broken before we could wash in the mornings. We were confined to school for days on end, not even able to take the walk to church which pleased most of the girls if not me. Instead, we had to sit quietly, studying our Bibles until evening where there was Catechism and then one of the teachers might read a story from the Scriptures, or from Reverend Carus Wilson's horrid little book of fables which he'd written to remind children how wicked they were. Recreation was spent huddled in the walkway, which acted as a tunnel for the icy easterly wind or running for warmth along the pathways that the gardener cleared through the snow from time to time. Even those girls who detested exercise were restless and the teachers found fault everywhere: an untidily made bed, an irritating cough, lessons poorly learned. But I was top of my class in all subjects except one—Margaret being a little ahead of me at ciphering still—and it was a matter of pride to me. (Jane Sykes was a very pleasant girl but remarkably slow in all things.)

There was history and geography and grammar, and I was surprised to find that the more I learned the more my mind made space for new ideas. Knowledge was like the mountain I had seen on the horizon that day, a vast and unknown territory waiting to be explored. The only time I got into trouble was when I had too many questions and forgot to control my tongue.

One morning when the teachers were particularly bad-tempered, Miss Andrews made Maria stand in the corner of the schoolroom with a sign reading SLOVEN around her neck. My sister had come down to breakfast with a crooked collar and a missing button on her pinafore. *I don't care for your airs and graces, Brontë*, Miss Andrews had said, *or that sullen look.* Margaret swore that Miss Andrews had only become a teacher because she was jilted at the altar by her childhood sweetheart. No-one else wanted her, on account of the fleshy bobble at the end of her nose and the way she hissed her s's: *sssssullen ssslovenly*, so she'd turned into an ogre. Margaret was given to exaggerating though, sometimes lying outright, though she swore this particular story was completely true, that her aunt who lived in the next village to Miss Andrew's family knew all about it. Jane Sykes liked to point out things Margaret said that did not add up, but I thought a good story did not have to be entirely true, would sometimes suggest other incidents that might also have happened. For the rest of the morning's lessons, Maria stood in the corner of the schoolroom, hands behind her back and her head slightly bowed, displaying no sign of airs or graces. No-one would have considered my eldest sister pretty, but something more than empathy kept drawing my eye to her during that hour of punishment. Always pale, the spots of colour on her cheeks gave her a rare glow of health today, and her high forehead looked as smooth as marble in the grey, morning light.

At recreation, Charlotte interrupted our game of skipping, her eyes ablaze.

'How dare Miss Andrews make Maria stand all that time!' She dug her fingers into my arm. Her face looked tight, had the greenish, turnipy tinge it always took on when she was ill or angry, and which made you see what she would look like when she was an old lady. I looked around. There was Maria beneath the covered walkway, with a book in her hand and a small smile on her lips. Elizabeth was keeping her company, but there was no need. Maria was completely absorbed by her reading, despite the wind that was tunnelling along the passage, whipping at her hair and at the pages. And Miss Andrews was forever hanging signs round necks—I'd thought it a better punishment than blows from the switch which she also favoured.

Weeks passed and then the snow melted away, leaving only icy caps on the fells to the north, and in sunless hollows. Snowdrops lifted their dainty heads above the dark winter soil of the garden plots and on the hillside the sheep rose and fell across the stony ground like dirty mops. We woke one day to a world that was sunlit and golden-green, buds bursting on the tree branches and new leaves unfolding, fresh and hopeful as morning. This was the secret that the trees harboured all winter long when the world had seemed a dead and dark place. At recreation, I saw pink growth sprouting on the rose bushes that edged the courtyard, and in the flower plots, tips of green pushed up through the dark soil, small and determined. Lambs started to appear on the fellside, legs trembling, pure white fleeces. They leapt after their siblings, tottered back to their mothers, the valley echoing with their complaints. Soon the hedges would be clouded with blackthorn blossom, and when Margaret and I poked a hole in the ice on the beck at the foot of the garden, we saw movement in the blackness below. By the following day the ice had quite melted, and I thought of the story Papa once told us about a poet called Coleridge who loved to throw himself down the sides of mountains, letting the land take him where it would. I'd always imagined him laughing to himself at such freedom, at the madness of it, all his poetic words churning inside him and then bursting forth as he tumbled, and this was the sound of the beck as it broke free from the chains of winter and rushed down the hillside. The coughs that had rattled around the dormitory every night faded away, and everyone said spring had come early this year, until one morning we woke to find that fog had rolled down the fellside and settled over Cowan Bridge like a pall.

CHAPTER 3
1825

Fog caught in the trees, muffling the sound of the Leeds to Kendal coach as it passed. It sounded like a ghost carriage, or else we were ghost girls, the ghost building we lived in swallowed up by the mist. The windows of the schoolroom dripped with condensation and every morning when we dressed our clothes felt damp and chill. On Sundays, Tunstall church emerged from the fog like a ship lost at sea, and poor Charlotte's feet were rawer and more swollen than ever. Everyone talked endlessly about the cold, the miserable journey to and from services, but I was perfectly happy. The walk never troubled me and without any effort on my part, I seemed to have become the school pet. The older girls liked my questions, and the way I elbowed my way towards the hearth every evening, where they kept the best seats for themselves. If I was lucky, one or other of them would lift me onto their lap and stroke my curls, and it was worth being babied, finding something new to prattle about, just to be near the warmth of the fire.

For the rest of that month, the thick, unmoving fog weighed down on us day after day, rubbing us out. The coughing in the dormitory started up again, and then Mellany Hane, who was in Charlotte's class, came down with a fever and vomiting. When the doctor examined her, he found an infectious rash and ordered that she be moved to the sickroom to prevent the contagion spreading. The next morning the fog lifted slightly. Standing on my bed to look out of the window, I saw that the fields down here in the valley were still sodden and sorrowful-looking, but the hillsides were bright green, even in the weakest of sunlight. After so many colourless days, it hurt my eyes to look, but in a good way. A girl named Cecily Weekes fell ill that afternoon. She had the same symptoms as Mellany, as well as a cough and an infection of the stomach. Next was my own classmate, Jane Sykes, who collapsed while attempting to name the oceans on the big globe that stood at the front of the schoolroom. She cried out as she fell, hit the floor with a soft, crumpling sound, her red plait falling to one side, tethering her to flagstones. By the following day, ten more girls had been taken ill. A storage room was converted into an extra sickroom to cope with the numbers and Miss Evans excused two of the teachers from their duties to help nurse patients. It was strange to see them carrying trays of food, or hurrying to and from the washroom, sheets bundled in their arms, instead of standing in front of their classes. The smell of vomit and excrement hung in the corridors and stairwells. I was thankful that my sisters and I suffered no more than the usual winter colds, though Maria's cough was lingering longer than usual.

'In a time of crisis, we must all do our best to help one another,' the headmistress explained, standing to address us at breakfast one morning. Her eyes looked darker than ever and there was a greyness to her face I had not seen before, like someone much older or very tired. According to Charlotte, who seemed to know everything, she stayed up half the night, tending to the most distressed girls. 'There'll be no lessons, but everyone is to keep themselves busy with private study. This unfortunate situation is no excuse for anyone to fall behind.' She blinked in that deliberate way of hers, held down her lids for so long I thought she'd fallen asleep.

In the schoolroom, Maria explained where I'd gone wrong with my ciphering, stopping to cover her mouth when a bout of coughing came on, while Elizabeth unpicked and then showed me how to re-stitch the mess I'd made of my new tucker. We wondered what Branwell and Anne were doing at this very moment; how our old servant Nancy Garrs was finding married life and whether Aunt was taking to Tabby Aykroyd, who'd come to replace her. Sometimes I'd feel a sudden, hard longing in my chest and think that I could hardly bear to wait for the summer holidays. Would the moors and becks still look the same? Would Tom still let me scoop him up and hold him like a baby, purr vibrating through his light bones? I missed the clean, outdoor smell of him, the miaow that did not quite work. A coach rattled by on the road beyond the boundary wall. I listened until it was absorbed by the hills, and the idea of home felt impossible, as though the days of fog and sickness had snuffed out that other life for good.

Cecily Weekes' father came from Wakefield to collect her, though none of us saw him arrive or leave. A few days later, Margaret's parents came. They had heard about the contagion from a relative who lived in nearby Kirby Lonsdale and were angry that the school had not informed them. I'd never had a friend before now, only my sisters and Branwell, so I was sad to say goodbye to Margaret. I liked her sharp chin and the laughter that got her into trouble too often; the way we'd decided to become friends without asking. Within the week, the dormitory was half-empty. More girls had been moved to the sickrooms and parents arrived even when their daughters were unaffected, wanting to remove them from the miasma.

'I told you this place was unhealthy,' said Charlotte, scowling at me as she held her feet to the stove in the schoolroom one morning. Her chilblains were better but her mood worse. 'No-one listens to me.'

'Of course we do,' said Elizabeth, putting an arm around her shoulder. Maria smiled and then tweaked her ear and called her a regular little Cassandra.

At last, halfway through February, the fog lifted and stayed away. The sun shone hard and bright for a whole week and each morning there was a good, sharp frost. By that time, the teachers were too exhausted to bother with anyone who wasn't sick, had even stopped enquiring about our private studies. It became clear that we might do as we pleased, so long as we didn't make too much noise in the garden, with the sickrooms being so close at hand. Among those of us who were still well, a holiday feeling reigned, the schoolroom becoming a playground. Girls yelled across the room to one another, threw balls with no care for the windows, or pushed back the tables and benches for skipping games or plays. One of the older pupils said how strange that the Reverend Carus Wilson did not come to visit the afflicted, and everyone laughed. We walked over the fields in whatever direction we wished, clambered over walls and stiles, breathing crisp cold air into our lungs after all these weeks of being confined in the school buildings; began to talk of the sick as though they lacked strong constitutions.

'We should climb the fell tomorrow,' I said, jumping down from my bed. At night, when the dormitory quietened, I could feel the presence of that rise of land to the north. It pressed on my imagination in the darkness, and in the daytime my eye was often drawn by its mass, the surface broken to scree in places, something harsh about it reminding me of home.

'We ought to be studying,' said Charlotte, who was sitting on her own bed and looking at her most turnipy today. The dormitory was the only place we could work in peace nowadays. 'It's further than you think. Don't forget that it still gets dark at four.'

I was not stupid enough to forget such a thing. And how did she know how far I thought the distance? 'Papa wouldn't think twice about it,' I said. 'Or Branwell,' I added, knowing this would needle her. I appealed to Maria, jiggling her arm as she tried to work beside me: 'I'm tired of dull, flat fields.'

'Charlotte's right about the distance,' Maria said, looking up from her French grammar. In the clear morning sunshine, you could see the bones beneath her skin. Then a slow, serious smile. 'But we could walk part of the way if you like.'

I said nothing but hugged myself in excitement. Even Charlotte wouldn't be able to resist the temptation to carry on until we reached the top of the fell when there might be a whole range of mountains waiting for us on the other side. We would chase the horizon into unknown parts of the world, just like proper explorers.

The next day, we followed the beck upstream and away from school, grass crunching beneath our feet in the spots where the frost hadn't yet melted. As the ground started to rise, we discovered that after all these months away from home, we were unused to proper walking. Even Maria struggled for breath, though she had the longest legs of all of us. We soon grew hot and uncomfortable from the effort of climbing, had to stop to take off our shawls.

'We'll have dinner when we reach that crag,' said Maria, pointing to a grey outcrop about a third of the way up the fell. I was starting to wonder if we could reach even that point, but then our breathing fell into a rhythm and our bodies remembered how to move up a hillside: steadily and surely. Cowan Bridge grew smaller beneath us, the sky a deep shade of blue above. We spotted the Leeds to Kendal coach on the road below, a toy coach passing a toy school, and could just make out the sound of hooves, faint on the breeze. Our chatter and laughter rang out across the empty slopes, our only company the sheep who watched us approach and then skittered away. The wind grew stronger as we climbed, tugging at our hair and carrying our voices away. When we reached Maria's crag, we took shelter from the gusts and unwrapped the slices of pie that the new cook had given us—the old one had finally been dismissed when Miss Evans caught her drinking gin instead of preparing breakfast for the invalids in the sickroom. The pie had proper pieces of meat and potato in it and even Charlotte agreed it had been seasoned properly. I ate a whole slice and half of Elizabeth's too when she insisted that she wasn't hungry, and thought how simple it was to be happy, here on this hillside with my sisters, with the wind singing in our ears and the world unrolling at our feet. I wished only that Branwell and Anne could be with us.

'It'll take no time at all to climb to the top,' I said, lying back and tipping my neck to look. Above me, the sky spun.

'You know it will,' said Charlotte, as Elizabeth ran to rescue the paper in which the pie had been wrapped. She folded it carefully and put it in her pocket.

'Just to that next crag then,' I said, pointing to a limestone ledge that promised even better views of the countryside. Maria glanced up at the sky. It was almost clear, just one or two clouds drifting over the tops. The sunlight swung across the fellside in arcs, turning the thin grass from green to gold. Her grave face lit up with a smile as she caught my excitement, the bubble of freedom about to burst in my chest.

We were hungry again by the time we turned back, and the fell was already half in shadow. The wind dropped as we lost height, but the air was so cold that it brought on Maria's cough.

'That way looks quicker,' she said, spotting a path running at an angle to the one we'd taken on the way up. We crossed the fellside to reach it, the light fading fast. This new route was rougher underfoot. Charlotte turned her ankle on a loose boulder and began to cry. Far below us, we could see the lamps being lit at school, window by window beginning to glow.

'We'll be late for supper,' said Elizabeth in a low voice. All of us remembering that downhill was as hard as going up: the rocky ground jarring the bones of our ankles and shins, and the cold making us clumsy. Charlotte stumbled again on a jutting stone, was saved only by Elizabeth catching her from behind. Maria led the way, but she had a pain in her side which meant she had to keep stopping to bend double.

'Just a stitch,' she said, straightening. We rubbed our hands and stamped our feet against the cold. 'Come on.'

Beneath the outcrop where we'd eaten our dinner, the sheep had gathered, a pale glow against the violet dusk. We hurried past them, pushing on towards the valley, and at last we were climbing over the final stile and crossing the field that led back to school.

A large pot of something stood on the table at the front of the dining room. Steam was rising from it and there was a good savoury smell in the air. A loaf of bread was ready for cutting too, but there was no queue of hungry girls and no-one to serve them. Instead, everyone was gathered around Miss Andrews, the teacher Charlotte hated most.

'What's wrong?' Elizabeth asked a girl in the class above mine, who was crying. The girl wrapped her arms around Elizabeth's waist, firm as a young tree, and sobbed still harder.

'Where have you been, girls?' The teacher's voice sounded distant, as though she was only pretending to be angry. She had grown thinner in the last month, I noticed, cheekbones pushing up against her flesh like the rocks beneath the surface of the fell. Without waiting for an answer, she said, 'The doctor has just left us. I'm sorry to tell you that little Jane Sykes died this afternoon.'

Chapter 4
1825

Children died all the time at home. In a bad winter, Papa might take several funerals at a time, tiny coffins jiggling up the hill to the church all in a row. Children who had spent all their short lives in poverty, had breathed the hot, unhealthy air of the woolcombers' cottages from the day they were born. The worst days made Papa angry. He'd come home exhausted and uncommunicative, then write to the newspapers about the conditions his parishioners were forced to live under. On an unseasonably warm day, we walked across the fields to attend Jane's funeral at the church in Tunstall. She'd been an orphan, her only family an elderly uncle who lived too far away to collect her body or attend the burial. I watched the coffin lurching into the earth, the scattering of dirt on raw wood and it seemed to me that I cared more about Jane's death than she would have done. My classmate had always taken things as they came, neither complaining nor rejoicing. I'd liked her solidity; how predictable she'd been, a counterpoint to Margaret's nervy exuberance. When the funeral was over, we walked back to school in silence. I kept my head down, surprised to see my feet still moving over the surface of the world as if nothing had changed. Beneath her freckles, Jane's skin had been as white as the bone china cups in Miss Evans' study. The sun had seemed to shine right through it. I'd thought her indestructible though, with her sturdy limbs and thick-set body of a country girl, that heavy plait hanging down her back like a rope. Now I imagined it caked in mud, a streak of orange in the soil, the creatures of the earth swarming.

Maria came in late to breakfast one morning, when the rest of us were just finishing, and Miss Andrews did not pinch her arm or threaten her with the switch.

'I'm going home,' she said, coming to our table. With over half the pupils ill or returned home, there were no more rules about sitting by class at mealtimes. 'Miss Evans thinks it's best.' A shaft of white sunlight illuminated the alcove where she stood, like a saint in a niche.

'You're not sick?' said Charlotte, eyes widening.

Maria shook her head. 'Only this wretched cough keeps on. And the pain in my side from when we climbed the fell.' She shifted from toe to toe. 'Doctor Field says I can come back after Easter when the weather's settled.'

'Oh,' cried Charlotte, her face crumpling. 'You lucky creature!'

A rare smile from Maria. 'I can't wait to see dear Haworth again.'

Lessons began again but the doctor said we should also bolster our constitutions—already strong, none of us having come to any harm with the fever—with afternoons at leisure. With Maria gone home, Charlotte and I had to think for ourselves. Elizabeth was good at rubbing bruised knees or settling a disagreement, but she could not make adventures happen like Maria, who always knew if we should be explorers or fugitives or natives or castaways. Without her, our games frayed around the edges, and we would wander off through the trees that lined the beck, where the wild garlic was pungent and the wood anemones formed a delicate, starry carpet. I liked to lie face down on the bank watching the small brown fish twitch through the sparkling, dark-pebbled water, pulled this way and that on invisible threads. The beck sang its cold song and the swallows flashed down to scoop up water and the insects that floated above the surface. I liked the elegance of their forked tails, the indigo gloss of their back feathers. Charlotte preferred to read her book in the shade of a lichen-covered alder, while Elizabeth sat among the dog violets and gentle yellow cowslips with her face turned up to the sun, content with no occupation at all.

Easter came and we walked to church, the earth springy beneath our feet, though a cold wind was coming down from the fells. To our surprise, the morning service was taken by the curate, and when the Reverend Carus Wilson preached in the afternoon he seemed in a great hurry to get through his sermon. His family pew stood empty and for once he did not stop to fire the usual questions at us after the service, sweeping past without a glance in our direction. In his black cloak and breeches, he looked like a stout crow, his beaky nose jabbing the air.

'I do believe he's frightened of us,' said Charlotte, watching intently as the minister climbed into his carriage, a look of disgust on her face. Then she smiled, registering victory over a man who had, until now, terrified her. 'Imagine Papa behaving like that.'

'I don't believe the Reverend is a good man,' said Elizabeth as the carriage sprang forward. It was the first time I had heard her speak ill of anyone.

But one evening Miss Evans gathered everyone round with surprising news of the Reverend's generosity. Tomorrow, she told us, all those who were well enough would travel to a place called Silverdale on the Lancashire coast, where Reverend Carus Wilson had a holiday home he'd said we might use. She herself would remain at school, tending to those still in need.

'Sea air, girls!' she said, clapping her hands together. There was something forced about such excitement in one whose nature was normally so composed. She looked grey as granite after all the weeks of caring for sick people. I wondered how old she actually was; whether she really knew what to do for the best.

Elizabeth was also to miss the trip, we learned. She'd spent the last week in the sickroom, her cough not improved enough to risk the journey.

'We ought to stay too,' said Charlotte when we visited her on the morning of the trip. The comment came from nowhere—we'd only come to the sickroom to take our leave. She pressed her hands together in holy fashion, which was something Maria sometimes did, but not in such an annoying way. Outside the sickroom window I could see a fat, orange sun muscling its way over the horizon. 'Or at least wake her to say goodbye.' But Elizabeth hadn't even stirred in her sleep, and I was halfway down the corridor by then, having heard the coaches that Miss Evans had hired to take us to Silverdale.

The sun rose higher in the sky as we set off, softening to pale gold. On either side of the road, the hedgerows churned with haw blossom and sparrows flung themselves from branch to branch, singing their cheerful, artless songs. I leaned forwards and lifted my face to the sunlight and before long, the bumping of the coach wheels and the growing distance between us and Cowan Bridge began to dislodge something that had been fixed in me since Jane Sykes had died. Even Miss Andrews seemed to relax, made no objection when a couple of Charlotte's classmates began to sing. Charlotte did not join in, but the mild May air drifting through the window smoothed her brow and blew the green, winter tinge from her complexion.

I sensed the presence of the sea before it came into view: a freshening that quickened my blood and woke the sleepiest of girls dozing in the coach. The land began to flatten, the skies widened. Gulls circled and complained overhead. They were more densely built than land birds, I saw, made to withstand tempests. As the coach slowed I watched one of them drop onto the roadside and begin pecking at a piece of rubbish. He was ugly, with a heartless eye, but I liked the way his legs were painted to match his curved yellow beak. Then we turned a corner and I thrilled to see a vast bay opening out beneath us. The end of land was not at all as I had imagined, looked nothing like the pictures I had seen in books. There was no surf pounding against black jagged rocks, or ships careering through the waves. Water did not spout from whales as big as boats. Instead, a wide stretch of buff-coloured sand reached out to the headlands that jutted against the sky on either side of the bay.

'There!' I seized Charlotte by the arm and pointed to a dense bluish line merging with the sky on the horizon. Between the sea and the solidity of land, I could see horse-drawn carts threading their way around shining pools, where water birds stood quite still, like lookouts, or sat suspended on the surface. I had not known the world could be so wide, that it could glitter in the sunlight like a diamond, though Aunt always insisted we had the sea in our blood. She and Mamma had grown up in Penzance, a town that sighed and shifted, perpetually nudged and sucked at by water.

'Will we walk on the sands today?' asked a classmate of Charlotte's. She pointed to a party getting down from one of the horse-drawn carts out in the bay.

Miss Andrews sat up very straight. 'We'll take a guided walk tomorrow, but no girl is to go on the beach unsupervised. Several rivers converge here—you will all draw a map later—and there is quicksand and a powerful tidal bore. People can be stranded on the sandbanks and children have been sucked down beneath the sand before they can be rescued.'

She eyed our little party as if this outcome would not be wholly unwelcome, and then we were turning into a driveway and passing wide, well-kept lawns planted with fine old trees. Ahead of us I saw a house built of dove-grey brick, with a slate roof and large windows reaching almost to the ground. It had a friendly, comfortable air which made me think Reverend Carus Wilson could not spend much time here.

Excitement spread among us as we entered the building and the housekeeper led us up the wide staircase. We were to sleep in proper bedrooms instead of a dormitory! Charlotte and I were given a large room overlooking the gardens, with one vast bed and a smaller one beneath the window. Both had smooth white pillows and sage-green counterpanes that matched the curtains. The furniture was dark wood, highly polished, and the walls were papered in primrose yellow. Sunshine fell on the carpeted floor, so soft beneath my feet, and through the open window that same salt-sharp smell was carried on the breeze. We had high hopes for tea, but the Reverend's generosity stopped at the kitchen and the food was as plain as ever. Afterwards, I left Charlotte to walk along the neat gravel paths that edged the flower beds and ran across the open expanse of grass to an ancient Lebanon cedar tree at the far end of the garden, where a high wall divided it from a wood beyond. I sat on the far side of that immense trunk and stared up through the branches, which layered themselves to the sky. The ridged bark pressed into my back, and I remembered those sands sculpted by a ghost sea, like the fingerprint of a giant, and could not wait for tomorrow to come. That night, I took the smaller of the two beds, beneath the window. Muffled giggles came from other rooms, a shout of surprise. Miss Andrews called for quiet from somewhere close by. Outside, the stars hung in clusters, little white fires blazing across the heavens. I heard the wind stirring the trees and somewhere beneath that sound, a low rhythmic murmur that was the call of the sea. As I drifted to-wards sleep, I thought of what Miss Andrews had told us about quicksand. I pictured little children running across the bay, a kite swooping and dancing high above their heads, and then the ground giving way and the hands of the earth, cold and grainy, closing around small ankles. Not letting go.

After breakfast, Charlotte beckoned me to follow her back upstairs. I followed her past our bedroom to the end of the landing where she pointed to a tiny doorway set into an angled wall.

'I noticed it last night,' she said, voice hushed though everyone else had gone to explore the glasshouses. 'Couldn't stop thinking about it.'

It opened now onto a narrow stone staircase with no windows which curved to the right as we climbed, the steps so tall that we had to stretch our legs. We came to another door at the top, this time with a key in the lock. Charlotte opened her eyes wide and then turned it. I followed her into an attic room, the darkness broken by a dazzle of light from a series of windows just beneath the roofline. The first thing I saw, once my eyes had adjusted, was a double-fronted dolls' house in the corner of the room. Charlotte spotted it at the same time and ran to open the front, which was secured by a clasp. How forlorn it looked when we crouched down to peer inside, rooms empty of furniture and occupants, dust furring the floors and the roof tiles.

'Every inhabitant smitten by a terrible plague!' said Charlotte, forgetting to be miserable for once.

Through another door, we discovered wooden trunks organised neatly against a wall, a stack of oil paintings and a mirror, clouded with age and dust, on the wall opposite. We pulled out old-fashioned dresses which had been packed carefully between layers of soft paper in one of the trunks, held them against ourselves. They had high waistlines, smelt of perfume and dust, of lives folded away forever.

'Mamma would have looked like this.' I held one against me, but it did not help me remember her. In the next room we found odd pieces of small furniture, an easy chair, a nightstand, an old mangle; we even found a bedstead in the final room furthest from the stairway. Charlotte said some evil member of the Reverend's family must have been locked away here to die. I said that it would be a strange thing, bringing them on holiday when they were so evil, but Charlotte thought it just the sort of thing he *would* do. We found a hobbyhorse too, as well as a set of quoits, a chessboard, and a box of Venetian masks with ribbon ties.

'We should make up a play,' said Charlotte. She chose a mask for herself and then handed another to me. But once we'd put them on we fell silent, suddenly scared by those smooth, blank smirking faces.

A bell was ringing somewhere in the depths of the house. We put the masks away and hurried back down the little stairway, making sure to close the door behind us. At the bottom of the stairs in the main hallway, a man was standing with his back to us. Miss Andrews was there too, hands spread as if explaining something. Her expression looked wary, almost fearful, but that could not be right because the man she was talking to was Papa. We flew into his arms and there was the familiar Papa smell of him, the scratch of his jacket against my nose.

'Your father is come to take you home,' said Miss Andrews.

Charlotte burst into noisy tears, wrapping her arms around Papa's waist again, and burying her face against him. 'Thank you oh thank you.' Her voice muffled by his clothing.

'Hurry to pack,' said Miss Andrews. She looked past us, to the dining room where the other girls were clattering about. The ticking of the hallway clock bothered me for some reason, like a persistent itch on my skin, a fly buzzing past my ear.

'Now?' I asked, stepping back from Papa. What about the plan to go walking on that great sweep of sand this afternoon? That magical place where the land ended and the sea had not quite begun, and your footsteps might be firm, or else the world might dissolve beneath you; where the sky snapped open, and the sea was a smoky promise on the horizon. Then I understood that we were going home. To Haworth, and our parsonage on the windy hillside, and Branwell, and Aunt, and Maria and Anne. 'What about Elizabeth?'

'I shall arrange for your belongings and—' said Miss Andrews.

'Elizabeth is already at home.' Papa half turned towards Miss Andrews and then seemed to change his mind. I didn't understand, knew only that he would never normally interrupt a lady like that. 'Arrived yesterday with only a servant to accompany her. I suppose it was the best that could be done.' His mouth stayed open in a strange way when he'd finished speaking, like a dog panting from exertion, as if there was more to say. Then he turned towards the door. 'I'll wait outside.'

There was screaming and it was not mine. That word clanging in my head, *died, died, died* and Charlotte's mouth a black hole with terrible sounds coming out of it. What would the coach driver think, I wondered? And why had Papa waited until we were nearly home to tell us? There was a reason for everything, but I could not work it out. Papa was talking faster and faster now, as if Charlotte's screams might be smothered with words. 'Too ill by the time she . . . every possible medicine . . . poor Maria . . . suffered too much, so patient . . .' To my horror, I saw his eyes filling with tears as he told us about her funeral. Only then, his words starting to make sense. Maria, my clever, serious sister, gone. Forever. And then, somehow, all three of us were clinging together in a clumsy, broken huddle. We were far from the sea by then, but in my mind I could still hear the gulls shrieking as they wheeled above the coast road.

Branwell was waiting for us, a small red-haired figure standing at the entrance of the inn, his face a splodge of white against the greyness of Keighley. While Papa went to make arrangements for our boxes to be sent on, I prayed for my brother to make some remark about Charlotte's appearance. Surely her cranium had grown too big after so much learning? Wasn't she in danger of toppling over, the rest of her being mouse-sized? In reply, she would accuse him of being more dancing puppet than boy, a creature barely in control of his own limbs, and everything would be normal then, Papa's words a terrible mistake. But Branwell stared down at his shoes, a strange sort of embarrassment settling over him, while Charlotte seemed only interested in watching the millhands on their way home from work. At last Papa returned and we set off to walk the four miles home. Cottongrass bobbed and swayed on the riverbank. I saw a patch of snakeroot, like little pink bottlebrushes. As we left Keighley behind us, the leggy meadow buttercups lifted their faces to the sky and the moors rose all around us, consuming the mills in the valley bottom, a land as familiar to me as the features of my own siblings. Except that the whole world was different now.

'We'll never go back again?' I'd asked eventually, when Charlotte had stopped screaming. In the corner of the carriage, she moaned quietly, her head in her hands. I'd wanted to scream too, but when I opened my mouth, nothing happened.

Papa had already explained how he'd been planning to come to Cowan Bridge to tell us what had happened to Maria, when Elizabeth had arrived home, ashen, exhausted. Shocked by her appearance, he'd set off immediately to collect us. I knew school no longer mattered but it felt important to be clear about absolutely everything from now on.

'You can keep up your studies at home, Emily,' Papa had said. 'I'll help both of you. Anne too.'

Tiredness had overcome him then. He slept with his head back and his mouth half-open. He snored a little and then stopped and for the first time I understood that he too would someday die.

We walked up the steep curve of Main Street, past the familiar shops and the tightly packed cottages. I looked straight ahead of me when we reached the church where our family vault lay, but as we turned onto Parsonage Lane, I had a sudden vision of Maria reading to us from the rocking chair beside the fireplace, the newspaper held properly like a grown-up. I pictured her silver hairbrush and mirror, gifts from her godparents, always at odd angles on the nightstand; her blue shawl draped carelessly in the closet, and it was like a blow to some tender, unprotected part of me. How she had loved the books in Papa's library, taking them from the shelves with such reverence, turning the pages so carefully. Even Maria's hands had looked clever and serious. Our sister had been the authority in all things, and I did not understand how the world could work without her. She was gone from this life and my legs were made of stone or wood and not flesh, but there, at last, was the house and I could see Aunt hurrying down the lane, her bonnet flapping in the wind, and running behind her, face as sweet and open as a pansy, was dear little Anne.

We found Elizabeth asleep on the little sofa in the dining room, her embroidery abandoned on the coverlet—a few dark elderberries stitched at its edge, purple thread hanging over the frame. We saw what we'd missed before, how thin she'd become, the pallor of her complexion, but her smile was full of joy when she awoke to see us, and the new servant, Tabby Aykroyd, had already taken charge of her recovery. Tabby had iron-grey hair in a tight bun on her neck and such an air of capability that we took to her immediately. In the days that followed, we became used to the sound of her bustling about the house before dawn, setting fires and scrubbing the doorstep and hallway in readiness for a new day. She administered bowls of bread and milk to give us all strength—it wasn't just Elizabeth who needed feeding up apparently—and kept a pot of beef tea simmering on the range for the same purpose. And it was Tabby who suggested that Papa should carry our sister into the garden on days when the weather was fine. While Charlotte read to us from *Ivanhoe*, Elizabeth lay on a blanket with her head on a cushion, helping whenever Charlotte struggled with a word or with the rhythm of a sentence. No-one looked in direction of the church, but when a dried peony slipped into Charlotte's lap, dark as a bruise, she stopped mid-sentence and we did not ask why. Maria had pressed it between the pages last summer. Charlotte put the flower back in place, then closed the book. A blackbird bounced across the lawn. The sun grew hotter, and we moved the blanket into the shade of the cherry tree. Elizabeth dozed beneath the fresh green leaves, while butterflies trembled on the June air.

Two weeks after our return, I came out onto the landing one morning to find Papa in the doorway of Aunt's room. I spoke to him, but when he did not answer or move, I ducked beneath his arm and entered the room. At the bedside, I saw Aunt on her knees with her face buried deep in the covers. Her false front of curls had come loose, lay half-adrift on the white sheets like a rare creature on display in a museum. Her dress was rucked up too, showing layers of petticoats. Aunt, who was forever trying to school me in manners and what she called normal behaviour! I did not understand why Papa stayed frozen in the doorway behind me, not asking what was wrong, not going to her assistance. Then my eyes moved past Aunt and settled upon Elizabeth, now sharing Aunt's room so that she could be tended to at night. My sister was lying on her side, facing the doorway, with eyes closed and her mouth open. On the pillow beneath her, a gush of blood, bright and fresh as a guelder berry.

Raainah,' shouted Anne, holding her nose with one hand, pointing with the other.

I slid down from the table, went to look. Ghost of my breath on the glass of the dining room window, fading, returning. There were thick black clouds over Brow Moor, a few heavy drops of rain splashing on the garden path.

'Sit down, Emily,' said Aunt. 'I've told you. And there's no need to shout, Anne.'

'Who-aar care-aaaars?' said Charlotte, holding her own nose. She shrugged and then dropped her hand. I saw her eyeing the mutton chop on her plate, already stripped to the bone, her gaze shifting to the blue and white platter in the centre of the table where the last of the chops was waiting. Yesterday at tea-time, Branwell had made her cry when he caught her slipping two slices of bread into her pocket. Now he was pulling faces at her from the opposite side of the table, his bright hair brushed close but already springing into madness.

'Finish your dinner,' Aunt said, looking at my plate which was almost untouched. 'And for pity's sake, stop talking in those ridiculous voices. It's gone too far now.'

Charlotte pinched her nose harder this time, whitening the skin. '*Emilaaar* doesn't taaalk at aahhhhhhl.' She let go of her nose to point at me. 'She could if she wanted.'

'What is the matter *now*, Anne?' said Aunt. Anne was nudging her plate away an inch at a time. Her legs began drumming against the chair which meant trouble was coming. Aunt's voice softened then because Anne was her favourite. 'What is it?'

Anne shook her head, her baby-fine curls swinging violently. Then she pursed her mouth and held her breath until her cheeks went red which was her latest trick. 'Don't do that,' said Aunt. I wondered what would happen if we were to make her cry.

'Youaah meaaan pleaseaaah stopaah,' corrected Branwell.

'For the love of God!' Papa's chair crashed to the floor. He was on his feet, arms in the air, the bulk of him blocking the light. A revelation or a miracle? We followed his gaze, all eyes turning to Charlotte, half-hunkered now beneath the table and gnawing like a dog on the last mutton chop, her face slick with grease.

'Enough,' said Papa. I watched his big hands flexing, clenching. Outside, the rain was coming hard now, dripping from mossy walls, blurring the boundary between garden and the graveyard. 'That,' he said seeming to address the greasy smudge of grey beyond the graveyard which was the church, 'is enough.'

A month since Uncle Morgan had come from Bradford to preside at Elizabeth's funeral. He was not really our uncle but Papa's great friend since they were young curates. We'd followed the bobbing coffin to church, past the villagers lining the path to the door and Charlotte had thanked them, being the eldest now. That gave me a strange, dizzying feeling, like the time I woke up to find I could not keep my balance, that the world would spin madly whenever I tried to move. It was an infection inside my ear, painful enough, gone within the week, but Elizabeth would be dead forever.

When the men set the coffin down awkwardly, I felt Papa flinch beside me. For once, he'd joined us in the family pew, folding his legs into the limited space, eyes ahead, silent tears running down his face. Aunt comforted Anne, who cried inconsolably at one moment, but could be distracted by a trick of the light, the promise of a story after tea. Cold was all I could feel, striking up through the stone floor of the church, travelling up through my ankles, my knees. The flesh on my face felt solid, frozen to my bones. Charlotte and Branwell were huddled together in one corner of the pew, small mice curled into one another, dependent on one another for warmth. I tried to move toward them but came up against Charlotte's elbow. She was listening intently to the service, though she'd always thought Uncle Morgan too loud, pleased with the sound of his own voice. I pictured her strutting up and down the hallway after his last visit, cheeks puffed out, hands supporting an enormous, invisible stomach. Papa had pretended to be cross but could not help laughing at her sing-song accent, the long-winded anecdote she'd told. Laughter seemed a strange thing now, something that belonged to other people.

As the service went on, I found myself staring at Elizabeth's name, newly-carved above our family vault. I needed a sign, a magical revelation, a secret contained in stone that would make sense of what had happened, but the lettering was just raw, random gashes, and there, immediately above it, were the words the mason had carved just weeks earlier: MARIA BRONTË. My eldest sister who was no longer my eldest sister. When it was time to pray, I knelt and closed my eyes, but I could still see the mason's mallet rising and falling, his chisel angled precisely into the stone, the cuts sharp and irreversible, and now Uncle's sonorous voice was disturbing the stone dust, making it rise once more. It drifted along the nave, carried on the dark, currented air towards our pew. I opened my mouth to pray and I felt it swirling about me, those coarse inert particles accumulating, searching out a new home.

Our Father, who art in Heaven
Hallowed be thy name

By the time that Elizabeth's coffin was lowered into the vault, the stone dust had lodged itself deep in my throat, stopping up all my words.

Papa went to Leeds one day. The next morning Branwell burst into our room, still in his nightgown.

'Papa bought me a present!' He held up a small wooden box like a trophy, hopped across the room following the stream of sunlight on the floor, and then leapt onto the end of our bed, landing on my feet. I'd been lying there for some time, not caring about moving. I considered pretending to be asleep still, but then Anne came scrambling up beside Branwell, her blonde curls hanging loose over her shoulders, wide awake though only moments ago she'd been snoring in her own little bed. Charlotte sat up next to me.

'For me too.'

Branwell whipped the box from her in a tantalising way, while Anne bounced up and down on the bed, her feet still small and plump as a baby's, toenails like little moons. I opened my eyes just enough to see that the box was made of golden wood, with darker stripes running through it. It glowed in the sunlight. Despite myself, I felt the urge to reach out and touch it. With the air of a magician, Branwell slid back the lid, which was inlaid on a set of grooves, then angled the box to display its contents. Inside, lined up as if on parade, was a set of wooden soldiers. I opened my eyes properly then, counted twelve soldiers in all, three of each kind, painted in bright, new colours.

'The Duke of Wellington!' said Charlotte, snatching up a fine-looking soldier, dressed in black and red with gold epaulettes.

'To *borrow*.' Branwell took a soldier dressed in black and white uniform with gold buttons for himself. 'Then this cunning fellow is Napoleon Bonaparte.' Charlotte pulled a face of disgust and put her hand back in the box. Seeing that they were about to divide the rest of the men between them, I bolted upright and grabbed a soldier dressed in green. He looked thoughtful, not like a soldier at all. Reaching for the little notebook and pencil I now carried everywhere, I wrote in it, and then turned the book around to show them: *GRAVEY*

'Well, Anne better have one, I suppose,' said Charlotte, frowning. She picked a soldier dressed in grey, and then took the notebook from me. At the top of the page, she wrote THE DUKE OF WELLINGTON and NAPOLEON. Glancing again at Anne's soldier, she wrote *Waiting Boy* at the bottom of the page. She bit the end of the pencil then added: *Servant to the Duke.*

'But we must talk like Christian children now,' said Branwell. 'Papa says.'

'I already am,' said Charlotte.

Branwell had owned sets of soldiers before, most of them too battered and broken for use, but from the moment the new soldiers arrived, he cared only for them. His first idea was to stage Napoleon's escape from Elba, using the kitchen dresser as a rockface and the bathtub for the Mediterranean Sea, but Tabby Aykroyd said it was a waste of water and that he would get in her way. Charlotte thought the Battle of Waterloo was a much better plan, because it would involve all the soldiers and stop Anne complaining about being left out, but we all knew it was because her Duke would win the day.

'Wellington never would have won without the Prussians,' said Branwell, and then with one of his bursts of enthusiasm, came up with the idea of using the staircase to recreate the Mont-Saint-Jean ridge. Charlotte and Anne were to organise the Duke's troops, massing them on the top landing, while he and I would take up position on the middle landing, in front of the grandfather clock, and begin pushing up from the south. Charlotte didn't see why she had to have Anne on her side, so Branwell said she could have me instead, but that didn't please her either. After a minute, it became clear that what Charlotte really wanted was to fight alongside him, which didn't make any sense. All the arguing made me very tired. In my notebook, I wrote *NOT PLAYING* and went to the dining room instead.

Recently, I'd taken to lying on the floor between the fireplace and the window with my arms outstretched. I would stay in the same position for hours sometimes, even when Tabby started sweeping around me and the dust got in my nostrils. In my imagination, I was gagged and bound upon a rock, must live out the rest of my days alone in the middle of the ocean. I needed no company, but it was nice to have Gravey lying beside me today. I closed my eyes and tried my best to ignore the excitement out on the staircase—I imagined the wash of the waves, the crying of vultures overhead—but then Branwell was calling for me, in urgent need of dried peas for his *Grande Batterie*. Gravey and I gave up on isolation, our life of abandonment on the rocky island and fetched the jar of peas from the pantry. Then Branwell and I unleashed the onslaught without warning. It went on until Charlotte was hit in the eye and started crying, which went to show, Branwell said, that girls were no good at war. She stopped crying immediately, began drumming her feet to frighten everyone with the thunderous roar of heavy cavalry, and then brought on von Blücher's Prussians—Anne's dolls— to reinforce her flank. The battle ended naturally at dinner time and when we came back, the devastation was sad to see. Men lay groaning on their backs, one soldier had lost a leg, another an arm, which Charlotte managed to reattach. We cleaned up the blood, administered laudanum with teaspoons to dull the pain, piled those who had perished into a corner of the landing. One of Prussians had been hit by a musket ball and had a cracked nose which made Anne cross.

'We ought to remove the teeth of the dead ones before we bury them,' said Charlotte. The corner of her right eye was bloodshot where one of my peas had landed, giving her a wild, piratical look. 'People pay good money for a healthy mouthful.'

CHAPTER 7
1825

The Twelves, as we came to call the new toys, or sometimes The Young Men, were English sailors shipwrecked in Ashantee, on the west coast of Africa, which was a dry patch of grass in the corner of the garden. All that summer, they scaled mountains which were the garden walls, crouched in the thorn bushes to conceal themselves from the natives, even accompanied us on our daily walks up onto the moors. On one particular outing, we were so occupied conducting a funeral service for the dead after a ferocious battle in the heather, that none of us noticed the sky turning violet and brooding, the silence that always came before a storm broke. When the first peal of thunder came and the wind flattened the purple moor grass, we gathered up the Twelves and ran to the shelter of some of the large, overhanging rocks which broke the moor's surface here and there.

'Look!' cried Branwell. Across the valley, high above Stanbury, a fire had broken out in the tinder-dry heather. Almost immediately it was doused by an immense downpour which moved across the hillside like a grey curtain. Another crash of thunder shook the earth. Charlotte screamed in terror and Anne burrowed backwards against the rock. I lifted my face as lightning flickered across the horizon, touching the ground in bright forks. I wanted the rain to drive down harder, for the wind to whip the earth into new, fantastical shapes, the world to burn in an inferno.

Despite our attempts to take shelter, the storm soaked us

down to our underwear. We came home dripping and Aunt fretted to Papa about our safety, wished we would play in the garden instead, but Papa said the moor was as safe as anywhere if we were all together, that it was good for us to be *away from things*.

The next day Charlotte said the lighting had brought The Twelves to life and this set them apart from the other toys. We no longer needed Branwell's set of Turkish musicians, or Anne's dolls, had no use for a skipping rope or the skittles. We should lock them away in the cellar for some other family to discover in a hundred years' time. Neither did it matter if her Duke of Wellington had sustained a fatal injury in pursuit of Napoleon, and that Branwell had insisted on burying him beneath one of the gooseberry bushes in the garden on our return. Charlotte had dug him up because she was now the Genie Tallii, with the power to restore life whenever she pleased. Branwell said by rights the Duke's bones should be ground down for fertiliser, like all the other men who died in the war, and that she ought to be tired of her precious, saintly Wellington by now. Due to the lightning's transformative powers, Napoleon was not actually Napoleon anymore. His new name was Rogue, but sometimes he would be called Sneaky too, if it suited Branwell, and everyone would just have to get used to it. Charlotte said this wasn't possible, that you had to stick with what you'd chosen and make the best of it. They argued back and forth until I was very tired. I was on the point of going to lie down on the dining room floor when I felt a strange sensation, something pushing up through my chest and all the way into my throat. I turned to Anne who had her hand it the air, trying to get Charlotte's attention, and pointed to Gravey and Waiting Boy who were standing side by side on the kitchen dresser.

'I'm sick of those two.' The words arrived in my mouth like hard, round pebbles, threatened to take up all the space. I stopped for a moment, needing to be sure that my breath could find a way around these unfamiliar objects. Then I pulled Anne closer and whispered the news in her ear. Our men were not boring old soldiers anymore, but Sir William Parry and Sir James Clarke Ross, real-life explorers.

'Emily's speaking!' shouted Charlotte, jumping up with a look of triumph on her face. She'd just finished brushing the last of the dirt from the Duke of Wellington, restoring him to his old self. 'I told you she could.'

On a wet and windy afternoon, when Aunt had refused to let us step outside, Charlotte fetched an end of wallpaper from the cellar, cut it into tiny pieces and then set Anne—the best of us with a needle, despite her age—to sewing the pieces together. A secret book where we would record the adventures of our Young Men.

'They might not survive to tell the story for themselves,' she explained. But it soon became clear that Anne and I would not be allowed to write in that book, or any of its sequels produced over that summer, even though our men were important ex-plorers, had only ended up in Ashantee when they'd taken a wrong turn on their way home from searching for the North-West passage. We were useful only for reminding the other two of parts of the story they'd forgotten, or details such as meals eaten after the battle and when was bedtime. It was Charlotte and Branwell who took it in turns to write the day's adven-ture, each of them making sure to criticise the other's soldier for errors of judgement or foolhardy behaviour. Around the same time, Branwell started to work on *Branwell's Blackwood's Magazine*, which was meant to entertain The Twelves with book reviews and poems after a hard day subduing natives. After the first few issues, he grew bored and gave the whole thing over to Charlotte, who immediately changed the name to the *Young Men's Magazine* and reported that the quality was much im-proved by this change of editor. She insisted on reading her articles aloud to him each evening, even when he was busy with much more important things like Greek translation—Papa had bought him a copy of *The Iliad* for his birthday, was teaching him a little each day. There was no point Charlotte even wanting to look at the illustrations, he said, because Greek was something girls could never understand. While they argued over that, and who should rule the capital of Ashantee, a glittering, crystalline metropolis which was to be called Glasstown, I lay down on the floor with my arms stretched out so that everyone had to step over me if they wanted to pass, woke up only when Papa came in to say that he had a great surprise for us tomorrow. We bothered him until he lost his temper and sent us to bed straight after prayers, but the next morning, even Tabby Aykroyd must leave off washing the breakfast things to come out into the garden. We waited patiently this time, fearful of annoying Papa again and being sent inside. Aunt stood with her shawl wrapped tightly around herself, shivering in an accusing way, but for once she did not complain of the morning damp.

'There!' said Papa suddenly, pointing in the direction of Keighley. Rising up from the Worth valley, I saw an enormous red balloon. Beneath, and seeming to hang by four fine threads, was a square basket. The balloon was drifting towards us, still gaining height.

'A man!' squealed Anne, pointing to the basket.

'He's waving to me,' said Branwell.

'To everyone,' said Charlotte. She looked down at Anne, who was jumping up and down beside her and calling to the skies. 'He can't hear you.'

'That is the celebrated Mr. Green,' said Papa, smiling with delight at his gift. 'He'll travel all the way to Colne in Lancashire before landing.'

'Will he have his dinner up there?' asked Anne. For one so small and delicate of appearance, she always had an interest in the next meal. Papa's answer was drowned out by a roar. Tabby gasped and clutched at Aunt's arm as a great flame exploded beneath the balloon, just as it passed over our church.

'He's simply heating the air inside the balloon to keep it buoyant,' explained Papa.

'It doesn't seem natural,' said Aunt, frowning into the sky. I thought that the basket carrying Mr. Green looked insignificant, an afterthought. 'If the Good Lord had meant us to fly, he would have given us wings.'

'Like the angels,' said Anne.

But for once Papa did not want to talk about God's ways, was too busy marvelling at the age of ingenuity we lived in, explaining air density and currents, the fact that the earliest balloon flights had remained tethered to the ground.

'I don't think Mr. Green truly knew where he would land,' said Charlotte that evening, when the four of us were gathered around the kitchen fire. 'Perhaps he carried on drifting all the way across the Atlantic Ocean. Will have to land at the North Pole.'

'Where he'll fight the natives and be chased by ferocious Polar bears,' said Branwell.

'Or make friends with them,' insisted Anne. I said nothing but I spent the rest of the evening drawing a map of the Arctic, decorated around the borders with sledges and bears and people dressed in fur hoods fishing through holes in the ice. That night I fell asleep imagining myself flying high above Haworth, alone and untethered, the moors unfurling all the way to the horizon. In my dreams I could travel in any direction and all the maps were in my mind.

The next morning, Papa discovered Charlotte reading a copy of *The Lady's Magazine* and threw it into the fire. She cried because she could never bear anyone being angry with her and then went up to the bedroom for the rest of the day, didn't want to speak to anyone, even when Sir William Parry and Sir James Clarke-Ross came to visit with a cup of tea. The magazine had belonged to Mamma, the last of a bundle that had been sent all the way from Cornwall when she married Papa. The trunk containing them had survived a shipwreck and the pages of the magazines had still borne the marks of the sea. Aunt's voice was clipped all morning which meant she was angry. The stories they contained were perfectly fine, she said, had been good enough for her own sister, but Papa was unrepentant, said it was just the sort of nonsense to rot a young mind. Branwell was in a rare uncommunicative mood too. Usually, it was easy to distract him from his studies by asking him to invent a game or find something exciting to read to us from the newspaper, but Papa had been bad-tempered with him too, something to do with a poorly prepared composition and general laziness. No-one could expect him to be a scholar, he explained, if he had to entertain his little sisters for hours on end. For the rest of the day, he carried his *Iliad* around with him to demonstrate his point.

Left alone, Anne and I spent the afternoon planning a new voyage of exploration for Sir William and Sir James. The two men had tried their best to settle as ordinary citizens in Glasstown. They'd been honoured with ceremonies by the city dignitaries, given glittering mansions that towered a mile into the sky, and even taken wives (the Glasstown women were renowned for their beauty) but at a meeting in a low tavern frequented by sailors, they secretly agreed that it was no good. With every flagon of ale, they'd grown more mournful, each of them gazing out across the docks where great ships were being loaded for departure. Finally, Sir William had confessed how much he missed the ocean wave. He longed for the empty horizons, he told his friend, the blur of the future. It was impossible to breathe in Glasstown with its rules and by-laws, its ordered streets, and shiny, perfectly finished surfaces. Hurrah! cried Sir James, thumping the table and calling for more ale and a brace of capons to celebrate. We began listing provisions required for their voyage: sacks of barley and potatoes, barrels of dried fish and salt pork and hard biscuits, hammocks, lengths of new rope, musical instruments, and books to keep the men entertained. Anne added a handsome parrot to the list, thinking it would give the crew some common ground if they needed to parley with pirates along the way, while I drew a black kitten named Lord Lucifer Mouser who would keep the rodent population in check. By the time Charlotte came downstairs again at tea-time, her mouth still tight, eyelids puffy from crying, Sir William and Sir James had set sail from Ashantee, leaving behind the band of Young Men forever. Our very own stories would be set on the island they'd discovered in the North Pacific, far away from Charlotte and Branwell, a place where the inhabitants cared nothing for Glasstown or the Twelves and their exploits. We named this new land Gondal.

CHAPTER 8
1830

I t's snowing again,' said Charlotte, going to the window. I looked up to see that the light was already fading though it was only three in the afternoon. The church was a dark mass beyond the graveyard, blurred by the flurries of snow, the green-grey tint of the sky. 'And the wind's getting up.'

I put down my pencil. For the last two years, we'd been taking lessons in drawing. I'd been trying to capture the muscular build of a brown hare, the shading of its ears, but I knew Charlotte well enough to guess she had not come into the dining room to report on the weather. 'I'm going to school after Christmas,' she said. She'd left the door ajar and the draught from the hallway caused the fire to expand and then climb up the chimney in protest. 'Near Dewsbury. I didn't want to say until it was settled.'

I stared at the fire, at the holly which we'd brought in from the lane that morning. Anne had woven the branches into a crown for the mantelpiece, the glossy leaves and crimson berries bringing festive cheer to the room.

'Papa made proper enquiries,' she hurried on. 'Roe Head is small and select and close to my godparents at Mirfield. They already know the sisters who run the school, have promised Papa that they'll keep a close watch over me.' She paused to take a breath. Though she was months off her fifteenth birthday, I'd already outgrown her by a foot, and even Anne looked likely to overtake her soon, no matter how greedily Charlotte ate. Her little hands twisted the front of her dress, as if trying to form it into a different garment. 'I don't want to stay here forever. None of us can.'

'Papa teaches us everything.' Which was almost true, except for drawing as I said, and music which Mr. Sunderland the organist came to teach. Recently I'd started learning Latin, using my own Bible for translation. And how could Charlotte say that she didn't want to stay here when there was no more perfect spot on the whole earth than this house cradled by the moors? This village wedged into the jaw of the hillside, the narrow, blackened cottages shouldering one another for space like ageing teeth.

'It's not enough. Aunt says we'll only find positions if we can show we've had proper schooling. Because there's so much competition nowadays.'

'Branwell isn't made to go away to school.' I sounded like a petulant child, despised myself for it. I did not need Charlotte to explain that it was different for our brother, had always known that we must one day become teachers or governesses, the only respectable occupations for girls like us. I'd tucked this knowledge away in some hidden part of my mind though, covered it in sheets like antique furniture stored in an attic. All these years I had been perfectly happy at home with Tom the cat and Grasper, our ancient terrier, and a young tawny owl named Sir Walter Scott that I'd found injured on Penistone Hill, one of its legs hanging powerless beneath it. I was nursing him to health, feeding him on meat scraps from the kitchen until he was well enough to soar free again.

'I'm to enrol for a year and then prepare you and Anne after that.' She smiled. 'You'll definitely be able to go as well, just later.' The fire crackled and shifted. Charlotte glowed with unconcealed excitement as though she'd brought me a precious gift. As if Cowan Bridge and our two dead sisters had never existed.

I fetched my cloak and went out alone before anyone could object. In the last year, Aunt had taken to reading out loud to me from the newspaper, her voice loaded with significance. The stories were all the same: women who had put themselves in the way of danger, young ladies who took foolhardy risks and then found themselves subjected to ungentlemanly behaviour. She said the moors were too lonely for a young girl to go walking alone, especially with so many of the farms abandoned since the mills took over. The only people you might encounter *up there*—she'd raise her chin at that point and glance suspiciously towards the window, hoping to catch a collective of vagabonds plotting unspeakable deeds on the garden path—were strange sorts, travellers and drifters, people who lived outside society. When I asked why she didn't trouble the others, she said that Anne was still a child, and Charlotte might as well be—that neither of them cared for wandering off on their own like me.

'Remember Sally Westhope,' she'd warn, knowing that I didn't. The story was familiar though—the milliner's daughter who'd gone missing and was discovered on a boggy stretch of land towards Oxenhope two days later. She'd been face-down when they found her, her dress and petticoat, it was whispered, up around her waist. There was little point arguing with Aunt, but I did not see why Papa and Branwell could roam wherever they wanted, taking the loneliest of paths with only their own enjoyment in mind, and no thought for danger. Why God's wondrous earth should be available only to them, while I must learn to conceal my existence, to fold myself out of sight, into the smallest possible space.

When I reached the top of Penistone Hill, I stopped for breath and looked back down into the valley. Nothing was straightforward with Charlotte though she looked so small and malleable. What was true one day—that school was a dangerous place, that the world beyond our home was perilous—was no longer so, simply because she had changed her mind. The truth according to Charlotte had proved as slippery and treacherous as the ice at the edge of a beck in early spring. I walked on, Haworth Moor stretching into the distance before me now. In summer it was a purple, rolling carpet, alive with the hum of bees, but at this time of year it was a more muted landscape, dun and grey and black against a sky of wintery blue. There was still colour to be had—clumps of coarse copper grass, the silver underside of the heather, exposed by the wind—but you had to look harder to find it. More than a year, Charlotte had said, before she and Papa thought I might join her at this new school. I pictured the two of them planning my future for me before I'd even known it was in question, then had a sudden vision of myself shaking my sister until her teeth rattled. I strode out still faster. By the time I'd passed the farmhouse at Top Withens and then skirted the boggy area around the base of Delf Hill, I'd escaped her. I walked on until I came to one of the small becks that threaded down the hillside here, stopping to push back my bonnet. Anne and I had spent an hour in this exact spot last summer.

'That rock,' I'd said, pointing to a stone in the middle of the water, 'is Gondal.' I'd stretched out on my front to observe it from eye level. The rock was bright and spongy with a forest of moss.

'This one's called Gaaldine,' said Anne, finding a smooth, flat stone nearby.

Islands that grew in our imagination, occupying all of our time. Gondal was a land of moors and mountains, with a king named Julius Brenzaida who did as he pleased, taking a wife for himself, and also a lover. He was a wild and conniving man, who had his eye on conquering the neighbouring Gaaldine, which was a tropical island with palm trees and giant crabs running along the shoreline. There had been sunlight on rushing water that day; swallows swooping over the glittering surface. I walked on more slowly now. All this was mine, but for how much longer?

I was just approaching the deep crease in the hillside that was Ponden Clough when something struck my cheek. I looked all around and then above, though there were no trees on this stretch of open moorland that might have shed a sharp twig or a nut. I checked on the ground but whatever had hit me had disappeared into the tussocky grass that grew hereabouts. I rubbed my cheek and saw a faint streak of blood on my finger. At the edge of my eyeline, I caught a movement in the bare heather. At first, I thought it was a grouse, waited. Then I saw a head of brown curls and dark eyes, my own self emerging from the earth. I stepped off the path and strode straight towards the crouching figure, but the boy was already gone, leaping over the mounded heather towards the lip of the clough. Determined to tackle him, I broke into a run, but by the time I reached the clough he'd already started down its steep side. He was barefoot, goat-sure, dressed in rough, country clothes the colour of mushrooms. I wheeled around, looking for an object to throw in retaliation. Finding nothing, I started down the hillside after him, in the direction of the flat-headed gritstone outcrop which was called Ponden Kirk on the map in Papa's study, but which Tabby called the Fairy Cave. A narrow tunnel ran through that jutting rock, she'd told us, all the way from one side of the outcrop to the other. It was too dangerous to climb down to—the hillside was slippery even in the height of summer—but anyone who passed through the tunnel would be married within the year. I'd lost interest at that point and returned to my sketch, a noble profile of Julius Brenzaida.

I was close enough now to see the fissure in the rock like a narrow doorway, my feet slithering beneath me as I descended. The boy was standing right by the entrance, grinning over his shoulder at me. He was older than me, perhaps by four or five years. His hands and feet looked too large for his body, and he had that stretched look which meant he was about to turn into a man. In my haste, I lost my footing on a ledge of rock that ran with water, saved myself from tumbling to the bottom of the clough only by grabbing a handful of long, coarse grass. It cut into my palms, burned my skin. By the time I'd scrambled down the last few feet to the Fairy Cave, the boy had disappeared inside the entrance. I could see the shape of him though, blocking the light ahead of me. I went inside and the rock was clammy to the touch, cold as death. I pushed forwards, fingers feeling my way, prodding beak-like at the stone. Ahead of me, I could hear him moving and then I couldn't. I stopped and for a moment I felt sure that we occupied the same space, that I could hear his light breath, smell him on the air, damp, animal-like. I scrambled towards him and then I broke through into the winter sunshine on the far side of the cave and my knees were damp and my hands had turned to ice. I climbed to my feet in the cold, shattered light and looked all around me, but the boy had disappeared and there was nowhere left to go.

Charlotte left us in the middle of January, a wretched-looking creature sitting very upright in the cart which Papa had hired, her face dwarfed by her bonnet. Mirfield was too far for her to travel home for weekends, so we would not see her again until the summer holidays. Watching the cart set off, I told myself that it would be a very long time before it would be my turn to go. Aunt had on several occasions made much of the expense involved, and part of me still believed that the world would change in some remarkable way to prevent it ever happening.

In the beginning, I was a poor, scared creature, Charlotte wrote. *I am sure you can picture it.* Even with his glasses on, Branwell had to squint to read the letter. *There are only a small number of girls here, all of them hearty, well-fed beings who delight in games and running around. They were impatient of me at first, could not understand why I rushed to finish my work in order to continue with my own studies; why I did not want to set down my books and catch a ball with them. They pressed me on the matter but soon learned that it was hopeless, the ball flying past me on every occasion. I do not understand the point of games. They seem the perfect way to ruin a period of recreation. Why must one always be running up and down and growing hot in the face instead of observing, considering? Mostly they are girls of wealthy families who do not need to trouble themselves greatly about the future. Yet kindly enough they have now grown accustomed to my oddities, and Miss Wooler who is the head-mistress, and her sisters who help run the school, take care that everyone is in good health and spirits. I have made two friends! Ellen Nussey is a good, gentle girl who arrived a short time af-ter me and took pity on my homesick tears. Her family are from Birstall and are in the cotton business. Mary Taylor is a hard-headed and sharp-tongued girl from Gomersal. She has a younger sister, Martha, who is also boarding at Roe Head and has a lively, endearing nature. Mary says that I am ugly and that, though I am well-informed, my arguments are not always sound. I like her very much. I only wish Emily could be here with me; I think she would be happy.*

Here Branwell broke off and finished reading in silence, which we understood to mean that the rest of the letter was private business about The Twelves, or their newly discov-ered territory which they'd named Angria. He barely noticed Charlotte's absence, he assured us at least once a day, but one morning he rose before dawn so that he could walk all the way to and from Mirfield, which was nearly twenty miles away, to see her.

Charlotte's next letter was even more cheerful.

The other girls have grown accustomed to my odd ways, helped in part, I believe, by my friendships with Ellen and Mary, both of whom are well-liked. It takes little to impress schoolgirls: some little bit of knowledge that I have stored away—a poem, some event in ancient history, a passing acquaintance with an art-ist's most famous works—seems to astonish them, though they, in turn, are equally astonished by my lack of understanding when it comes to grammar or the most rudimentary ciphering, which still seems the most baffling of subjects! I now see that our lessons at home were more comprehensive than any curriculum devised for young ladies. Would you believe that not one of these girls has heard of Herodotus? The names of Ovid or Virgil spark something in their minds—perhaps they have heard their brothers or fathers mention them—but they have no acquaintance with their works, even in translation. I have told them nothing of Glasstown or Angria of course, but when we are gathered round the fire in the evening, they press me for stories to entertain them. I like to shock them with some of Tabby's wilder tales and sometimes I frighten them with ghostly stories that I invent as I go along. One night a girl became hysterical with fear and I got into trouble with Miss Wooler. She is rarely cross with me for long since I am now top of the class and have every intention of remaining there!

I returned to Ponden Clough often that spring and summer, searching the horizons in the hope of seeing the boy rising out of the heather again. Once I climbed down to the Fairy Cave itself, sat by the entrance all afternoon watching the sun swing across the sky, but the boy didn't appear. I'd intended to teach him a lesson, to retaliate in some unthought out way, though the cut on my cheek had long ago healed. I went home at dusk feeling empty and restless all at the same time, as if I'd lost the centre of myself out on the moors. I thought about asking Tabby if she knew anything of the boy but decided against it. I didn't want her asking questions I couldn't answer or speaking to Aunt.

Each time Charlotte came home for a holiday I looked closely at her for signs of suffering, but there were none. When her three terms came to an end, she chose not to come straight home but went to stay with Ellen Nussey in Birstall for a fortnight. The following month Ellen came to Haworth for a week. Aunt was delighted with such a ladylike and well-mannered guest, who was an example to us all, but Anne and I were shy, not being used to strangers in the house, especially one who wore expensive-looking dresses and had such pretty, soft ringlets. Ellen was easy and undemanding though and it was plain that she and Charlotte took great pleasure in one another's company, though the two of them were quite different in character. Miss Nussey happily joined us on our daily walks, and Branwell, who was shy of no-one, chattered and laughed in his usual fashion, spilling over with questions about Ellen's family and home, her time at Roe Head; with anecdotes and local gossip, lines of poetry, snatches of song. He pointed out the best views, gave a quick lesson in natural history, told her about his organ lessons and the boxing club he'd joined. When Ellen admired the picture of Bolton Abbey hanging in Papa's study, Branwell became excited.

'A day trip!' he said. 'We can hire a phaeton, stop for breakfast at the Devonshire Arms. Picnic by the Abbey. I'll arrange everything!'

Sometimes I thought our brother had enough ideas and words for a whole family. There was almost no need for the rest of us.

As pleasant as Ellen was, I began to feel uncomfortable after she had been with us for a few days. I grew silent at mealtimes, felt the old urge to stretch out on the dining room floor and close my eyes. On her last full day with us, I took myself off to a corner of the graveyard where I could not be spotted from the house and spent a few happy hours working on a new idea for Gondal, the story of a young prince who'd been swapped at birth and grown up as a shepherd boy.

Have you given up on becoming an artist?' I asked. The moon was full, washing the bedroom with an eerie light. Charlotte didn't immediately answer, so I gave her a sharp nudge with my elbow.

'What?' she said in an aggrieved voice, though she could not have been properly asleep. She always snored when she was lying on her back.

This morning, a letter had arrived from Miss Margaret Wooler confirming my place at Roe Head school for the next term. When Aunt handed it to me, I read the first few lines, then threw it away in a panic and headed up to Penistone Hill by myself. Charlotte had long since finished her own schooling. As time passed, I'd started to believe Papa had changed his mind about sending me next, made sure never to mention it. It was only when I returned to the house at dinner time, that I learned Miss Wooler had also offered my sister a teaching position, that her salary would help cover my tuition fees. It was not Charlotte's fault that I must go away from home, but I was still angry with her. If she hadn't talked so glowingly about Roe Head for the last three years everyone might have forgotten about the idea.

Notwithstanding Charlotte's nostalgia for her schooldays, she had seemed happy to be home, at least until recent months. At first, her mornings had been spent teaching Anne and me—she took more pleasure in imparting her superior knowledge than I could stand at times—while the rest of the day she kept busy with writing. She'd taken up drawing again too, working on tiny portraits of the Angrian aristocracy, as well as multiple profiles of Anne—the only one of us patient enough to sit for her—and a series of delicately wrought pictures of wildflowers and little birds. As well as these, she set herself to making painstaking copies of the engravings of Bolton Abbey and Kirkstall Priory which hung in Papa's study. Branwell had sniffed at these efforts and then, with a sudden change of heart, suggested she submit them for last summer's Exhibition of the Royal Northern Society for the Encouragement of Arts. When her entry was accepted, she was frantic with excitement and fear, hardly slept in the days leading up to the Exhibition. The whole family had travelled to Leeds to see her work on display, but how tiny and insignificant Charlotte's little sketches seemed, in the same room where the great JMW Turner's work was on show. I'd tried to concentrate on the neat, feminine lines of her work, but all I could sense was the presence of those paintings of his, like thunderclouds building at the edge of my vision. Since the Exhibition, I'd noticed her becoming restless, her moods tending to pessimism.

'It's given up on me,' Charlotte said, stiffening beside me now. 'You know my drawings didn't sell.' She shifted to another position. 'Anyway, Branwell's preparing for the Royal Academy now, so we can't afford my extra lessons.'

'You really want to teach then?' Though Charlotte was often nostalgic for the happy year she'd spent at Roe Head, I was still surprised that she'd accepted the post. All of us had given classes at Haworth Sunday School: Branwell impatient with the stupidity of the village children, Anne and I doing as we must, but everyone knew that Charlotte lived in terror of her turn coming round. All those eyes upon her felt like a judgement, she said. Her voice shook and failed, her knees threatened to give way, and the pages of the Bible swam before her eyes and made no sense at all. I'd always assumed that she would prefer a governess position when the time came, with just a small number of charges in her care.

'Not particularly.' She wriggled beside me again, then turned over her pillow, seeking a more comfortable spot to lay her head. 'But it's hard to settle at home when you've lived independently. You'll feel that too. And Miss Wooler and her sisters are fond of me. I know they'll be patient with my efforts.' She waited for me to reassure her, but I had never met Miss Wooler or her family, did not feel like being kind. A note of defensiveness entered her voice. 'I have to earn a living somehow, and I'd rather be at Roe Head, with people who care for me, than have to make my way alone in some stranger's house.' She was silent for a few minutes and her breathing began to thicken. Just when I thought she was about to snore, she propped herself up on her elbow and started again. 'You know, all the time I was at school I had a purpose, a place in the world. Oh, I'm sure they thought me an oddity, but it was the first time I'd ever felt truly visible. At least a teacher can make her own mark, not be overlooked.' She rolled onto her back again and gave a sigh so great that it resonated through her small frame. 'Sometimes I feel as if I'm disappearing here.'

Roe Head was just as Charlotte had described it in her letters: a dark-sand coloured house with bow windows on all three storeys, set far enough back from the road to give it an air of peaceful seclusion. It was surrounded by sunny fields, with views down the Calder valley towards woodland. Miss Margaret Wooler herself came out to greet us, a middle-aged woman, with a square, masculine face, benign features and greying hair. Though her manners were reserved, she was plainly delighted to see Charlotte, seizing her by the hands as she stepped down onto the driveway. The headmistress took us straight to an airy room overlooking the gardens where we were to have tea with her sisters, all of whom taught at the school alongside her. I was amazed to see how animated Charlotte was during that meal, speaking as naturally as she did at home, keen to share news of

Ellen Nussey and Mary Taylor with their former teachers. I was left in peace until the meal drew to a close.

'I shall teach you myself until you are ready to join the rest of the class,' said Miss Wooler, turning to me. She pronounced her words with old-fashioned care, giving each its full weight. 'This is my practice with all new pupils, so that we can address any areas of weakness.'

Charlotte answered for me. 'Emily's been well schooled by my father.' She smiled with a touch of self-consciousness. 'And more recently, by me.' Outside, a little brown butterfly rose and fell against the bow window.

'I won't detain her long then.' The headmistress's voice was firm but kind. Her eyes, beneath a wide brow, had a teacherly wisdom.

At supper that evening, Charlotte joined the teachers again, while I was directed to a nearby table where the school's most senior pupils were seated. I saw immediately that none of the girls were more than twelve or thirteen years of age. Tomorrow would be my seventeenth birthday.

'Why aren't you a teacher like Miss Brontë?' asked one of them a minute or so after I'd taken my place, a bold-looking girl who had been holding court among her peers till then.

'I'm not yet qualified,' I replied.

The girl stared at me. Her eyes were dark beneath black brows and so deep-set they almost disappeared into her head. She shrugged and looked away. A moment later I heard her whisper, 'Perhaps she's an idiot.'

'Hush!' said another, giggling.

By the end of that meal, I understood that I was among privileged young ladies, all of them marked by a confidence that came from lives spent in ease and security. They were mostly the daughters of mill owners or cloth merchants, Charlotte had said, but surely these girls had never set foot in those workplaces in their short, comfortable lives? When bedtime came, I remembered with a strange fondness another dormitory, with mean blankets and water freezing over in the jugs on the nightstands. I pictured those rows of clergy daughters in their shabby brown pinafores and worn shoes, hair arranged plainly. Even at a young age, before sickness and death had slunk into that bare room, they'd had a grey, hungry look about them, future sufferings etched on their faces. Here at Roe Head, the girls fell asleep quickly, contented snoring rising all around me. Full stomachs, pretty, snub noses that had never been troubled by the sewage-stink of open drains or public privies, the meat-rot heat rising from backyards and alleyways.

'I shouldn't break confidences,' said Charlotte, hurrying down the garden to find me, one evening a few weeks after our arrival. 'But Miss Wooler says you're making wonderful progress since you joined the main class.'

This short period after lessons, when the whole school was at recreation, was the only time in the day that we could be alone together. Even then, as the newest teacher, Charlotte must supervise the pupils, so our eager conversations were constantly interrupted. She looked around now, checking on her charges. The younger girls were gathered on the paved pathway by the house, where the seniors were trying to master a dance step, the long windows of the ground floor rooms serving as mirrors for them to admire their reflections. 'We could both be teachers by next year.'

'Here?' I asked. My sister looked tight faced with weariness and a ridge had settled between her brows. When she was not supervising pupils, all her free time was spent preparing lessons.

She shrugged. 'Or somewhere else. I'm not convinced any of these girls listen to a word I say.' She laughed joylessly. 'I can't decide if they're deaf or just dense.'

'I wish Anne could come,' I said, watching the trees for a

barn owl which hunted at this time of night, its face a blank disk in the twilight. Perhaps then I could find happiness in this place, just as Charlotte had when she herself was a pupil a few years ago. The Misses Wooler had made it plain that they regarded me almost as an equal, an acknowledgement of my age and my relation to Charlotte, and while one or two of the more daring girls passed comment on my height, my natural reserve, they were too wary of me to go further. I'd defended myself from girls twice my age when I was at Cowan Bridge. Of what then would I complain? That the schooldays were long, that I was unused to applying myself for hour after hour? (Charlotte worked harder still, and the quicker I learned, the sooner my schooling would be done.) That I longed for home? Homesickness was for children, too feeble to fend for themselves. It would be shameful to call this misery by that name, yet every minute of the day reminded me of home—the sun angling across the unreachable hills in the distance, the sound of happy voices in another room, the grey brick of a building I passed on a walk, a black cat strutting along the boundary wall.

I was sick at heart and it was just the nature of things. At home I did not speak often, but my words had always mattered. Here, my sentences dropped like stones into a well, their ripples lost in the murk. August came and from the windows of the schoolroom, I could see the distant moorlands turning purple. The world swooned, bathed in sunlight, but a small, cold rock had lodged itself in my stomach and there was nothing I could do about it. One Sunday, the Reverend and Mrs. Franks came to visit us from Huddersfield. They were some of Papa's oldest friends, from the time when he and Mamma lived at Thornton. We all took tea with the Misses Wooler and I did my best to look happy, knowing they were sure to write to Papa about our well-being, but my awkwardness and misery only increased as the meal went on. I could feel stoniness spreading to the rest of my body, cold tendrils pushing into my veins. By the time we came to say goodbye my lips had calcified, and I could not speak at all.

As soon as they were gone, I went straight to the empty classroom, knowing that writing was the only thing that would free the words snarled up inside me, but to my horror I could not find my way to Gondal. The world where Anne and I had spent so many delightful hours had vanished, the pathways quite grown over. I tried again the following day, with a sense of growing terror, but no islands appeared on the flat, featureless oceans, no towers and turrets punctuated the skyline. I could not even picture the face of Julius Brenzaida though I'd drawn him countless times. After that the days at Roe Head were interminable. I gave up trying to find Gondal and longed only for nightfall, for sleep which was a bottomless black pool from which I never wanted to return. But the mornings kept on coming, daytime hooking me like a fish, dragging me to the surface. The stoniness found its way into my limbs. I struggled to raise myself from my bed each morning. All was order and sedateness and contentment in that place, yet I could not breathe, and it was not the devil and it was not God, it was something in the nature of me, in the nature of Roe Head, though to another's eye it would look like perfection: that sunny valley, the verdant woods in the distance. I lay on my back on the grass one evening as three swifts wheeled overhead, black arcs against a deepening sky, tails divided. They darted and swooped around the whisper of a moon, their voices high and wild, and when they had gone, the sky seemed empty. Sometimes a place imprisons your mind, your spirit, and there is no telling why.

Once, about the time Charlotte had left for Roe Head for the first time, I'd come across a dog standing in middle of Parsonage Lane, close to our gate, a black, scruffy-looking mutt with no collar. I'd called to him, but he shrank away when I approached, retreated to the far side of the lane. His legs were trembling beneath him, and his head lolled to one side.

'Poor thing,' I said softly. 'Wait there.' I went through the yard and into the back kitchen where I filled a small bowl with water from the pump. When I returned, the dog had crossed back over the lane to stand by the gutter. 'Here, boy,' I called, taking care not to slop the water. He looked up as I approached, something wild in his eyes. 'Are you hungry?' I'd just put some leftover brisket in the storeroom. 'Have a drink first.' I placed the bowl down where he'd settled himself now, nose to the ground. I saw the wet red of his mouth first, tongue like raw meat, and then his teeth clamped down on my forearm and the water sloshed over the setts and ran down the lane in rivulets. The dog huddled away from me, yellow teeth bared, drool hanging from the corners of its mouth. I stood, bracing myself for another attack but he skittered down the lane, back towards the village. I looked down. The sleeve of my dress was ripped, the brown fabric reduced to threads and a piece of flesh was missing from my forearm. I thought how strange it was to see the inside of your own body, when only moments ago it had been hidden away in the dark. The hole in my arm gleamed and then, as if it had only just registered the injury, began to pool with blood. I caught a glint of white that could be tendon or could be bone, steadied myself against the wall. It was my own fault. I should have waited for the dog to come to me. Hunger and the smell of meat on my hands must have turned him savage. You could not blame a beast for following its own nature.

I thought of the drool stretching from the dog's mouth. Pictured that strange, skittering gait. Wrapping the sleeve of my dress tightly around the wound, I went back inside. Closing the door that led from the kitchen to the hallway, I took two clean tea cloths from the dresser, turned back the sleeve of my dress, then wrapped one of the cloths tightly around the wound. In seconds, the snowy material had bloomed deep red. I put the smallest of the flat irons—the one we used for collars—on the range to heat, then pushed the second cloth into my mouth.

The neatness of the iron's fit struck me just before the sizzle of hot meat, burning flesh. Violent white pain bursting. I bit down and then I was on the floor, the iron lying just beyond my reach, the tea cloth no longer in my mouth. I tried to move. My head was spinning, my forearm thrust into hellfire. I could smell my own flesh, cooked. I vomited on the scrubbed flagstones, once, twice, then forced my breath to slow, shutting myself off from the pain, from the foul smell. I lay on the mercifully cold tiles praying that no-one had heard me or caught the odour on the air. At last, the ragged edges of my breath smoothed and I allowed myself to look at the wound again. I saw a blackened mess of coagulated blood, burnt shreds of flesh at its edges, like some horrible, gaping mouth. My vision began to break up again, black spots before my eyes. Another wave of sickness came. When it was over, I found a fresh cloth and wrapped it around the wound. Then I cleaned up the vomit and gathered up the soiled cloths. The iron sizzled again as I put in under the pump, washing away my blood and flesh.

The pain was so intense that I could not eat any supper, feared I might be sick if I forced anything down. When Anne looked at me with concern, I pretended that I had a stomach-ache and went to bed early. That night I dreamt my arm had been severed at the shoulder—the relief of that clean break, then the realisation, even in my dream-state, that it was still attached. I dreamt of dogs that were not dogs but wolves with amber eyes and fangs that dripped yellow poison. I sensed some great force at work in my body, fanning the flames, willing them to burn hotter, to cast out the infection from my blood, from my ragged, singed flesh. The fever stretched my dreams in still stranger directions, the Gondals setting sail on an ocean that undulated and shuddered like a vast blue jelly, arriving in a tropical land so humid that the jungle interior dripped all day long, a constant,

maddening sound in the men's ears; where fruit swelled to immense proportions and creatures grew in strange new ways,
mouths where beaks should be, feather and paws and fins all
mixed up in one beast. Julius Brenzaida perched on his throne
a mile up in the air, commanding all of the Gondal troops. Time
passing. The quality of light changing. By morning the fever
was gone. I drank down a glass of water in one go, cold and
mineral and cleansing.

Somehow, I managed to conceal the injury from Anne, but
when Charlotte came home at the end of her first term, she
caught me at the nightstand with my sleeves turned back.

'You could have died!' she said when I finished explaining.
She stared in horror at the wound. By then, it had shed the
bloody scab to reveal new skin beneath, shiny and pink, but the
dip in my arm still looked alarming.

'I did not,' I said.

The bell was ringing now, signalling that evening recreation
was over. I got to my feet and brushed the grass from my dress.
Once I had healed myself, purged all bad things from my blood.
Why could I not do the same now?

Charlotte came looking for me one afternoon, found me sitting beneath an ancient oak at the far end of the garden, trying
to concentrate on *Paradise Lost*. The sky was the rich blue that
only comes in autumn. Sunlight fractured through the canopy
of leaves above me, and the damp, mossy tentacles of the oak's
roots held fast to the earth, joining the underworld and Heaven
in a way that ought to have made my spirit glad. It did not
touch me. Stone was beginning to creep over my surface. Soon
I would be quite encased.

'Are you ill?' said Charlotte.

I shook my head, lay down my book. Everyone knew that
I had the strongest constitution of all the family. The problem

was that my soul was dying, but I could not voice such a ludicrous idea when I was living in a place of ease, comfort and learning. It seemed a weakness of character, to be incapable of finding happiness here.

'Miss Wooler thinks you're homesick. I suppose she's seen it enough to recognise the signs. I was unhappy myself at first, but then I met Ellen and Mary.' She glanced around to check on her charges and then sat down on one of the oak roots. 'There'll be new girls coming soon. Companions nearer your own age. Other people to talk to.'

I didn't need companions or conversation but the tenderness in her voice wounded me. I bit the inside of my cheek. The blood tasted like metal. It seemed to me that any capacity for friendship must have been left behind me long ago, back in the schoolroom at Cowan Bridge. How freely the words had come to me then, falling from my mouth without a thought behind them. My sisters had died, and it was a knife to my tongue, but still the words had swirled and multiplied inside me, wild and melancholy. Now they lay quite still, inert in the darkness. Nobody perished of homesickness, but I began to fear I might die, felt my thoughts becoming strange, my vision skewing. There was nothing physically wrong with me, I reminded myself. I worked harder still at my lessons, dreamed of smashing my fist through that glittering schoolroom window, of rubbing my wrist along the glass splinters until the blood ran, proving to myself that I was still alive.

Food arrived in front of me. The girls nearest were excited about the harvest supper planned for the following week.

'But where is his *heart*?' I heard Charlotte saying, addressing the entire teachers' table nearby. 'You say it exists, but I can't find it in a single volume of his works.'

Her face was pink with the effort of expressing herself so publicly. She looked like a child seated at a table of adults, so tiny that a kind passer-by might scoop her up and place a cushion beneath her. Yet I could tell that she was happy, eating her food at a normal pace instead of wolfing it down or gazing covetously at other peoples' plates. I stared down at my own dinner which was untouched. Girls cawed down the table at one another, chattered like noisy magpies. When the bell rang everyone stood and the room tilted and receded, rushed back at me. I grasped for the edge of the table and then my vision turned black. When I came to, I found myself lying on the floor, Charlotte appearing in a circle of faces above me. It was peaceful on the cool floor. Outside the window, I could see just a few white streaks of cloud. The back of my head was tender. Did I hit it on the bench or the floor? It seemed important, in that moment, to know.

Charlotte sat on the edge of the bed and took my hand. 'You're to go home. Miss Wooler and I have discussed it, and everything is settled.' Again, that ridge between her eyes. Probably one of her bilious attacks was in the offing. I shook my head. 'You're fading right in front of me, Emily.' She looked away from me, pursed her lips. 'It's difficult to watch. You've stopped speaking again.'

'I talk to you.' I thought of pushing myself up on my elbow but couldn't summon the energy. 'Miss Pearson almost passed out in church last Sunday.'

'She suffers with her monthlies. It's not the same thing.' Charlotte shook her head. 'Miss Wooler says you've learned so much already, that you'll still be able to teach later.' She stared down into her lap. 'If that's possible.'

My copy of *Paradise Lost* lay open on the little bedside table. I thought of Satan cast out of Heaven by the angels, tumbling to earth like a firebolt. He could not live there. It did not fit him. I said nothing. If I opened my mouth, my voice might rise up and destroy the entire world and once I began, I would never stop.

S kin and bone, girl,' Tabby complained, gathering up the loose fabric at the back of my dress. 'We'll see about that.' Anne sat opposite me, the skin around her delicate nose red and peeling, eyes watery from coughing, but her gaze as warm and gentle as spring sunshine. 'Your Aunt says you're to rest in bed today.' Tabby's fists thumped as she knocked back the bread dough. 'And Anne's not to put a foot outside with that cold.'

I had on my boots and cloak before she'd time to rub the dough from her fingers, breaking into a run down the hallway. I stepped out into a ghostly world. The night before, when I'd arrived home, the fog had been curling along the valley, skeins of mist hanging over the fields. It had clung to the banks of the river, dampening the air, creeping up through the village, blurring the lamps in the windows and shop fronts on the lower part of Main Street, so that everything had looked both familiar and unreal, Haworth suspended in a dream-like state that matched my own. Now I saw that the fog had almost wiped out the church, just a patch of wall remaining visible at the base, and in the graveyard, the headstones floated in a shifting white sea, one moment visible, the next dissolving as the mist swirled, brushing the earth with cold, particulate fingers. Sound was altered. I had to listen carefully to hear Mr. Grieve at work on a carcass in the backroom of the butcher's, the thunk of meat and bone; for the muffled sound of handcarts rattling over the setts on Main Street. On Parsonage Lane, the baker's girl chattered to herself on a doorstep, while her brother chased a rat into a hole in the wall. I made my way up the lane, noticing how strange my legs felt, as if the muscles and bones had forgotten how to work in unison, but as I left the village behind, I felt my stride growing stronger. A bedraggled sheep blundered out of the fog, its wool damp and greying like a sodden dishcloth. The rest of the flock set up a melancholy lament, their baaing drifting over the boundary wall; rain-slick stones; moss a spill of vivid green in the ghostly light. I thought of the bones of all the dead soldiers, ground down and spread across the fields of England. At least they were home. Water dripped from the trees and my breath came harder as I started to climb Penistone Hill. When the moor began to flatten in front of me, I kept on going, my feet finding the familiar ways without difficulty. Past Top Withins now, the dark walls of that lonely farmhouse looming out of the mist. Sound shifted again, becoming clearer. I skirted the base of Delf Hill, the ground sucking at my boots, and then the sun broke through and the fog rolled back and there were the Alcomden Stones rearing up before me like a Druid Temple, a game of knucklebones abandoned by the gods. As children, we'd clambered over those grey rocks, unheeding, Branwell and I scrambling up to the highest point to seek out the faint bumps of Ingleborough and Whernside on the northern horizon. Now, as I stepped into their shadow, my knees gave way beneath me and I found myself down on my stomach, my whole body cleaving to the earth. I tore at the damp moss, dug down into the soil with my fingernails, salt tears and the mineral grit on my tongue, and on my teeth.

Eventually my breathing slowed. I sat up, looked around me. Spiders had been at work in the night, weaving tiny webs all over the dripping, frost-blackened branches of the heather, thousands and thousands of webs stretching from branch to branch, from plant to plant as far as the eye could see, like some great civil project they'd had set about in the hours of darkness; fairy hammocks slung for the night. They glittered like spun-sugar in the sunlight, trembled beneath the dew, so that the whole world appeared to be vibrating. The stone that had been lodged in my stomach all this time shifted, its cold weight moving like the rocking stone that sat atop one of the monoliths in front of me. A red grouse barrelled out of the heather, complaining to itself. The stony fingers in my veins began to oscillate and then they shattered.

Returning home on one of the sandy paths that cut through the heath, I saw a man striding towards me, his clothes the muted colours of the moors, mudstone, bleached grass. He stepped to one side when he noticed me, pushing back his shirtsleeves as if they were an irritation. This was the only path hereabouts, so I had no choice but to keep on towards him. As I came closer, I saw that he was younger than I'd thought at first, in his early twenties at most. He looked at me in the way that country people do, with open but neutral curiosity. I might have been livestock straying onto his land, a tree twisted into unusual shape, a weather front coming in. His eyes were peat-dark, uncivilised. Remembering Aunt's warnings, I lowered my gaze as I passed, found myself looking instead at his forearms, tanned from outdoor work, and at the broad, long-fingered hands resting by his sides. Neither of us spoke and I walked on quickly, thinking of the time last summer when I'd gone to the study for a book and found some visiting clergyman there, complaining of the heat. Anxious to fetch my book and be gone, I'd moved around him just as he finished unfastening his cuffs, then pushed back his sleeves to reveal milk-white arms, wrists as puny as a sickly child's. The sight had revolted me, made me wonder how any woman could bear to marry and be subjected to that every day of her life. Afterwards I kept picturing him removing his shirt completely and then the rest of his clothing, until he was standing naked and foolish in the study, exposed, grub-pale, his clothing pooled across the floor. The more I'd thought of it, the more repulsive the idea had become. I pushed the memory from my mind now and walked faster. It was only when I looked over my shoulder and saw the man heading down towards Ponden Clough, that I knew him for who he was: the boy who'd once led me down to the Fairy Cave.

T he leaves of the cherry tree ignited overnight, a whoosh of pink and orange against the grey Yorkshire sky. If you looked carefully, you could still see the place where I once broke one of the lower branches by standing on it, pretending to be Charles II hiding from the Roundheads. We'd tried to hide the accident, covered the wound with black paint which we'd begged from the sexton, John Brown, but it had stood out like a flat, dead eye, and Papa had been angry for the rest of the day, because he'd planted the tree for Mamma when they first moved here.

'I've always been scared of going away,' said Anne, finding me at the window. Frost furred the edges of the glass, little cold hands creeping. In the hallway stood two trunks—hers and Charlotte's—ready for departure. 'Ever since Maria and Elizabeth.'

It was a shock to hear those names usually reserved for prayer time; to hear Anne speaking so candidly. 'Roe Head's a good school, I promise. Just because I couldn't—' I shook my head in frustration and left it at that. I could give a million reasons for the actions of the fictional characters I created, could not explain my own behaviour.

Anne's first letter home was brief, but the next was more expansive and by the end of her first term, she seemed to have settled. I kept myself busy with my studies and with Gondal. (Within days of returning to Haworth, I'd found my way back to that enchanting country.) I read the stories that Anne had written in my absence and tried to continue where she'd left off, chronicling the civil war which had broken out between the provinces of Alcona and Exina. In theory, the war was about possession of a fertile valley shared by the two regions but was actually caused by the behaviour of Alcona's young aristocracy who dressed flamboyantly and spent all their time in drinking dens and playhouses, were more interested in poetry and nights of oblivion than civic duty. Their degeneracy offended the virtuous nobility of Exina who feared the dissipation might creep over the border and distract their own youth, brought up under a Spartan regime and expected to devote themselves to the service of their province. I soon became distracted though, by Augusta Almeda who was the daughter of Julius Brenzaida, King of Gondal. Augusta was not a new invention, but Anne and I had intended to leave her in peace until she was grown up. She was not that kind of child though. Even in her youth, she had a head for politics, sniffing out conspiracies before they could come to fruition and laying them before her father, negotiating all the traps laid for her by the elderly statesman of Gondal who would use Julius's only child to further their own ambitions. They wheedled their way into her company, tried to put words into her mouth, but Augusta had her eye on her future as Queen of Gondal, was too clever to become a pawn in the games that others played. She made a trickster of time, was eighteen years old before I knew it, pushing her way into stories that were not about her. I'd meant her to be mild and good, a civilising influence on her father, but Augusta insisted on herself, was more Tudor than Hanoverian, with her eye for political manoeuvring, her ruthlessness when crossed. The people of Gondal watched her with trepidation and awe, enamoured by her beauty which made men reckless and desperate, half-scared of her taste for attending public executions. She won their love by persuading the King's council to introduce a corn dole and lower taxes for the poorest, to sponsor expeditions to new lands which would relieve Gondal's overcrowded cities.

By the time Anne was close to completing her year at Roe Head, even Aunt had stopped fretting about her youngest and dearest charge, so it was a shock to all of us when she was sent home ill. She'd been suffering bouts of vertigo, she told us, lying on the sofa in the dining room looking wan and exhausted. Later, when we were alone, she said it felt as if the earth was tilting too violently, trying to dislodge her. Papa consulted *Modern Domestic Medicine* and insisted on calling for the doctor, who wanted to know if she'd suffered a recent blow to the head. He examined her ears, her eyesight, but found nothing wrong. Over the next few weeks, the symptoms faded but Anne remained subdued, too tired even to think about Gondal. One morning when I'd been to the stationer to buy ink, I spotted her slipping into church though there was no service to attend. When I put my head round the door, I couldn't see her at first and thought I'd been mistaken. Then I heard a noise somewhere in that empty, shadowy space, noticed that the door to our family pew was half-open. Moving closer, I saw that Anne was on her knees with her hands over her face and rocking back and forth on her heels. I stayed frozen to the spot until I heard a sob, then I stepped back along the aisle and outside again. I made sure not to look at her when she arrived home, and it wasn't until a letter came for me from Charlotte that I learned the cause of her anguish. Charlotte's letters were usually addressed to Branwell, so that she could stray off into Glasstown and Angria business half-way through. He was too busy poring over the atlas today to mind about this change of practice. Recently, he'd decided against applying to the Royal Academy and announced that a tour of Europe would be better preparation for his career as artist. Since then, he'd spent half his time planning the best route across the continent.

'London first, of course.' His finger running down the

country. 'Across to France. Paris, and then the Alps for walking. Then I thought the Italian Lakes and all the way down the peninsular: Venice, Florence, Rome and Naples.' Athens too, to see the classical remains, Delphi, Olympia; places which already lived in my imagination, stranger and more splendid than they could ever be in reality.

All I know, Charlotte wrote, *is that she has been through some sort of spiritual crisis, started to believe that God was an adamantine, pitiless being who would not hear her voice. She thought he had turned against her or had always been against her, that there was no place in Heaven for her. I only know this because I happened upon her journal one day, quite by accident. I asked the Minister here to speak to her and thought her a little happier, but one day she came home in a strange state and could not rise from her bed for the next week. I began to fear that something might have passed between them, because he left for another parish shortly afterwards. If you could just reassure me, as soon as it's definite, that she's safe in body, I might rest again. Of course, I hope that I am wrong about everything.*

I was so furious that I was determined not to reply, could hardly believe that Charlotte would violate Anne's privacy in that way, and was now asking me to spy on her too. But when, several weeks later, I saw Anne going to the drawer for her monthly rags, I relented, sending the briefest of notes with the news Charlotte wanted. Her letters home became less frequent after that, and when she did write her mood seemed depressed. There was rarely time to visit Ellen Nussey or Mary Taylor, she complained, though her old friends often invited her, and Miss Wooler encouraged her to take a holiday. But how was that possible when she must work harder, try harder all the time? Once, with a few minutes to herself before bed, she'd sat in the schoolroom looking out over the garden in the shadows of dusk. She'd begun to imagine a scene in which the Duke of Zamorna—the latest title bestowed upon her old hero,

Wellington—had discovered a plot to overthrow him, was so happy to be immersed in Angria that she fell into a reverie. Miss Wooler, coming in to see who was sitting alone in the dark, had to speak several times before Charlotte registered her presence. Her next letter was brief. She'd handed in her notice, was coming home. *I think a governess position in a good family would suit me better*, she wrote. *Here I seem to be indispensable and yet invisible all at the same time. I can't write even a line during term—there is barely a minute in any day to call my own. Sometimes I think that the girls are unnaturally stupid, take pleasure in resisting the least bit of knowledge I try to impart. I almost come to loathe them.*

Just before Christmas, Tabby Aykroyd slipped on some ice on Main Street, shattering her leg so badly that the doctor said she could not work until it was completely mended. Anne and I volunteered to help with the housework, having already agreed between us that we didn't like the idea of a stranger coming in to replace Tabby. Aunt was against it, of course, but since young Martha Brown, the sexton's daughter, was unable to help until the New Year, and Aunt could not manage by herself, there was no other choice. I took on the heavier, dirtier tasks, as well as most of the cooking, and was surprised to find that the repetitive, mundane nature of the work allowed my thoughts to wander in new ways. As I pumped water, blacked the fireplaces, or scrubbed vegetables, I would find a solution to a Gondal problem without even trying. When Charlotte arrived home, she offered to help with the ironing and promptly burnt holes in one of the sheets and in the second-best tablecloth. After that she declared herself in need of a proper holiday and immersed herself in her writing, barely hearing or seeing as I stoked the fire or set the dining room table around her.

I was sweeping the hallway one morning, when Branwell came flying out of Papa's study, straight into the little pile of ivy leaves and drying berries I'd accumulated from taking down the Christmas greenery. 'Where's Charlotte?' I pointed him towards the dining room, not needing to check. He stayed a moment. 'I'm not bothering with Europe anymore. My teacher thinks I'm good enough to set up my own studio right now and shouldn't waste my time.' He practised a couple of dance steps along the hallway for my benefit. 'Papa's agreed. I should be able to get the painting done before I go though, if you'll only sit still for five minutes.' He twirled again, sending dust flying.

That evening, he herded us around the dining room table so that he could finish the portrait he'd started painting last year and only recently resumed. I hadn't wanted to sit for it on either occasion, but Charlotte had insisted, though she knew that modelling made me bad-tempered for want of movement and the annoyance of being scrutinised so closely. Branwell painted at his usual great rate, talking all the time about the wonders of Bradford where he planned to open his studio: the artistic community already established there, the recitals and plays he would attend, the galleries and concert halls in easy travelling distance. He might have been moving to Renaissance Florence, Athens in the age of Pericles, remarked Charlotte, to listen to him.

Notwithstanding the energy of its execution, I thought the portrait bad. It had a flat, leaden quality, the paint lying on the canvas like a body on the slab. I watched Branwell clearing away his things when he'd finished and thought that if I were him, I would not paint sedate portraits or copies of other people's landscapes for anything. I would use my brush to forge ridges and swirls, cloughs and moortops, becks and standing stones, the earth turning beneath my feet, my knife cleaving through pure colour. He had managed to capture an aspect of Anne though: the pursed-up look she'd had since returning from Roe Head, her mouth tight as a flower-bud, as though she feared something catastrophic might burst from her lips.

The morning after Branwell left for Bradford, Charlotte was pale and silent at breakfast, barely touching her plate.

'Is Ellen well?' Anne asked. Having finished reading a letter, Charlotte was now holding it in a strange manner, at arm's length and with her face turned away. 'Or is it from Mary?'

'It's not from either of them.' Charlotte lay down the letter by her plate. Her attempt at a smile only emphasised her misery. 'It is from Robert Southey. I wrote to him.'

'Southey?' I said. 'Not the Poet Laureate?'

Charlotte shook her head violently as if trying to loosen it from her torso. 'I wish I'd never—I don't know what I was thinking.' A flush was seeping up her neck.

'What did he say?' I asked. 'Surely, he wasn't impolite to an admirer?'

'Not in the least,' said Charlotte. 'That is the worst of it! I'd rather he'd not replied at all. I sent him some poems I'd written.' She squeezed her eyes shut. 'It was a plan that Branwell and I agreed for our writing before he went away. He was to go on submitting work to *Blackwood's Magazine*, and write to Wordsworth, while I . . . Oh, I can't believe I had the temerity—'

'Your Angrian poems?' I found it hard to conceive that she would share those with anyone, let alone a poet of Southey's stature.

'It's only the opinion of one man,' said Anne. She placed a hand on Charlotte's arm.

'It is *Southey*!' Charlotte's voice catching in her throat. 'As a matter of fact he was kind about my writing.' She picked up the letter again and turned over a page. 'He says I have the faculty of verse.'

'Well, that's something!' In the drear morning light, Anne looked ethereal, delicately pretty.

'The point of his letter is to warn me of the danger to myself.'

'What can he mean?' I craned to look at the letter for myself. 'Has Wordsworth responded to Branwell?' How strange to say those two names in juxtaposition, like peering through a chink in a wall—never-before noticed—to discover a new land lying on the other side.

'He hasn't sent it yet,' said Charlotte. 'I think he was counting on a reply from *Blackwood's* first, but they never do respond, no matter how many times he submits to them. You know how Branwell is though, downcast for an hour and then he's hatched the next plan. He's already sent verses to a few of the newspapers.'

'It's probably not as discouraging as you first thought,' said Anne.

Charlotte looked down at the pages, then found what she was seeking. '"Write poetry for its own sake . . . Not with a view to celebrity."'

'That's not so . . .'

She raised her voice over Anne's. '"Literature cannot be the business of a woman's life."' She dropped the pages to the table with an air of finality.

'I don't agree,' I said. 'What of Mary Shelley . . . Miss Austen?'

'Miss Austen didn't have to earn her own living, Emily. Southey's point, and he's quite right, is that someone in my position can't afford to indulge their love of writing. He says it is an unhealthy distraction from reality. Papa said much the same to me the other day. Stupidly, I told him I'd rather spend every day writing than go back to teaching oafish children.'

'Not all of us were oafs,' said Anne, with a smile.

'Anyway, I should be applying for a new position. We all—' She stopped herself just in time, her eyes flicking away from me.

'Why should Southey's word be final?' I said, too intrigued by what she had done to feel the familiar flush of humiliation when Roe Head was mentioned. 'He's just a man, like any other. Papa too, though he means well.'

Charlotte pushed her chair back from the table, and then stuffed Southey's letter into its envelope. 'Oh, how much easier to have been born a man, even a poor one! Think of the free-dom Branwell has compared with us, with a million professions to choose from! I used to think teaching a noble career, but one is no more than a workhorse, barely tolerated.'

'If you were to find an agreeable family though,' said Anne. 'It must be easier to make a difference with a small number of children than an entire class.'

'True,' I said. 'They can be horrible *en masse*.' I thought of the hordes of children at Sunday School. 'Yet almost human individually.' I smiled to myself, feeling unaccountably light-hearted. Robert Southey knew nothing of me, had barely acknowledged my sister, but in that moment I felt a sense of liberty and recklessness, ambition even, that defied everything the great man had counselled.

It rained persistently. We woke each day to a steady thrum, the rush of water down the gutters and then the wind would get up, begin to squall testily around the house. By midday the rain thrashed against the windows and the sky pushed down on the hills with a look of permanency.

'The usual,' said Charlotte, blinking up at me every time I asked what she was working on. In her writing desk I could see pages and pages of new script. Scattered among them were the numerous sketches she'd made of the Duke of Zamorna, his patrician profile emerging from the constraints of his military costume, black eyes, dark, foppish curls. When not writing, she wandered round the house, unable to settle to any other task, finding advertisements in the newspaper and then despairing that none of the positions were suitable. This new energy—which seemed to spring from a kind of concentrated misery—began to affect me also. I grew restless, dissatisfied with myself when I had been perfectly happy before. I attacked the domestic chores as though they were the source of the problem, and they distracted me for a few hours, but every time I tried to settle to Gondal work, I found it impossible to keep my mind on the narrative. I felt hemmed in by my own self, newly shamed by my failure at Roe Head. One afternoon, I picked up a newspaper which Charlotte had left open at the advertisements page. That evening, I stayed up later than everyone else to write a number of letters, brief and taciturn even by my standards, almost certain that no-one would respond. When, just a week later, a reply came for me, I opened it at the breakfast table, in front of Aunt and my sisters. The same reckless impulse made me hand over the letter as soon as I finished reading it.

'You're nearly twenty years old, Emily,' said Aunt, meaning that I ought to have found a suitable way to earn a living before now. Meaning that life was hard for everyone.

'Will you take it?' said Anne. The concern in her eyes frightened me.

'I don't know.' I found myself in a panic. 'It's not for a few months yet.' I thought of Augusta Almeda who could not be written in any given direction, her adventures spilling over the page just as they pleased. Flushed with life, my heroine strode through her world like a Titan, remaking it to fit her desires, caring only for herself.

'Look at the salary!' said, Charlotte, running her eye over the pages. She dropped the letter on the table. 'You absolutely must.'

The moon was high, flooding the room with an unsettling wash of light, and sleep would not come. I heard the clock chime midnight and then one o'clock before I felt that first sinking towards unconsciousness, then was jolted awake by a noise. Charlotte lay with her back to me on the far side of the bed. I thought her asleep, dreaming scenes that made her tremble in fear, was about to wake her when I heard her whisper 'Zamorna!' I knew all there was to know about men and women—had seen the pictures that Branwell kept underneath

his mattress, which shocked and excited me at the same time—
but I'd thought this other thing private to me, descending only
when night rolled down from the moors and the wind groaned
around the house, knew only that it was the same impulse that
had driven me to clamber down the hillside and into the Fairy
Cave, though I had not understood why at the time. Dark eyes
watching me from the path side. The boy now a man. Was Anne
in its thrall too? I thought of her prayers at bedtime, soft and
fervent, hands clasped to her breast. Praying was not the same
thing at all, and yet watching her, it seemed so. And what if
Aunt, even now . . . I turned away from Charlotte and covered
my ears with my pillow, forced my eyes to close.

There was nothing truly bad about the months I spent teaching at Miss Patchett's School for Girls. Unlike Charlotte, I had no fear of standing before a class to deliver a lesson, my professional status acted as a shield to my inner existence, requiring me to give nothing of myself away. My voice remained low, but it was firm, carrying to the back of the room with the authority of knowledge, which was not surprising when the curriculum was so unchallenging. I did not warm to my pupils, nor they to me, but I'd not left home seeking friendship and a certain chilliness in the classroom was useful for maintaining order. The other teachers were well-established at the school and took little notice of my arrival, other than to ensure that this newest member of staff should take on all the out-of-hours supervision of the girls. Within a week of arriving at the school, which was situated at Law Hill, near Halifax, I understood that this was to be a joyless, thankless existence, but for the first time in my life I was earning a wage and it soon became clear, even to the exacting Miss Patchett, that I was capable of hauling her pupils if not to intellectual enlightenment, at least to somewhere in its general vicinity. If there was no room for happiness in this world, no middle-ground between the wild freedom of childhood and the weight of adult responsibility, then I told myself I must become used to that. Still, my heart leapt when a letter arrived from Anne. She'd also started her first job, as a governess at a place called Blake Hall.

I was lost in the beginning, but the family made much of my arrival and the house is very comfortable. The children are good at heart though a little too high-spirited. I am not to punish them directly if they misbehave but must instead report the matter to Mrs. Ingham so that she can discipline them herself. I thought this a good arrangement at first, since harshness doesn't come naturally to me. The difficulty is that they are naughty from the moment they wake until after their bedtime and I cannot trouble Mrs. Ingham all day long without seeming incompetent. You would lose patience with them in an instant—I do not have the courage. Please don't tell Charlotte—I know she believes governess work is far less arduous than the classroom, yet it doesn't seem so to me. Dearest Emily, I am determined to succeed! There is little time to write and I'm afraid the poor Gondals are quite neglected . . . I hope you are finding time to visit them often.

The months ground on. I rose at daybreak, spent all day teaching, stayed up until eleven at night, preparing lessons or on duty, and there was nothing truly wrong except this: how is a soul to survive when there is not an hour in the day to walk alone and breathe the green air of the distant woods; when the seasons turn and you may only stand at the schoolroom window, like an insect caught in a jar; when every hour is allotted from dawn till dusk, the lessons so simple that they barely tax the brain to deliver them? From the hour of waking until I fell into bed, there was barely a minute to write a letter home, to think or to dream. The school had its own music room equipped with a piano—a solid instrument, built of dark wood and quite unlike the little cabinet piano at home. I would have liked to learn its ways, to feel out its character, but there was no time to find solace there. I lavished too much attention on an undernourished little mutt belonging to the housekeeper, saving half of my meals to feed him.

Anne wrote again, her normally neat handwriting spilling over the page:

I'm so worried—this morning, the children would not stay in their seats during lessons but kept running to the window to see if their parents were returning from their trip to London, though they are not due back until tomorrow. I pleaded with them, threatened them with punishment. At first, they ignored me completely, and then they made a game out of it, cupping their hands to their ears each time I spoke and looking around the room and then at one another in puzzlement, as if they'd heard only a mouse squeak. This only stopped when they began arguing about who ought to receive the best gift from London and the little girl lost her temper and flung her Bible at her brother—who'd gone back to watching for his parents at the window—tearing a page right across. I did a terrible thing then. I locked the nursery door and tied them both to their chairs with the cords from their dressing gowns, paid no attention to their crying and threats for the rest of the lesson, even when the little boy upset his chair in his effort to free himself. I merely righted him and kept on with my teaching. I didn't free them until the gong rang for dinner when they ran sobbing from the room. They were quite unrepentant and are sure to tell their mother as soon as she returns, which means I will be dismissed, or at least severely reprimanded. I will accept any punishment that comes my way; am afraid only of myself. I have always abhorred violence, but when I unloosed the little boy, I saw that his wrists were raw from where I'd drawn the cord so tightly. Oh Emily, I so wanted to be like a gentle Mamma to my charges, for them to obey me out of love, and never to fear me—I must go now—I hear the pair of them calling for me from the hallway—I long for your company—for home.

I could not sleep that night for thinking first of Anne, and then of Charlotte who was soon to take up a governess position herself. When sleep finally came I dreamt I was running through open countryside in the darkness, bare feet moving through the bog grass. I waded through streams, clambered up steep hillsides, reached the summit of a rocky peak just as the moon slid out from behind a cloud. Then I saw that I was high on the moors above home, could just make out the shape of the village in the valley below. I started to run faster then, so fast that I knew that I must stumble at any moment. Then I woke in the darkness of my little room to one side of the main school dormitory and lay there so grief-stricken that I could not breathe. I felt the blackness of night pushing down on my chest, compressing me, pushing me into a smaller and smaller space until I felt I must collapse in upon myself. The glass in the round window above the end of my bed bulged towards me like a giant eyeball. I wanted it to implode, for the shards to lodge in my flesh, to pierce me like a saint. I went down to the garden in my nightgown, with my feet bare, and stayed there till dawn, a cold wind whipping the sky to a curdled, pink mass, the dew trembling precariously from each blade of grass. Birds screeched from the shadowy branches, and it sounded like the beginning of madness. I returned to my room and lay down on my bed. Sleep came as dark as death and when the morning bell rang, I could no longer speak.

I went home and nobody asked me why. It would have been easier if someone had shouted at me, berated me for my weakness, anything but the resignation in Papa's eyes, Aunt saying nothing, just shaking her head and going up to her room. I went to the dining room and lay down on the floor between the fireplace and the window. The next morning, when I tried to leave the house, terror rose in my throat the minute I was out of sight of those solid walls. I retreated, closing the door behind me, tongue turned to stone.

I was proud of Anne's efforts, harboured a secret hatred for those Ingham children and their mother. She remained resolute in all her letters but less than nine months after she'd left, she returned home. In a shaking voice, she explained that she'd been dismissed from Blake Hall for being unable to control the children.

'What did Mrs. Ingham expect?' said Charlotte, sympathetic for once. She had been home herself since the autumn, her own post having been a temporary one. 'I've come to see that there is a class of women who are all good-breeding and kindness on the surface, but with something low in their characters which is only exposed when they deal with those they consider their inferiors. At least teachers are held in some esteem and their work is circumscribed. A governess is a nothing! One is expected to shoulder all responsibility, to be grateful for any task that the rest of the household finds unpalatable, yet with no power. It's as well you've never thought of it for yourself, Emily.' She looked at me. 'You'd never stand it.'

'I don't believe it was ill breeding on Mrs. Ingham's part,' said Anne, drawing her fine brows together though her expression remained equable. She took out her sewing box. 'More a wish to protect her children from any kind of unpleasantness. She lost two children in infancy and another two before they were born, so perhaps it is to be expected.'

'It will do her other children no service to grow up without discipline or constraint,' Charlotte persisted. 'You might have found a way to communicate that to their mother.'

'In which case she would have been dismissed at an earlier stage still,' I said. 'You cannot blame Anne for Mrs. Ingham's poor behaviour.'

My instinct to defend Anne was sharpened by Charlotte's assertion about what I could or could not stand. She barely noticed the work I did around the house now that Tabby was growing older and less able to manage. Even with young Martha Brown to help me, there was plenty to do, but unsalaried labour had no value in Charlotte's eyes. And I didn't believe for a minute that she would have found the courage, in Anne's position, to stand up to an employer herself. Her own letters home had started out cheerfully enough but were soon full of complaints about the isolation of her position, a lone figure accepted by neither family nor the other servants.

'I will do better in future,' said Anne. She bent to give Keeper a tentative pat and then thought better of it. He'd been with us for eight months now, was yet to decide if this new arrival was family or not.

Keeper's mother had been lying on the floor of the barn with a resigned look on her face, front legs splayed to keep her balance while her puppies squirmed and wriggled, pushing their wrinkled black snouts against her belly. The farmer's hand had closed around a puppy that was still nudging for a place. It had a sweet, scrunched face, made no protest when it found itself in the air, just licked the farmer's hand with a tongue as pink as the hams in Mr. Grieve's shop window.

I shook my head, then pointed to the puppy who'd twice displaced this one. He was head-deep now, suckling at his mother, legs scrabbling to keep off his siblings. When the farmer pulled him away, this second puppy flung open its paws in protest, back legs immediately flailing. He was the colour of a biscuit, with soft black ears and black folds around his muzzle and above his eyes so that he appeared to be scowling.

'See how angry he is, Papa,' I'd laughed, as the farmer handed him to me. I knew right away that this puppy would never settle in my arms. Small as he was, I had to keep shifting him from one hand to the other to keep a grip on him. I could feel the warmth of milk in his belly, the thud of his heart through his stocky little body.

'Mastiffs, they are.' The farmer could not make up his mind to it, on the one hand wanting to be rid of the puppies yet unsure if this was the right kind of dog for a young lady. Probably, he was picturing some foolish lap dog with snappable bones.

'He'll be tame for me,' I said, my tongue working perfectly well for once, though I barely knew the farmer. With his brown, weathered face and knotty hands he was more tree than man. I let the puppy down onto the ground. He leapt at my ankles, attacked the laces of my boots. 'I shall call him Keeper.'

From the beginning, Keeper followed me everywhere, even out to the privy where he barked and threw himself repeatedly at the door until I came out. He raced up and down the stairs, skidded across the hallway, got under Tabby's feet as she worked, tugged at the ironing, chewed the table legs, urinated on a pile of laundry. He paused only to gulp down the scraps I prepared for him first thing in the morning and each evening. The only thing that quietened him was the sound of the piano. Whenever I played, he would sit beside the stool or stretch out with his nose to the rug, snoring to himself, the music soothing the wildness in him. Keeper heeded nobody's voice but mine, barely turned his head when anyone else attempted an order.

'Emily, will you take the little divil out!' Tabby would say, when he'd drooled over the kitchen floor, left footprints over the newly washed front doorstep. At first, I walked him only to Chapel Field and back, but soon he grew stronger, his shoulders and torso broadening into a slab of solid flesh. Strangers were wary of him, thought twice before bending down to pat his bony head. By the time he was a few months old, even Aunt conceded that no-one was likely to bother me with such a companion by my side. We walked in all weathers and when we stopped to rest on one rare sunny day, I drew him with his nose buried in the grass, chin resting on his paw, trying to capture the wrinkles of his shoulders, the subtle changes of tone in his coat, from sand to ripened wheat to black. Together, we sought out the highest reaches of the moors, where the sparse dwellings were empty, half in ruin, weeds clambering up the walls as the earth reclaimed the space, Keeper scrabbling on ahead, paws slipping and sliding on damp stones, his brass collar glinting round his thick neck. Returning to circle me, gone again. It was hard to know whether he was reassuring me or rounding up the sole member of his flock. The only people we ever encountered were travellers taking some old route across the hills, packs loaded on their backs, or the occasional hill-farmer—men with faces that were older than their bodies, half-hidden by shaggy beards. Dressed in indeterminate shades of mud and bark and leaf, they'd emerge, silent, eyeing me a little too long for comfort. But with Keeper by my side, I could never be afraid. Like Diana with her hounds, we would tear to pieces any foolish Actaeon!

Eventually, Anne found another position, as governess to the children of a Reverend Edmund Robinson at Thorp Green, which was near York. At first, she wrote of new difficulties—there were four children in her care, and she had never lived anywhere so grand or so far from home—but to my relief, it soon became clear that she was beginning to win her charges over. Charlotte said little in response to Anne's news, but I noticed her searching the newspaper advertisements again. Around the same time, Branwell wrote to say that the portrait studio had been a mistake: there were too many other artists already established in the Bradford area. He informed us that he'd taken a job as tutor to a family named Postlethwaite in

Cumbria, so it came as a surprise, just a month or so later, to hear his voice in the hallway one afternoon when Charlotte was reading, and I was busy hemming sheets.

'It's nothing to concern yourselves with,' he told us a little later, jabbing at the fire with a poker and causing it to flare up. 'Why are you huddled round a fire on a day like this? The position did not suit me, that is all. Mr. Postlethwaite and I had a discussion and came to a mutual agreement. There was little point in delaying after that. A bit of local trouble too.' Another jab at the fire. 'Besides, I'm not sure tutoring is the way to support my writing. You can't imagine how many hours in the day were devoted to giving or preparing lessons.'

'I was a governess,' Charlotte reminded him.

Just that morning she'd told me that she'd been offered another position, this time at Rawdon, which was situated near Leeds.

'You hate being a governess,' I'd said when she came to find me in the yard. I began beating the study rug harder to drive out the dust.

'I didn't like living with those people. This new family may be quite different.' Charlotte sneezed and took a few paces back. 'There are no teaching positions at present, and I must begin something.'

I'd thought about reminding her that she didn't enjoy teaching either, then wondered at the strange kind of world we inhabited, where all our personal talents and idiosyncrasies, our particular abhorrences or attachments, must be channelled into one of these two occupations; where we must be wrenched from the home we loved in order to earn the sparsest of incomes.

'As I've explained to Papa,' Branwell said now, 'I've a much better scheme in place. They need good people for the new Manchester and Leeds railway line. I've already applied for a post at Sowerby Bridge.'

'As a railway clerk?'

'I'll be in charge of my own affairs for once—I'm too old to be running around to another man's bidding—and the salary is surprisingly good too. I'll have peace and quiet when I want it, with Halifax just down the line when I need company—it's pioneering work, when you come to think of it!' He smacked his hand on the table in sudden excitement, then paused for breath.

Charlotte picked up her book. 'Your classical studies will prove remarkably useful, I'm sure.' Then: 'It is a living, I suppose.'

W hat do you think I have?' said Charlotte hurrying into the kitchen. Without stopping to take off her shawl, she dropped a package on the table. My hands were thick with pastry dough, so she opened the package herself and propped one of the cards it contained against the mixing bowl, so that I might read it without touching.

The Misses Brontë's Establishment
FOR
THE BOARD AND EDUCATION
OF A LIMITED NUMBER OF
YOUNG LADIES,
THE PARSONAGE, HAWORTH,
NEAR BRADFORD.

Terms.

	£. s. d.		
BOARD AND EDUCATION, including Writing, Arithmetic, History, Grammar, Geography, and Needle Work, per Annum	35	0	0
French German each per quarter Latin	1	1	0
Music Drawing each per quarter	1	1	0
Use of Piano Forte, per Quarter,	0	5	0
Washing, per Quarter,	0	15	0

Each Young Lady to be provided with One Pair of Sheets, Pillow Cases, Four Towels, a Dessert and a Tea spoon.

A Quarter's Notice, or a Quarter's Board is required previous to the Removal of a Pupil.

'I had Mr. Greenwood make them up for us,' said Charlotte. It was difficult to know if the hectic colour in her face came from excitement, or from the brutal wind that had been howling around the house for the last two days, though it was the middle of July. 'We must ask everyone we know to distribute them. I'll write to Ellen before I go back. Mary Taylor too. I've kept the fees low because we are so remote.'

'Any sensible parent would think that an advantage,' I said. I gave the pastry a quarter turn and dusted the rolling pin with more flour. On the range, the meat for my pie was simmering gently. 'The air is healthier here.'

'The important thing is to attract some pupils in the first instance,' said Charlotte, barely listening. Her thoughts were running ahead of her, into the future. 'Once we've some income, we might think about extending the house. We can always increase our prices later.'

The idea had come to her at Whitsun when she and Anne were home for a holiday, but she'd had no time to put it into action until now.

'Anne and I might manage most of the teaching,' she'd explained, the night before the two of them were due to return to work. 'We'll need to make some alterations, of course. And we must persuade Aunt. None of it can happen without her investment and you know how careful she is with money.' The caution in her words belied her excitement. She'd circled the dining room table twice, then darted to the window and back again, a skittish marionette. It was a long time since I had seen her so animated.

'A school of our own,' said Anne, a gentle fire igniting in her eyes. Her face was drawn, and she was too thin. She insisted that her employers treated her with kindness and affection, but I knew what it cost her to live so far from home and among strangers. Even more so since the arrival in Haworth of William Weightman, the only one of Papa's curates we'd ever been able to tolerate. Within days of taking up residence, William had become a friend to all. He was charming and attentive to each one of us—even I managed to exchange a word or two with him, and, like everyone else was half in love with his beauty— but more than once I'd caught him gazing at Anne on her visits home, noticed the flush on her cheeks as she perceived this.

'Branwell seems remarkably settled at his little station so we might use his room,' Charlotte went on. 'Emily, you might give a few hours a week to help with music lessons, but the house will not run without your direction, certainly not if Aunt ever decides to go home to Penzance.'

I nodded, not yet ready to speak. The thought of filling the parsonage with chattering schoolgirls was abhorrent, but I could see that Charlotte's scheme had advantages: the opportunity to make decisions for ourselves, the three of us living and working together, here in our own home, for the foreseeable future. With Martha growing more capable by the day and Charlotte, Branwell and Anne all working, it was becoming harder to defend my own lack of paid employment, even to myself. The thought of it had begun to mar the pleasure of my daily walks, even finding its way into my dreams of Gondal which had become full of failed expeditions and disastrous schemes, prisoners racked with guilt for their misdoings. I'd spent the last few weeks trying to find a new story for Rosina, the wife that Julius had abandoned when he fell in love Geraldine Sidonia, the mother of Augusta Almeda. I wanted Rosina to take a lover from the neighbouring island of Gaaldine, for the two of them to plot Julius's assassination, but she couldn't seem to stop feeling useless and sorry for herself.

'I shall carry on working for a while longer,' said Charlotte. 'If I can bear it. You too, Anne, so that we can save as much as possible before we open.'

'I could teach drawing as well,' I'd said, a rare expansiveness coming over me. I might not mind the company of a child or two on an occasional walk either, so long as they had eyes and ears to notice what was around them and did not pester Keeper or expect me to talk. 'What will Papa think about it? You know how he hates his routine to be disturbed.'

'I will deal with Papa,' said Charlotte, her voice ringing like an axe on stone.

Within a day, she had persuaded Papa of our plan and Aunt had agreed to invest in our Parsonage School.

'It was remarkably easy,' she said. 'I bowed to Aunt's good judgement in all matters and then reminded her of the need for clean sea air and proper society in one's old age. All these years of being bound to Haworth.'

'You really think she'll go home?' said Anne, looking troubled. We were silent for a moment. Though we teased Aunt for her fussy, exacting ways, her little snobberies and affectations, she had been part of our lives forever. It was hard to imagine this household carrying on without her.

Now, with a means to advertise our school, the plan began to feel possible. We hurried to send the cards to everyone we knew before Charlotte and Anne returned to work. The list was not extensive, but Ellen wrote to say she had pressed the information on all her acquaintances, and Reverend and Mrs. Franks promised to spread the news among their circles. Even Miss Wooler said that she would recommend us to any family unable to afford the fees at Roe Head, which was remarkably generous—she had once hoped Charlotte would return there to take up the Head Teacher position. I received a couple of enquiries in the post, and replied by return, but nothing came of these. Autumn passed in a flurry of ochre and russet and Charlotte's letters from Rawdon grew despondent.

We should have fixed on another location. I thought of Bridlington at first, somewhere with more life. It's no surprise that families would think twice about sending their daughters to such a lonely little spot. Think how bleak it is in wintertime.

It's hardly lonely, I replied, in the briefest of notes. If anything the village was too crowded, the streets and alleyways teeming with men, women and children on their way to and from the mills every morning and evening, carts rattling up and down Main Street all day long, the horses straining at the steep incline, thud-thud as the dray wagon was unloaded, pink and white carcasses being shouldered into the butcher's, the long, complaining queues for the water pump, for the public privy. *And I'm not moving to Bridlington.*

You have been too long at home, wrote Charlotte. *Can see no fault in it.*

Her next few letters were mainly about her dissatisfaction with her employer, Mrs. White, who seemed at one moment to offer friendship, as though the two of them were almost equals, and the next to treat my sister with more contempt than if she were the lowest of scullery maids. She was an intolerable woman, Charlotte said, of very little breeding. She enclosed a page from a letter that Mary Taylor had written to her. Though the death of Mary's father the previous year had left the family with some financial difficulties, Charlotte's old schoolfriend had managed to find enough money to travel in Europe. She wrote that she and her little sister Martha were now attending a school in Belgium, for the purpose of improving their French and learning some German. She had not quite settled on teaching as a career, she wrote, was even looking into the notion of emigrating to New Zealand where, apparently, opportunities were less codified, especially for women.

I tucked the page away in Charlotte's writing desk for when she returned home, which was sooner than expected. She arrived late one evening in early December and went straight to bed, citing one of her headaches. It seemed that Mr. and Mrs. White had decided to take a week's holiday in York and had not required her presence. In the days that followed, her mood remained subdued. She did not once speak of our school plans, and I suspected she was working herself into a depression or imagined state of ill-health. If Anne had been home, she would have tried to coax her out of such self-imposed misery, but I had long since learned that these moods lifted eventually and of their own accord, requiring no intervention from me. An invitation from Ellen to stay at Brookroyd over Christmas could cure all of Charlotte's complaints in a moment.

'I can read for half an hour at most, and only then in full daylight,' she announced one afternoon, throwing aside a copy of *The Lyrical Ballads* I'd borrowed from the circulating library in Keighley. 'If I carry on like this, I shall lose my eyesight altogether!'

'It's gloomy today,' I said. I glanced up from my drawing, a sketch of a blackbird for Martha Brown who was fond of creatures.

'I have seen so little of the world,' she said, flicking at the spine of the book. 'How strange we must seem to God, looking down on us. The earth He gave us stretches in all directions, is full of riches, yet all we do is run around in the same little circles, like poor little mice, scratching an existence.' Her gaze shifted. Outside, the sky was an impenetrable grey, the rain coming in sullen slaps against the dining room window. 'Every day the same hills, the same valleys.'

'The bad weather is passing,' I said. 'You'll feel better by tomorrow. Perhaps we will receive news of our very first pupil.'

'Emily.'

'Yes?'

'I have a different plan.'

PART 2

Ostend was clean air and wide beaches backed by sand dunes. The town itself had an open, sprightly air and though it was winter time and other visitors were sparse, the sun shone and the two days we spent there felt like a holiday. But on the morning that we left, there was an icy chill in the air and the early coach was crowded.

'There are no hills,' I said to Charlotte. I stared out at countryside as flat and unyielding as my mood. Papa was already asleep in the corner of the carriage, his phrasebook open on his lap.

'Not in this part of the country.' Before we'd left home, Charlotte had read everything she could find about Belgium. 'A lot of this coastal land was reclaimed from the sea. But there are hills further south apparently, in the Ardennes region.'

'The forest is beautiful there,' said Mary, then carried on reading, knowing better than to expect a response from me.

Though Mary was accompanying us to Brussels, our destination was not the Château de Koekelberg, where she and her younger sister Martha were studying. The fees there were too expensive for us, and even Charlotte's more economical scheme had required backing. I'd seen the letter she'd sent to Aunt, persuading her to invest in this latest plan. It was artful, full of praise for Aunt's sound business sense:

You always like to use your money to the best advantage . . . you are not fond of making shabby purchases . . . when you do confer a favour it is often done in style . . .

The thrust of Charlotte's argument had been that a period of study abroad would give the two of us a thorough grounding in French, as well as an opportunity to learn German and possibly even Italian. With these accomplishments we would be far more likely to attract pupils to our little school. This was not, she'd assured Aunt, a notion she had happened upon herself, rather one that had been pressed upon her by those with greater knowledge of such matters.

My friends recommend me . . . if I desire to secure permanent success . . . by hook or by crook . . .

Knowing that Aunt was unlikely to fund all three of us, Charlotte had proposed that Anne should remain in her well-paid employment at Thorp Green for the time being. If all went well, she might benefit from the same trip later. Charlotte had already written to Mary to ask if she knew of any teaching establishments less expensive than the Château de Koekelberg; had also applied to a Mrs. Jenkins, the wife of the British consul in Brussels, for similar advice. By the time Aunt replied to her at Rawdon, suggesting that she might make some enquiries, Charlotte had already settled upon the *Pensionnat Héger*, an establishment situated in the old quarter of Brussels. Which was why, at the age of twenty-four years, I found myself on the wrong side of the North Sea and on my way to school again.

Man didn't really belong here, Charlotte went on, craning round me to look out of the coach window. The inhabitants must work day and night to hold back the sea. I made no reply. It was not that I'd expected Belgium to look like home precisely, but I'd never imagined a place as alien as this, with its flat brown fields, the slack-watered dikes threading round their edges in neat lines, the uniformity of the embankments. Charlotte was still talking, insisting that it was a matter of great ingenuity, this reclaiming of the land, but to my eye there was something deadened about the resulting landscape. Nature had been defied, robbed of its true purpose, resulting in this place

that belonged to neither sea nor man. A family at work in a
field lifted their heads as our coach passed, pausing their labour
for a moment. In the greyish light their faces had a blank, silty
quality, as if, half-formed, they'd only just raised themselves out
of one of the muddy dikes. Before we'd come away, Papa had
traced our route across the pages of the atlas in his study. Now I
pictured myself being nudged along that imaginary line, further
and further from home. Once, when I was small, I'd hacked an
E into surface of the dining room table, earned a severe punishment from Aunt who'd thought it the behaviour of a savage.
Even now I could not explain why I had done it, but I remembered the feeling: it was the same one I had when my feet carved
their own pathways through the moorland heather. *I am here.* I
thought of Keeper, the sorrowful folds of his doggy face as he'd
followed me to the end of Parsonage Lane and I was tempted
to throw myself from this coach. I was more at sea here, in this
carriage packed as tightly as a coffin, than in all the hours spent
on the crossing to Ostend. And yet here was Charlotte sitting
across from me in the grip of some strange energy, almost trembling with excitement at the sight of this new world.

Before we'd come away, she'd shown me the rest of Mary's
letter, the words which had proved the catalyst for this whole
journey. It had been written with Mary's customary directness,
full of sharp observations and abrupt questions for Charlotte.

*What do you plan to do if this school of yours doesn't work
out? You surely won't try for another governess position? It is
plain that you do not have the constitution for it. But it is no
good, my dear Charlotte, languishing at home either. Knowing
you as I do, I can firmly say that your spirits will never lift until you've made the world take notice of you in some way. You
cannot bear to be overlooked, underestimated. These months of
travel have opened my eyes and I am now determined to gain my
independence even if that means travelling to the other side of the
world. I will not be reliant on another to sustain me in this life*

*or forced to choose between teaching or some wretched governess
position. Why should I be constrained by England and English
ways?*

The coach jolted over a pothole, nearly dislodging Charlotte
from her seat. I felt a sudden pang of tenderness for her: almost certainly she would have one of her bilious headaches by
nightfall.

Our first few days in Brussels were spent exploring the wide,
verdant avenues of the *Haut-Ville* with Papa, admiring the gra-
cious mansions of the rich that lined them, the expensive-looking
shops and restaurants with plate-glass windows and scalloped
canopies. At the heart of this quarter of the city was *Parc de
Bruxelles*, its cool green walkways, bandstand, and smart cafes a world away from the *Basse-Ville,* the old part of the city
which lay just beneath it, which was disordered and pungent by
comparison, streets so narrow that they excluded the sunlight,
alleys that led nowhere, hawkers crouched over their wares before flat-fronted houses with stepped gables, squares crammed
with second-hand shops and tiny taverns selling dark beer and
little plates of fried food. The old town was a spider's web that
had been torn to shreds and then reformed in some haphazard,
half-remembered way, while for all its spaciousness the *Haut-
Ville* had a toy-like air about it, everyone moving in courteous,
pre-agreed patterns, English voices to be heard as often as
French or Dutch.

The *Pensionnat Héger*, where we were to study, was a newish
building of unremarkable design, in an ancient part of the city
just beneath this oasis for the leisured classes. The *Haut-Ville*
could be reached by a steep flight of steps almost opposite the
entrance to the school building, but you would not guess its
presence from here. The whole of *Rue d'Isabelle* had a subter-
ranean quality, like a recently excavated site. At the entrance to
the *Pensionnat*, we were greeted by a servant and then taken to

the living quarters of Madame *Héger*, a dark-haired handsome woman who was trailed by a number of small children.

'Your girls will be my only English pupils this year,' she told Papa over coffee and miniature cakes decorated with delicately feathered icing. She spoke English with the precision of a foreigner, notwithstanding her heavy accent. 'Mademoiselle Charlotte wrote that she is already fluent in French. Emily too.' I felt her looking at me, seeking a response.

'My sister doesn't speak,' said Charlotte hurriedly. 'I think I mentioned in my letter? Only to family, or people she knows very well.' Whatever Charlotte had written, it was clear from Madame *Héger*'s expression that she had not understood this. Before the question had time to form on her lips, Charlotte had supplied the answer. 'Or in a formal setting—she's delivered lessons before.' Which was true, but hardly the full picture. Perhaps I imagined the flash of scorn in those fine, dark eyes because Madame *Héger* made no comment, addressed Papa again.

'My husband has offered to tutor them in French for an extra hour each day, once they've settled, to ensure they do not fall behind with their other studies.' Monsieur *Héger* she explained, was a master at the *Athénée Royal*, a school for boys situated next door to the *Pensionnat*, already taught literature to the young ladies here . . .

I had no trouble speaking once Madame had shown us upstairs to the dormitory that took up the second floor of the building and left us alone to unpack.

'The lessons are in French? Surely Madame *Héger* is mistaken.' At the Château de Koekelberg, where Mary and Martha Taylor were studying, English was the first language. Not once had it occurred to me that the *Pensionnat* would operate differently.

'It's the best way to learn.' Charlotte began folding her

chemises into one of the drawers we were to share for our belongings. 'How thoughtful of Madame to give us this cur-tained-off area for ourselves, away from the young ones.'

I stared at her. 'How on earth am I supposed to learn any-thing? You know how poor my French is. I'd never have agreed to come if you'd told me.' I waited for an explanation, but she bent over her trunk, carried on taking out items of clothing and placing them on the rail that had been provided for this pur-pose. I wanted to sweep them back down, march downstairs to Papa who was about to go off to visit the site of the Battle of Waterloo, demand that he order a coach to take us straight back to Ostend.

'You'll progress fast, you always do.' She glanced in my di-rection at last, then looked away just as quickly. She gave a small shrug. 'What choice did I have?'

'We already had a plan! If we'd kept on advertising, we'd have found some pupils eventually, without you dragging me half-way across Europe.' I dared her to meet my eye. 'I can't believe you would deliberately mislead me, just to get what you wanted. It's hard enough when—' I gestured vaguely, angrily towards my own mouth. 'You *know.*'

'I truly didn't mean to, hardly thought of it . . .' Her voice grew higher as it always did when she lied to herself or others. She pressed her palms together. 'It will be different this time. We can learn together, support one another. It might help you find your voice—'

'Why not bring Anne?' I knew the answer before I'd fin-ished speaking. Anne did not count.

'She's happier now.'

I wanted to argue, but Anne *had* sounded so in her last let-ter. *The children have stopped talking over me all the time and running to their mother to complain whenever I set them a task or instil some gentle discipline. If I could only encourage a thirst for knowledge in their young minds, guide them towards virtue over self-interest, I would never complain of loneliness or long-ing for home again. I do believe I've overcome the worst of my self-doubt now, and that our little school might become a reality sooner rather than later.* I'd smiled at this, wondering if her new optimism had more to do with William Weightman than any improvement in her young charges.

Charlotte spoke with candour now. 'I wanted *you*. I knew you wouldn't come if I told you.'

'You were right.'

She began sorting stockings into pairs, placing them on top of the wooden chest.

'What now?' I asked. Her head was lowered over her task but there was no mistaking that sniff and her shaking shoulders. She swept aside the pile of stockings and then dropped onto the bed.

'Oh, please don't be angry with me, Emily! I honestly thought I'd go mad if I had to stay at home any longer with nothing happening.' She wiped her cheeks with a handkerchief embroidered with her initials.

'You've no patience—never did have.'

'We can't risk our school failing.' Her little face was suddenly fierce. 'It's our only chance.'

'Why can't you just let me *be?* Always snapping at my heels about something. It's my own fault, I suppose.' I threw my hands in the air. 'I'm stupid enough to listen to you, always go along with everything you suggest—' I stopped, noticing that she'd grown very still. Out of the corner of my eye I caught movement beyond the curtain, which we had only partially pulled across the section of the dormitory where we were to sleep. I followed Charlotte's gaze. A girl had entered the room through the far door, was now rummaging for something in a small chest next to one of the beds. She was tall but slenderly built, no older than ten or eleven years at most. As she closed the top drawer, then opened a second, she turned her head a fraction in our direction, though she did not appear to notice us. A shaft of holy sunlight from the half-open window pinned her to the spot and I felt my breath thicken in my throat. The girl was wearing a dress of French blue with matching ribbons, but she might as well have been dressed in a shabby, brown pinafore and thin shoes, had a handkerchief embroidered with an M hanging half way out of her pocket. I stared at her high, white forehead, her hair which glowed in the sunlight. One of us must have made a noise then, because she straightened and looked straight down the dormitory towards us. The light faded and she was just an ordinary schoolgirl again, herself.

I dropped my hand from my throat and looked down at Charlotte. Her handkerchief lay abandoned in her lap and the tears on her cheeks had dried. She returned my gaze, seemed to grow in stature.

I unpacked my belongings and went downstairs to say good-bye to Papa.

CHAPTER 16
1842

T he ground floor of the *Pensionnat* was arranged around three sides of a courtyard and contained classrooms, a refectory and the living quarters of the *Héger* family. The fourth side of the courtyard, furthest from the *Rue d'Isabelle*, opened into a garden which promised to be beautiful in summer. Since it was February though, only the bare bones were visible: leafless trees lining the gravel walkways, vines and shrubs traced in black over the walls and arbours, the plants in the borders cut back to soil level, tucked away for winter. The bells we could hear were from *Cathédrale St. Gudule*, said Madame *Héger* as she lead us at pace along the icy pathways, a red cashmere shawl laid lightly over her shoulders; they sounded different from English bells, like stone on metal. The winter light made everything appear too sharp. Already, this city, this whole country, felt like an out-of-kilter dream. At the end of the speedy tour, Madame pointed out the *Allée Défendue*, a walkway to the side of the garden only to be used by teachers, since it was overlooked by the adjacent boys' school, where her husband taught.

Notwithstanding this rule, it soon became clear that the regime at the *Pensionnat* was more relaxed than at any English establishment. We learned that many of the girls returned to their own homes at the end of each day, that the periods of recreation were longer and more frequent. There was a feeling that discipline only just held. The pupils made little effort to contain their disdain for the eccentric and peculiarly dressed

Mademoiselle Marie, the least popular of the three resident teachers, or their enthusiasm for one or two of the young masters who visited to teach drawing, singing, music and German. Mealtimes were noisy affairs, the girls sitting where they chose and helping themselves to stews heavy with meat and potatoes, sauces that were strange to our English palates, smoky sausage, seeded bread, cakes studded with dried fruit or caramelised apple, or filled with glossy yellow custard, sweetened cream.

That first morning I managed an arithmetic lesson well enough, able to follow the sequence of numbers in the book I was given and understanding, for the most part, what was required. A geography lesson came next, Mademoiselle Marie pointing to the Americas on the large globe at the front of the classroom. Charlotte sat beside me taking notes, a look of intense concentration on her face. Familiar words floated past me like bubbles:

voyage

ressources naturelles

I grasped them, tried to hold them in my mind but more words came crowding in, piling up and burying those little pockets of clarity, turning sense into nonsense. An image of Keeper flashed into my mind and for an appalling moment, I thought I was going to cry. Sensing my distress, Charlotte nudged me and pointed towards her notes, written in English, but there was no time to copy what she'd written. A history lesson came next, and it was only thanks to the fact that Papa had talked so much about the Napoleonic wars when we were young that I had any idea what was being described. I bit down hard on my lip. I hadn't cried since Tom the cat was run down by a cart on Main Street. I'd held him as the life went out of his body, carried him to the little grave that Branwell had dug for him in the garden, my tears soaking into his dusty fur. By the time we broke at midday my eyes were burning and my thoughts were scrambled. I sat through that meal without speaking to

Charlotte, while all around me words were being flung out in long, incomprehensible strings. The mistress supervising the table addressed Charlotte once or twice in a mixture of French and English but didn't bother with me. I wondered if she'd been alerted to my taciturn nature by the headmistress. To my relief, the other pupils were busy talking among themselves and took no notice of either of us. By bedtime, I was exhausted in a way that felt devastating, dangerous to my being. I fell into bed, then could not sleep though the bed was wide, the covers soft and warm. I lay on my back, listening for the cathedral bells, wondered how Papa was faring on his trip to Waterloo. He'd looked as excited as a little boy this morning, as he set off to visit the famous battle site at last. I thought back to the history lessons he used to give us when we were small. Whenever we started clamouring for battle stories instead of boring old politics, Papa's face would grow very solemn. War was harmful to the spirit of a nation, he'd remind us, an unspeakable offence in God's eyes. That settled, his eyes would light up as he launched into detailed descriptions of battle tactics, strokes of luck, difficult weather, fatal errors of judgement, only stopping when Aunt came in to tell us all over again about her uncle who'd done nothing of interest at Waterloo except die of a fit before he'd even left his bivouac. Papa said war was even worse than civil unrest, which he also hated, though it sounded like a polite argument to me. Secretly, I'd always thought war sounded a lot more fun than peace and even Papa conceded that without Waterloo the wars in Europe might still be raging, our own dear Haworth overrun by the French.

The bells rang for eleven o'clock. Papa would be alone in a strange hotel room now, his little book of phrases and notes on pronunciation beside him. I could hardly stand to think of it.

CHAPTER 17
1842

T he cold in Brussels was different from anything we had known, though we'd lived all our lives in the hills of the north, considered ourselves hardy. Madame *Héger* said the wind came down from Russia, travelled over frozen seas and flat land to reach us. It whipped along the *Rue d'Isabelle* needle-sharp and deathly, crystals of snow flaying our faces. The school had a half-day holiday every Thursday, but we rarely went further than the *Rue Royale*—even dressed in our warmest winter clothes, it was not possible to stay outside for more than a quarter of an hour at most. Any longer and we began to feel as if fundamental damage was being done to our bodies. We huddled in the doorways of hotels, took shelter from sleet showers beneath the canopies of brightly-lit shops, drank cups of steamed milk and coffee in the bakeries, or in the less expensive cafes and wondered how it was that the *Bruxellois*, small and neat in their furs and cashmeres, could bear their climate so merrily. Still, I looked forward to these small escapes, the chance to be alone with my sister. We'd expected to have Sundays together, but to our dismay we'd received a regular invitation from the Reverend Jenkins to come to his home at *Chausée d'Ixelles*, which lay beyond the *Haut-Ville*. Mrs. Jenkins had welcomed us when we'd first arrived in Brussels, tried to persuade Papa to stay on with them instead of leaving straight away for his Waterloo trip. This new invitation was another act of kindness, and yet it meant giving up our only full day of freedom. After attending the morning service at the

Chapelle Royale we might have shopped for some small thing or other, found a quiet spot to read back at school. Now, the agony began even before we reached the *Chausée d'Ixelles* since Mrs. Jenkins insisted on sending her two sons to accompany us from the *Pensionnat*. We were some years older than them, the younger being a solidly built boy of about fifteen, and the elder no more than eighteen. The junior Jenkins was affable but had nothing to tell us about the city he inhabited, and it was plain to see that the elder boy found this weekly duty as excruciating as we did. Had Charlotte and I been at ease in society, capable of light-hearted words, he might have taken his cue from us and managed a conversation of some sort. As it was, he flushed to his ears and into his collar every time Charlotte plucked up the courage to venture a question about a building, a street name, his poor, pimple-ravaged cheeks burning with embarrassment.

There was no respite to be had when we reached their home either. What a disappointment we must have been to Mrs. Jenkins. She and her guests were used to fashionable young ladies, able to hold up their pretty chins in company and talk about nothing, but throughout those interminable afternoons, my tongue stayed resolutely locked, while Charlotte sat either in mortified silence, unable to meet anyone's eye, or else burst out with opinions of such vehemence that conversations tailed off, excuses were made to move away. From her perch on a couch so overstuffed that it seemed to reject her entire person, she would launch herself into the middle of polite conversations and then, frightened by what she'd begun, keep on going with an air of growing desperation, at the same time twisting her entire body away in an attempt to deflect attention from her person, a movement so peculiar that it had the opposite effect, drawing bemused gazes from the rest of the room. I was left alone for the most part, guests having been warned, I suspected, to expect nothing from me. I had never cared for the opinions of strangers, but despite the good heartedness of our hosts, it was here that I felt our otherness most keenly. I saw us as others must, Charlotte writhing on the couch like a mad little doll, I too tall for this dainty drawing room, my limbs ungainly in forced repose. Our dresses were plain and old-fashioned alongside those of Mrs. Jenkins' English acquaintances, all of whom had adopted *Bruxellois* style, their clothing neat and tailored to fit them perfectly. I noticed that Charlotte had already begun making small adjustments to her appearance: a new brooch purchased, the sleeves of her best dress altered, but I couldn't stand to wear sleeves so tight that they restricted all movement, saw no point in layers of petticoats that would be forever stained with peat at home. I did not belong in this world and even if I could find the words to describe it, these people could never understand mine.

A letter arrived from Papa. Charlotte passed it to me over the breakfast table without a word. Her *brioche* sat untouched on her plate. I read the letter quickly. There was a brief paragraph about his trip to Waterloo, another about the journey back to Haworth, before I understood Charlotte's silence, the hard look that had settled over her features.

I am sorry to tell you that Branwell has been dismissed from his post. There was some discrepancy in the finances which could not be explained. He is home now, by turns furious and depressed by the matter, which he maintains was not his fault. His friends are all in agreement and your aunt works hard to keep his spirits up. I had hoped he was settled into a living at last, but God has other plans for him . . .

'Branwell would not steal.' I threw down the letter. 'It will be some act of laziness on his part. Or he will have become distracted by some new idea, a poem.' I thought back to his previous position in Cumbria. 'A girl.'

'It doesn't matter now, does it?' Charlotte's voice was entirely flat. 'What is wrong with him? He can't seem to settle to anything. To be satisfied.'

'You can't blame him for the portrait studio. He wasn't to know there was so much competition. Anyway, you said the railway job was beneath him. Have you changed your mind now that it's over?' I caught one of our classmates watching me across the table, clearly surprised to hear me speaking in anything but monosyllables.

'I didn't say that, but if Branwell can't succeed, what hope is there for the rest of us?'

'We're here, aren't we?' Even in my irritation, it occurred to me how hard it must be to be our father's only son, the focus of the whole family's hopes for the future. Papa's own story was family lore, from his beginnings in a two-roomed cottage in Drumballyroney to the fact that he'd been running the village school by the age of sixteen; had gone on to win a place at Cambridge, leaving Ireland and his siblings behind forever. For the first time I wondered how we'd come to know all this when Papa was the opposite of boastful, always deflected attention from his achievements, unless enraged by someone who'd made the mistake of underestimating him. The great abolitionist William Wilberforce had sponsored him through university, apparently keen to smooth the pathway for an impoverished young evangelical, but I couldn't imagine Aunt sharing the story with us. She was more inclined to point out Papa's faults and peculiarities of behaviour, to worry him away from what she saw as eccentricity. It came to me only now that Mamma must have been the source of such mythologising; that Aunt must surely have been aggravated by her little sister's hero-worship of a clever but imperfect man.

'Anyway,' I said. 'You'll forgive Branwell in no time and think him a genius again.'

'It is the wastefulness I can't stand. Everything comes easily and yet it means nothing to him. I have to work so hard for even the smallest success.'

I saw it differently. It was true that Branwell had an aptitude for almost everything he embarked on, enjoyed almost any occupation, any diverting companionship; had so much excess energy that Papa had been relieved when he took himself off for a punishingly long walk, joined the boxing club. Yet it seemed to me that it came at a cost, that my brother's considerable talents became diluted, unfocused. I understood Charlotte's bitterness though: even at his most lax, his attentions scattered in all directions, Branwell was more likely to succeed than the average person trying their utmost.

'He can't help his nature,' was all I said. 'Any more than the rest of us.'

Charlotte made some indistinct scoffing noise, and I gave up on it. They might have been twins, this brother and sister of mine, forever competing with one another though they swore they were above such tiresomeness; hurt more by the other's failures than their own.

In this strange city far from home I began to fail. I was surrounded every day by beauties that I could see with my own eyes but could not feel: the surprise of the *Grand Place* after the narrow, crooked streets of the *Basse-Ville*, the gothic arch of the Cathedral, like lace frozen into stone. I rose each morning, washed, dressed and then stepped from behind that curtained-off area in the dormitory, trying to steel myself for the babble of foreign voices about to close in around me. From refectory to classroom to recreation, I moved in a dream. Despite Charlotte's hopes for me, her praise for my poor efforts at written French, I could not unfreeze my tongue, even in my own language. I sat beside her in silence while she tried to converse with the teachers or one or two of the older pupils. We were plied with food almost hourly, or so it seemed, at the *Pensionnat*, but I had no stomach for it. The food was too rich or too strange, all the darkness of Europe, of the dead past, contained in those heavy breads, the stews bitter with beer. On the *Rue Royale*, the wind carved my flesh close to the bone and I longed for Keeper, the ripple of his warm coat beneath my palm, the doggish smell of him, the click of his great claws on the flagstones. Here, the dogs were all tiny, shivering things that looked as if they'd been born too soon. Their owners— elegantly-dressed young ladies or grown men—had to carry these raw-skinned creatures across the park since their trembling, pliable legs could not transport them very far. I comforted myself with the thought that my darling boy would have gobbled one whole for his dinner.

At Château de Koekelberg Mary Taylor eyed me in that no-nonsense way of hers, while Martha was all charm and giggles and youthful fun, but none of it touched me. I pictured myself as a pinprick on a map, far from home, diminishing by the minute. Soon I would disappear altogether, swallowed up by Europe, while England, which had already broken free from that continent, would slide out of sight. When Anne wrote with news of a peasant uprising in Gondal I skimmed over the words. In my brief reply I made no mention of the rebellion, terrified in case that magical island had become invisible to me once again. Spring was coming, fresh green leaves bursting from unpromising buds all over the city, but a grey veil had dropped over my eyes. Sheltered from the wind, I walked the sunlit walkways of the *Pensionnat* garden feeling like the loneliest of exiles, the longing for home as raw as the flesh once torn from my arm. I wondered how I could survive another failure. I did not think it possible, would rather disappear, die even, only I could not bear to be buried so far from home.

M adame's husband was a dark, intense little man, with a volatile temper which terrified the normally unflappable schoolgirls he taught. I liked him all the better for it in this country where passions seemed to run lukewarm, and predictability was valued as an asset. His outbursts could be triggered by anything from a classroom door left to creak in the wind, or a persistent fly buzzing around his head, to the paucity of intellectual curiosity exhibited by his pupils, most of whom aspired to little more than rote learning and could not, by any means, be induced into a sensible discussion of literary works. He was the only teacher able to reduce those young schoolgirls to tears, at which point he would become aware of himself and produce an enormous handkerchief from his pocket. *Ne t'inquiète pas, ma pauvre*, he would say. Tears were dried and peace would reign until the next explosion.

Having witnessed these performances in the classroom, Charlotte was already fearful of the private lessons we were to take with him. At our first meeting—delayed for some weeks because Monsieur had to cover lessons for another teacher at the *Athénée* who'd fallen ill—he spoke slowly and clearly, holding up a book by someone named *François-René de Chateaubriand*. With a little help from Charlotte, I understood what he was proposing: in each lesson we were to read a passage from the work of a French author. When we were sure of the meaning, he would explain the merits and faults of the piece and then set an essay which we must write in the style of his chosen author.

'That's ridiculous,' I said to Charlotte, when she'd finished explaining. 'I can't write in the style of anyone but myself. It is a waste of time.'

A short discussion followed between Charlotte and our teacher.

'Monsieur says this is an excellent way to improve not only our French but the style of our own work.' Charlotte, already nervous, now had a pleading look in her eyes. 'He's used this method many times before.'

'By aping the writing of others?' I sat back from the desk. 'I see no point in the exercise.'

Monsieur began to talk again. I must have absorbed more of the language than I'd realised by then because I understood the gist of his complaint. Your sister, he told Charlotte, must not argue with her teacher when her French is so bad. When she does not even—he made an unmistakable sealing gesture across his mouth.

I made a noise which was not English or French but a universal utterance of disdain.

'*Je crois que* Emily—' Charlotte began.

Monsieur *Héger* slammed his fist down on the desk, jumped to his feet and directed a great torrent of French first at Charlotte, and then at me, most of which I now failed to understand, all his words rolling into one furious, extended noise. He flailed his arms, clutched at his scalp and then, in a fit of rage, threw his copy of *Chateaubriand* across the room. I felt a rush of air as it brushed my ear and then clattered to the floor behind me. I bent to pick it up, aimed it at Monsieur for fun, who flinched in anticipation, and then threw it out of the open window. A second later, I heard it thudding to the ground.

'Emily, please . . .' Charlotte's eyes wide with alarm.

I crossed my arms, knowing there was little point trying to interrupt someone in high temper, you must simply wait till they are done. But Monsieur's words had already tailed off, a look of growing puzzlement on his face. He stared at me, and it occurred to me that he was waiting for me to cry. Ignoring him, I turned to Charlotte again.

'Please explain to Monsieur *Héger* that I'm not used to my imagination being stifled in this way; that I maintain the uselessness of his method. I'm willing to try, however, if only as a matter of courtesy.'

How much of this Charlotte was able to translate, I could not tell. She stammered through some sort of explanation, to which Monsieur listened intently, his little black eyes narrowing. When she was finished, he turned to me again, his face devoid of any expression that might give away his feelings. I held his gaze and then he gave an abrupt laugh and left the room. A minute later he returned, carrying the book I'd thrown out the window. *Bien sûr*, Mademoiselles Charlotte *et* Emily, he said. *Maintenant nous commençons.*

Somehow this dispute broke through the greyness that had lodged itself in me. I felt a spark of something in my belly, a stirring in my blood. Monsieur *Héger* thought my French appalling? Very well, I would prove him wrong. Probably, he also believed English women incapable of conducting a logical argument. We would see. From that moment on, I spent most of my free hours studying, a dictionary at my side, even on our Thursday half-days. Charlotte fussed over me, worried that I did not take enough exercise, breathe fresh air, but I could tell that she was relieved to see the change in me. At mealtimes and during recreation, I began to listen properly, seeking patterns in the chaos of language all around me. I read the shop signs, plucked words and phrases from the air as we passed the *Bruxellois* on their promenades, stored away pronunciations, the particular music of the language, looked up unfamiliar words as soon as we returned to the *Pensionnat*. Still, there were days when I thought it all a hopeless quest. Words swarmed around me like angry bees and I longed for the flat Northern vowels that were so familiar to me. I'd go to bed tired and dispirited, my mind exhausted by hours of effort that had proved fruitless; wake with my energy renewed and a fresh determination, the memory of Monsieur's contempt still clear in my mind. I began to speak in his class, occasionally even at mealtimes, though only ever in French. The act of speaking in a foreign tongue liberated me and at the same time erected a protective barrier between the visceral, inner part of me which was my true self, and the world. By now, the Jenkins' had given up inviting us to their house after Sunday services. With the day to ourselves, we could visit Mary and Martha, or explore the countryside beyond the boulevards that contained the city, a soothing landscape of pastures and farmsteads. We talked of home, of our studies, of nothing at all and the quiet sunshine replenished me as we sat beside streams or followed pathways through cool green woods. The trees breathed their verdant secrets and I found myself daydreaming about Gondal again.

'You've a gift,' said Charlotte one morning after I'd helped her understand a shopkeeper's explanation about a delivery of lace collars from his other store. 'How quickly you learn!'

I studied harder, tried to think in French. The days passed and I began to eat again, to believe that I might survive.

CHAPTER 20
1842

A re you not scared of Monsieur *Héger?*' said Charlotte. We'd attended the morning service at the *Chapelle Royale* and were crossing the park with the intention of passing out of the city by the *Porte de Louvain*. Earlier in the week, our teacher had grown so exasperated with me, that he'd stormed out of the classroom, abandoning our lesson altogether.

'No,' I lifted my face to the early May sunshine. Monsieur's hands sliced through the air like a guillotine, proving a point, but he was a small man, with the soft, indolent body of a city dweller, and I could never fear him. All his power lay in his mind and while he had the advantage of years, of formal education, I knew my wit was as strong as his.

'I believe he's some sort of monster,' said Charlotte, closing her eyes in ecstasy. 'I work harder and harder to please him, and I am sure my work improves, but he takes pleasure in crushing me.'

'Because you allow it,' I said. More than once, she'd dissolved into tears in the middle of one of his lessons. 'You shouldn't indulge him.'

'Oh, I wouldn't dare to face him down as you do. But then you've never been afraid of wild creatures.' She laughed, finding pleasure in this idea of Monsieur. 'He's not all bad though. He treats Madame with respect and affection, and I've watched him play with his little children in a delightful way.'

'He's generous enough, once his temper's blown itself out,' I admitted. 'Which is why all the girls love him.'

Charlotte sighed. 'I'll never understand these Catholics. Not if I lived among them for a hundred years.'

'What's that to do with Monsieur?' I crouched to watch a butterfly with white wings and black markings that had settled on a sweet-smelling shrub.

'Only that he fits the mould in the way I expected, with his great passions and storms. Everyone else here seems to go on with their strange little rites and idolatry without thinking. I wouldn't mind so much if they seemed to care. There is something repulsive, almost heathen in their blind worship of objects.'

That night, Charlotte fell asleep beside me almost instantly, tired from our walk. No sound came from beyond the curtain, where the other girls slept, but moonlight was streaming through the window, flooding the room with unearthly light and making me restless. I glanced at my sister, lying on her back with her hands clasped across her chest as if in prayer and wondered if I could ever worship a man in the way one was supposed to. At home, the only males of our own age were Papa's curates whom we made a point of despising, while the young men we'd encountered here in Brussels, guests of the Jenkins for the most part, had seemed uniformly stupid, notwithstanding the benefits of education and the wealth required for European travel. I'd been silent in their presence and they, in turn, had shown no interest in me. No, I could care only for a man of substance, a man with the intellectual rigour of Monsieur *Héger*, though there was nothing in the least attractive to me in my teacher's squat body and dark features. That kind of mind would need to be housed in a form hewn from grit. I thought of the man I'd encountered on the pathway across the moors. The day before we'd left for London, I caught sight of him leading a horse into the farmyard at Top Withens. As Charlotte unclasped her hands and began to snore, I tried to seat him behind a desk, to dress him in city clothes but for once my imagination failed me. Over in the *Basse-Ville*, the bells rang out from the *Cathédrale St. Gudule*. I turned on my side, closed my eyes. There *was* no such man.

The warm weather had not yet broken but the sky turned a deeper blue each day, signalling autumn. As I waited for my coffee to cool a little one morning, my eyes moved across the refectory to where two of the Wheelwright sisters were giggling together over their breakfast *brioche*. At Madame's request, I'd started giving piano lessons to these little English girls. It was a waste of everyone's time since the younger girl had no ear for music and the other had double-jointed fingers which meant she would always struggle to hold her hands in the correct position. Still, their parents were willing to go on paying. I'd insisted that the tuition took place outside of my own study time, a decision which caused some tears since the girls were used to having their own way in all matters. Laetitia Wheelwright, the eldest of the sisters, was a sharp-nosed miss who could not hide her contempt for me whenever we met, though she herself did not take music lessons.

Charlotte dropped a letter on the table, covered her mouth with her hand.

'What is it?' I asked. 'Tell me quickly.'

'Martha Taylor has died. Of cholera.'

I stared at her in disbelief, at the scrawled note Mary had sent from the Château de Koekelberg. I pictured vivacious little Martha as we'd seen her last. What could such exuberance have to do with sickness and suffering? We hadn't even known she was ill. It seemed impossible that she should lie in a coffin now, stiffened by death.

'What on earth will Mary do now?' said Charlotte. 'She adored that child. We all did.' She pressed the note to her heart.

Martha's death cast a sombre tinge over the weeks that followed. On the first Sunday, we walked in silence to visit the grave, Mary's face determinedly set, giving way only as she stooped to lay some greenery on that fresh mound of earth. Charlotte held her by the arm until we took our leave of her.

'So far from England,' I said when it was just the two of us again. I could still hear Martha's fearless laughter, see her pointed little face so full of mischief. 'Imagine being buried in foreign soil, Charlotte. I could not bear it. My soul would find some way to return home.'

Another letter. Branwell wrote to say that William Weightman had died, also of cholera. He was distraught—in a short space of time the two of them had become great friends—but my first thought was for Anne. I'd been certain that an understanding had formed between the two of them before we came away, though Anne had said nothing to confirm this. Charlotte had been unconvinced. She maintained that Anne had not made her feelings clear enough; that William would need more assurance to speak out. Those amiable lips were silenced forever now. Aunt hadn't been well either, Branwell mentioned at the end of his letter. The doctor thought it was an obstruction of the bowel. The next morning, another note arrived from him, a hurried scrawl this time. Our aunt was dead.

'I never thought of Aunt as old,' said Charlotte. 'I wonder why.'

The sea was flat and shiny today, with barely a ripple to disturb the surface. It looked solid rather than liquid, a mirrored surface that might support the weight of a body rather than swallowing it down. It added to the feeling of unreality that hung over the journey. We'd calculated that Aunt had been sixty-five years old—a good age when you thought of the village women who died in childbirth, their bodies spent after the first ten or so pregnancies, the babies still coming; or else perished from the various contagions that tore through the densely-packed cottages. A good age too for a woman of Aunt's standing, who'd lived in relative comfort. Like Charlotte though, I had never considered her elderly. Had hardly considered her at all, I now realised. With her huge bonnets, her false front of curls and her permanently pattened feet, she'd been an oddity existing beyond the calibrations of time, like some strange fixture in an inherited house, so familiar that you stopped noticing it.

'Do you think she'd have agreed to come to Haworth if she'd known she'd never go home again?' I asked. As far back as I could remember, Aunt had liked to complain of leaving behind her beloved Penzance to look after her sister's little children. There was never any true heat in her words, and I didn't recall anyone taking offence at them. On the contrary, they had made us laugh at times when we had not felt like doing so. There was comfort to be taken from that regular litany; it imparted a sense of permanence, a pattern to our lives. Now, I was struck by the sacrifice she made, coming to help when Mamma was ill and then staying forever. 'There might have been someone waiting for her at home in those early days. She always said she was considered handsome in her youth.' It had taken death to make me see Aunt as a complete person instead of an adjunct to our own lives.

'I don't see how we'd have managed,' said Charlotte. She was quiet for a moment, gazing out of the window as another steamer passed in the other direction.

'She probably expected Papa to marry again, so she could go home.' I smiled at that idea. 'It's a wonder she didn't hate us.'

The joy of homecoming lasted no longer than the walk from Keighley and our reunion with Anne, who had obtained leave from Thorp Green; the solid wall of Keeper flying towards me down the hallway. Immediately I saw that Anne was very pale and had lost even more weight since we'd last seen her.

'Dearest William,' I said, drawing her to one side.

'Don't.' She shook her head and covered her mouth with her hand, 'I really believed . . .' Tears shone in her violet eyes and her soft voice was reduced to a bare whisper. It was Branwell who concerned me most though. We found him in the drawing room, where Aunt was laid out in her coffin, already looking like a poorly executed waxwork version of herself. I straightened her curls.

'She looks peaceful,' I said, turning to my brother. He was gaunt and white-faced, his hair standing on end like a red halo. A flash of memory came to me, wrenched from very early childhood, Branwell lying face down on the landing floor outside Papa's bedroom. He was crying inconsolably, tearing at his hair. Beyond the closed bedroom door lay our dead mother.

'I sat with her till it was over,' he said. 'It's not till you've seen someone suffering like that . . .' His eyes were lifeless. It was clear that he'd not slept.

'You've neglected yourself,' said Charlotte, smoothing down the hem of Aunt's dress so that it sat properly. She spoke more gently. 'We can't afford for you to be ill too.'

'She cared for me like a mother all these years, Charlotte. What do you expect? I couldn't leave her. She was screaming in pain, conscious to the end.' He shook his head, like a man waking from a dream. 'I begged God to put a stop to her misery, but no help came.' He stared out the window, towards the church. 'How can that be so? I used to think that death was just like sleep. You went to bed quite happy and did not wake again. My God, if good people like William and Aunt *must* be taken, then why can't it be that way?' His voice caught in his throat, and he dashed a tear from his cheek.

'You're exhausted,' I said. 'You need to rest.' He nodded, still gazing at Aunt's corpse. In many ways he was still a child, this brother of my mine, jumping like a frog from one idea to another, one scheme to the next. An outsider would think him resilient, blessed with boundless energy and enthusiasm. It was only we who understood how easily he was bruised by the world. 'You'll have been a comfort to her. Even if she couldn't express it.'

He nodded. 'The doctor said her insides were rotten, there was nothing he could do.'

I pictured the discarded core of an apple, brown and seething with maggots. 'They never can,' I said, suddenly full of rage for our mother, for Maria and Elizabeth, for dear little Martha Taylor lying in a foreign grave, so cheerful and optimistic that she would hardly have believed in the possibility of her own death, for William Weightman whose life had seemed charmed, but who had taken all Anne's hopes for the future with him. The anger faded. For a long time now, I'd thought of God's creatures as no more than seeds scattered in hope across the surface of the earth. An act of faith or madness, depending on which way you looked at it.

The next morning, I watched Branwell and the other pall-bearers shouldering the coffin with no apparent effort and then navigating between the headstones towards the church. How little space was required to parcel us in the end, and yet our minds could travel wherever imagination took us, could find solace even in a prison cell, in the soft feathers of a robin's breast, the glint of an ant's back. In her last agonies, I hoped that Aunt found herself carried over land and sea to her Cornish home.

The three of us were sitting around the fire in the dining room, having persuaded Branwell to attend a Christmas recital in the schoolhouse with Papa, which we hoped would lift his spirits. Tabby Aykroyd said he'd done everything for poor William in his final days and then refused to leave Aunt for a moment when she was suffering. Our preparations for the holiday had been quieter than usual, without Aunt worrying over every detail. Papa had seemed in a world of his own since the funeral, adrift without his companion of all these years. For all her fussing and odd fancies, Aunt had had a seam of granite running through her, had proved a source of comfort to each one of us. How scared Papa must have been all those years ago when she'd first come, grief-stricken and with six small children needing his care.

'I won't go back,' I said. The light was already fading outside, a sharp slice of moon hanging over the church.

'What?' Charlotte had been staring into the fire until I interrupted her thoughts.

'I'm not going back to the *Pensionnat* in the New Year. I shall stay here.'

'The *Hégers* will be sorry to lose you,' said Anne, her voice calm. So often, she sensed my thoughts before I'd expressed them, sometimes before they had fully formed in my mind. 'Their letter to Papa was so generous.'

'When did you decide this?' Charlotte glared at Anne suspecting, no doubt, that she and I had decided the matter between us.

'I don't know,' I told her. 'But I've made up my mind.' Keeper whimpered in his sleep, his chin resting on my foot. 'Papa needs someone to run the house now. I'm the best person for that.'

'But . . . you read Monsieur's letter for yourself. He couldn't have been more delighted by your progress. He thinks so highly of you! With a few months' more—'

'I've every intention of carrying on with my studies.' The tips of my fingers sought the *E* carved into the surface of the table. 'From here.'

I was already busy with Gondal work too, specifically a revised history of Augusta Almeda. When I first invented her, I had an image of our young Queen Victoria in my mind, but

Augusta's true nature would out. She'd refused to dilute her power by accepting offers of marriage. Instead, she'd taken lovers, from knight to stable-boy, persuading her father to throw them into prison as soon as they proved tiresome or began to harbour ambitions of their own. Now there was a new chapter to write, which began when Augusta's horse stumbled and fell as they jumped a boundary wall on her father's vast estate. (She was not permitted to ride alone, for fear of injury or kidnapping, but did so anyway.) The prince who'd been swapped at birth for a peasant child happened to be passing at the time and heard her horse's distressed whinnies. He leapt down from his own horse and then knelt to run his hands over the injured fetlock, all the time murmuring to the distraught creature. By the time he had finished, her horse was able to walk again. The boy was just on the edge of manhood, had been raised by a shepherd. Soon Augusta would discover his preternatural intelligence; that he was the only person who could truly understand her untameable nature.

'You want me to go back all on my own?' Charlotte threw her hands in the air and couldn't decide whether to cry or lose her temper with me.

'Not necessarily.' Keeper twitched in his sleep, edged closer to the warmth of the fire. Outside it had begun to snow. The wind had picked up too, swirling the flakes against the window. I could not, I realised, be happier. 'With Aunt's money we've enough money to start our school with a smaller number of pupils than we'd planned.' We'd received £300 apiece in the Will. 'At least in the beginning.' I looked at her. 'The *Hégers* will understand.'

'I can't believe . . .' Charlotte was on her feet now, pacing up and down. She swung round to me, struggling to control the emotion in her face. 'We didn't say goodbye! Not properly. I fully expected . . . Madame and Monsieur are like family to us.'

'They're very kind.'

'I never dreamed of going back alone, Emily.'

'Then stay.'

She looked around in a panic, as though our snug little dining room was a dungeon. 'I'm not ready yet. There's so much more I need to learn.'

'There's no reason for you to give up your studies for my sake. It's not as if you would arrive a stranger, and the Dixons are still in town,' I said, referring to cousins of the Taylor family who had taken a house on *Rue de la Régence*. 'We can wait till you return.'

'I think . . . I must go back. I can't bear to think I've seen Monsieur for the last time. And what about Madame, the children?' Charlotte had shown no more interest in the *Héger* children than I before now, but I let it pass. 'Branwell's sure to find something else soon—you'll be here without company all winter once Anne goes back to work.' She shivered, imagining her own loneliness. There was the sound of the front door opening, the stamping of feet in the hallway. 'If you're really sure then I must speak to Papa right away.' She put away her book and left me to the wind, the soft whirr of snow on the windowpane.

In the New Year, Charlotte returned to Brussels alone and Anne went back to Thorp Green. Shortly afterwards— and certainly because of Anne's influence—Branwell was offered a position in the same household, as tutor to the family's eldest child, a boy who had outgrown her teaching. My brother had brushed off dismissal from the railway as nothing more than an accounting error, but the loss of his great friend William, followed so quickly by Aunt's death, had plunged him into a state of depression. He'd spent most of Christmas locked away in his room, showing little interest even when Charlotte tried to engage him in their usual discussions about Angria. This new offer of employment had an immediate effect on him, like a flame catching paper, and I was pleased to see him leave for Thorp Green in buoyant mood, spilling over with plans for the enrichment of his young charge's mind.

With all my siblings away from home, I shut up the bedroom that Charlotte, Anne and I shared and moved my things into the room at the top of stairs, a tiny space that had served as our nursery, playroom and then a bedroom for occasional guests. That bare little room, with just a bed and chest for furniture, was all I needed, and its cell-like quality was useful for imagining the plight of Fernando and Oswald, the two Gondal noblemen I'd recently cast into jail for treasonous activities against the ageing Julius Brenzaida. On dark mornings in the dead of winter, I was first to rise, moving round the house in silence, lighting lanterns, clearing and setting the fires, fetching water from the pump, putting the kettle on the range. In the yard I fed the geese and the chickens, checked for eggs, watched the cold red dawn breaking. By the time I came in, Martha would be putting on the porridge for breakfast, Tabby coming to join us soon afterwards. Papa slept a little later these days, but would soon be at work in his study, writing letters and grant applications, or seeing to parishioners who would call by with one concern or another. The rest of the morning, I was busy with the house-keeping tasks that had once been the preserve of Aunt, study-ing too, with my textbooks propped up in the kitchen, until it was time to take Keeper out for his walk. I was mistress of my own kingdom, every hour of the day arranged just as I chose. If it pleased me, I need not speak to a single stranger from one day to the next. Sometimes, when I awoke and breathed in the achingly cold air of home or found myself going about my work with a quiet song on my lips, I felt something swelling in my chest. I recognised the feeling like an old companion, absent for many years, still wonderfully familiar. It was freedom, all the sweeter because I'd overcome that intense desire to abandon Brussels in those early months, to make the same tired, etiolated mistakes. Right up to her departure, Charlotte had urged me to change my mind, to return to Belgium with her, but for once I'd resisted and nothing bad had happened.

I thought about her often, sleeping in our little curtained-off area of the dormitory at the *Pensionnat*, shopping for gloves on the *Rue Royale*, lessons taken in private with Monsieur *Héger*, just the two of them now. At the same time, I found myself in thrall to a new force which sent me climbing up towards Top Withens every time I left the house. In that harshest of winters, even someone as familiar with the moors as I was could easily miss the path. I'd sink knee-deep in the snowy crevasses between the heather or lose my footing in the boggy ground beneath. I brushed the snow from my stockings, pulled my boots free of the sucking peat, then kept on towards that dark building on the horizon. As I drew closer, I'd smell the animals, warm and earthy, the peat-smoke that curled like question marks from the chimneys, but the gate was always barred, the footprints in the snow by the doorway already blurred by fresh falls, and there was never any sign of the man I'd seen entering the yard with his horse. Just once I caught the shadow of movement in one of the front rooms, where I could see a great fire burning in the hearth, the glint of copper pans hanging either side. I'd scrabbled in the snow, fingers closing round a stone that had fallen from the dry boundary wall. I wanted to fling it through the bright window, to smash my way into that snug room with a fire of my own in my veins, but the stone turned my fingers to ice and after a moment I'd let it drop, turned for home.

Charlotte wrote:

I cannot tell you how wonderful it was to walk along Rue d'Isabelle again! There was the dear, familiar sight of the Pensionnat, and Monsieur and Madame waiting to greet me as if I was one of their own children! That first breakfast tasted even more delicious than I'd remembered, though it was only the usual coffee and brioche. I had forgotten what a beautiful city this is, even now, when it is supposed to be spring but all in the garden is black and frozen and the cold feels as if it might be fatal to someone with my constitution. It was very strange to return without you and I do feel lonely at times, but I believe it was the right thing to do, that these extra months of study will pay off when it comes to attracting pupils to our remote little school. Monsieur and Madame wonder why I do not make friends with my fellow teachers—knowing them as well as I, you will quite understand why I don't seek companionship in that *direction!*

Evening-time was for writing. Augusta Almeda had dismissed all the simpering suitors who hung around the palace wanting to talk about their feelings, spent her time devising clever plans to escape the palace to be with the shepherd boy.

Together they galloped across the hills till dusk, urging their horses on. They climbed mountains, swam in a secret pool in a deep forest glade, feasted on purple berries which stained their lips, and never tired of one another's company except when he grew jealous of her past lovers, or she laughed at his rough ways, and then they fought bitterly. The story came easily, with just one thread eluding me. I'd planned that Augusta would teach her shepherd prince how to read and write, pictured delightful scenes of the two of them with their heads bent together over a book, a tender love developing, but as soon as I transported them to a domestic setting, they repelled one another like magnets. When the clock on the stairs struck midnight, I'd say farewell to the Gondals, happy in the knowledge that I would return to that kingdom of all possibilities tomorrow and the next night too. From the window, I wished a silent goodnight to Charlotte in Brussels, to Anne and Branwell at Thorp Green, to the silent souls in the graveyard and in the vaults of the church. Outside, the stars were cold little fires, the sky a dark prairie; behind me the quietening fire, the steady flame of my lone candle.

Mostly, I did not read over what I'd written, but one evening, when Papa was taking longer than usual to go up to bed, I turned back through my notebook and could not help noticing the influence of Monsieur *Héger*. I remembered him dropping our essays back on our desks, how he'd insisted on removing every extraneous word, every diversion from the thrust of an argument. The words on the page must be transparent, he liked to say, the reader should see straight to the thought, the image; *this* and *this* was an obstacle, glowering as he slashed his pen through line after line of a *devoir. It offends my eye!* Charlotte bore the worst of his wrath, sniffing quietly to herself while he destroyed some particularly florid piece of prose. In my case, he was more likely to point out a factual error or a misspelling, but occasionally I would have to defend my choice of word or phrase, if need be until the lesson came to an end or, as often happened, Monsieur lost his temper, which I also took as a victory. Against my better judgement, I had already conceded to his favoured teaching method—it would not do for him to prevail on every matter. Now though, with a distance between our opposing forces, I recognised a new clarity in my writing. I knew that it could not have simply dropped out of the sky, could just about bear to admit that to myself now that I was safe in my own world again. If I were Charlotte, I would have written Monsieur a gushing letter, praising him above all teachers. As it was, the idea irked me, and I resolved not to think about it again.

Happy as I was, it was a long and dreary winter. When spring finally arrived, the birds sang wildly in celebration, and on Penistone Hill the wildflowers burst from the gently-warming soil. Summer followed, the asphodels pushed their yellow spikes towards the sky and the first swallows returned. One morning Keeper came upon a leveret, asleep in the long grass, and sent it bounding. The sunshine was tempered by a cold wind blowing over the tops. On my way to Top Withens, I suddenly changed my mind and dropped down instead towards South Dean Beck, following its course until it met Sladen Beck at the indentation in the land we liked to call the Meeting of the Waters. Here was a secret valley, like the swipe of a Titan's thumb when the earth was still malleable, where we'd picnicked over the years, its steep sides woven by bracken and heather and bilberry bushes. I scrambled down the hillside into the valley and immediately found myself sheltered from the wind, hidden from the eye. Keeper chased his tail in the shallows of the beck, growled at the thin waterfall that stumbled from the high rocks and then went off to a spot at the far end of the valley, carrying the hambone I'd brought for his dinner. I took off my boots and stockings and paddled through the icy water which was a shade between green and rust. Around my toes swum tiny, almost-transparent fish for whom this was a whole world. Tadpoles punctuated the mineral-dark water, translucent, still jelly-like at their edges. I wondered if they were aware of my presence above them, if they sensed their half-formed state, the miraculous transformation that was coming.

When my feet turned numb, I sat on the bank by a stand of young, pliable alders and pulled up my skirts to let my legs dry. The spring sun warmed my skin and my limbs felt pleasantly lazy. I stretched out like a cat, was almost drifting into sleep, when I jolted upright, wide-awake. Standing on the edge of the valley and looking directly down at me, was the figure of a man. I dragged down my dress, the warnings Aunt had given so often sounding in my ears as I scrabbled for my stockings and looked around for Keeper. But the man was moving along the ridge now in the direction of Stanbury, away from me. I kept my eyes on him the whole time until he was out of sight, and then a feeling of disappointment settled over me. He'd been only an outline against the sky, but I knew for sure that he was the farmer from Top Withens. For once I did not understand myself. Had I wanted him to carry on watching me? To clamber down the side of the valley and approach me? I thought of all the times I'd climbed up to that lonely farmhouse in the hope of seeing him. Now I wondered what I would have done if we'd actually come face-to-face. I looked down at my pale legs, my feet, tender and exposed beneath the sunlight, and then lay back on the grassy bank and tried to transport myself back to our meeting on the pathway: the watchful eyes, those impatient hands pushing back his shirt sleeves. Long fingers. But instead came a vision of Monsieur *Héger* hunched and scowling at his desk, followed almost immediately by another: the sickly, mummified hands of Papa's visitor in the study. Repulsed, I turned on my front and closed my eyes, pressed myself against the earth until the sound of the beck rushed through me.

On a day when the sky pressed down ominously on the horizon, I received a strange letter from Charlotte. *I am lonely,* she wrote. *The city seems so desolate and dusty, everyone away for the holidays and the Pensionnat is quite empty. I walk the Basse-Ville and the boulevards all day long yet cannot seem to exhaust myself. I do not know what is wrong unless something bad grows inside of me, hidden from sight.* The letter went on to tell me how she had entered the *Cathédrale St. Gudule* one afternoon when the sun was punishingly hot, seeking the cool and quiet shadows of the nave. Seeing the confession boxes lined up in the side aisle, she'd been struck by a sudden urge to talk to someone, *anyone.* She had waited her turn, almost lost courage at several points, and then had to wait again once seated since the priest was busy on the other side of the box. When her turn came, she had no choice but to admit that she was a Protestant. The priest agreed to hear her, on the understanding that she would then visit him at his house for instruction in the true faith. Charlotte agreed, with no intention of going. She begged me not to tell Papa about this aberration, knowing how much it would trouble him.

Her unhappiness did not come as a surprise to me. Recently, her letters had become full of pessimism, her mood coloured by some ailment or other which was always a sign that she was entering one of her periods of depression. She did not like the new intake of pupils, could not seem to get along with the other teachers at the *Pensionnat,* though she'd managed well enough when I was there. Notwithstanding her urge to confess, she found herself claustrophobic among so many Catholics; felt something abhorrent and performative in their strange rites, their insistence on worshipping idols. Worst of all, she sensed that Madame *Héger* was becoming critical of her, no longer treating her with sympathy or as one of the family. The *Héger* children were losing their charm as they grew older. In Charlotte's opinion this was due to over-indulgence by Madame. Only Monsieur *Héger* treated her with kindness, but then days would go by when he barely noticed her, and she was quite alone in a city that seemed to negate her existence.

I paid little attention to the detail of the complaints, thinking it unlikely that much had changed in Brussels or at the *Pensionnat* since I'd left them. I suspected that Charlotte had fallen in love with Monsieur *Héger* and that she believed her love either unrequited or hopeless. Throughout my time at the *Pensionnat* I'd only ever seen Monsieur treat her with the affection he might offer a child or a relative. Had something happened since then? I pictured the two of them alone in a classroom, voices nearby. The excitement of it. Or was it just that Charlotte had turned little Monsieur *Héger* into a hero of her imagination: a Duke of Wellington, a Zamorna? All those epic stories, the idealised, obsessive sketches, unleashed on a *bourgeois* schoolmaster, the attraction of the mind overcoming any physical reluctance. It would have been comical if Charlotte's happiness had not been at stake. Even supposing Monsieur *had* come to care for her, I could not imagine him acting upon his feelings in a way that would risk his position in society or his livelihood. Knowing my sister though, a small act of kindness, a gentle word, would have been enough. Hers was a nature designed to worship uncritically, to seize upon a poor scrap of green in the most barren soil and imagine it a luxuriant jungle.

That letter made me uneasy, or perhaps it was just the weather. The heavy rain of the last week had been replaced with silence and a strange stillness. The sheep were static on the hillside, the water ran slack in the becks, and the cottongrass hung listlessly instead of bobbing in the wind. I was not used to my world sitting inactive beneath the sky, like a giant waiting room, and could not settle to anything. I hurried through the morning chores and then told Martha I was going for a walk. She was in the kitchen, mopping her brow as she ironed bedsheets in the damp, still air.

'It's a blessing ground's still wet,' she said, referring to the fires which burst across the heath sometimes during summer storms. But the skies remained leaden as Keeper and I climbed Penistone Hill and set out across Haworth Moor, no destination in my mind but my feet knowing where they wanted to go. When I reached Top Withens, I stood at a distance, watching the farmhouse and outbuildings but I saw nobody except a small, dark-haired child who was playing with a ball in the yard. I wondered if she belonged to the farmer and who her mother might be. How strange to think of a child growing inside your body, taking up more and more of you each day, nudging against your belly, snaking around your organs. Women yearned for that sensation, but it had always seemed as bizarre and improbable to me as the act that put it there in the first place. I remembered the man watching me intently from the lip of the valley; my bare legs stretched out in the clear, spring sunlight, the fine dark hairs at my ankles, my knees; the violent, empty, glorious ache after he'd gone. But I'd never seen him here at Top Withens again, no matter how often I crouched in the heather to spy. I thought about Charlotte's pitiful confession, all her repressed desires spilling out of her in that little wooden cubicle, in the presence of a complete stranger, and suddenly I was sick of myself and my own stupid imaginings. I called for Keeper, then turned my back on the farmhouse and scrambled up Delf Hill and down the other side as fast as I could. My intention was to carry on until I reached the Alcomden Stones, but Keeper started chasing a rabbit, so I followed in the direction he, and that white bobbing tail, took me. When I reached Ponden Clough, there was no sign of him. Then I heard a whimper. Looking down that steep hillside I saw that he was about halfway down, trapped on a ledge of rock too small for his solid torso. I whistled to him, but he gazed up at me and would not move. Another whimper. Without thinking I started down the side of the clough, using the coarse grass as handholds and calling to Keeper to stay where he was. The ground felt spongy beneath my feet from all the recent rainfall. It oozed under my weight, water trickling over the stones which were grey-green, slimy to the touch. I was almost alongside Keeper when he gave a loud bark which made me start. I misjudged my next foothold and when my boot slipped from beneath me, I found myself face down against the hillside, the smell of the earth in my nostrils. I dug my foot in again, gained purchase this time, was just thinking that it was a good thing my handholds had stayed firm, when Keeper barked again, with a new urgency, and then came scrabbling across the hillside from the ledge. Just as he reached me, the entire surface of the earth peeled away beneath us, like skin from an orange, and began to slide downwards. In the blur of panic, I seized Keeper's collar and tried to scramble back up the side of the clough, digging my feet in like spades, but we kept on moving downwards. Then a moment of clarity. Somehow, I threw the pair of us sideways, detaching us from that raft of sodden earth and grass that was now sliding towards the bottom of the clough. I lay on my side, the whip-like grass cutting into one of my palms, Keeper panting but safe now. The ground felt cold and wet against my cheek. I could hear the suck of water, the creep of a million roots, the blind progress of all the minute creatures contained in that dark, peaty soil. Pulling myself upright, I stared at what remained of the piece of hillside where I'd been standing only moments ago: earth which had been hidden from sight for thousands of years was now raw, exposed. A purple worm waved obscenely in the light, glistening like a fresh blood sausage. I watched it turn back on itself, its skin too tender for such a violent uncovering. By the time we'd clambered back up the clough side, the sky was dark. Keeper feared neither man nor beast but was not fond of a storm, so we dropped down to Stanbury and came back into the village along West Lane. Still the rain did not come.

Papa was in the study with a visitor from Bradford, a clergy acquaintance who'd come to advise him about a grant application. As far back as I could remember, Papa had been appalled by the lamentable level of education available to the local children, was now planning to set up a National School here in the village, which would also offer evening classes to the children who worked in the mills down in the valley. Even if the application was successful, Papa would still need to persuade local businessmen and landowners to donate. The meeting went on past supper, pausing only for prayers. While I waited for the visitor to leave, so that Papa could lock up for the night, I took Keeper out into the garden. The sky was darkening now, with no stars to be seen. The hills circled us, smudged an even deeper shade of black. A thin, warm wind had risen, was singing high in the old ash trees along the lane and rattling the branches of the cherry tree against the window of my little bedroom above the doorway. When I went back inside Papa was finished for the night. It was too late for his visitor to leave, so he would be staying in Branwell's room. When they'd finally gone up, I went into the dining room with the intention of writing for an hour or so but found myself caught by the sound of those branches against the glass, like the drumming of skeletal fingers. I left off writing and went to open the window, wanting to let a little of that strange, wild wind into the room. Across the valley, I saw a flicker of light. The storm was coming from west. The sky in that direction was purplish-black, and the clouds had a swollen, unstable appearance, like a pan of water about to boil over. Another fork of lightning split the sky over Crow Hill. The wind began to sigh. I rubbed my shoulder, remembering how the ground had given way beneath me this afternoon, the surprised look of the freshly exposed earth. By tomorrow, there would be a bruise to remind me of the fall. A memory unearthed too, from when I was very small. The day that Crow Hill exploded.

Nancy and Sarah Garrs, the sisters who used to help at home, had been there. And it was just Anne and I walking with them, so Charlotte must have been away at school by then. We ran ahead after we'd passed Ponden Hall and Nancy Garrs had called to us, said that we must turn back soon. We'd begged to keep on going, wanting to reach the foot of the moor at least, but Sarah pointed out the strange yellow clouds above Crow Hill, turning and rolling like someone was churning them. I remembered Anne closing her eyes and lifting her face, a small animal sniffing the air. Then the horizon turned black.

'A storm coming,' Sarah Garrs had said. Or something like that. As we turned for home, a fork of lightning divided the sky over the moortop. I saw the heather parting and swaying. On either side of the path, the wind began to rake through the trees. Lightning came again, followed by a crash of thunder, and then a groaning noise. I looked down at my feet and the ground shuddered beneath me, as though an invisible creature had clamped its jaws around the earth and was shaking it back and forth. I stared at my boot-tops, at the pathway which surely could not hold together, and then Sarah Garrs screamed. I looked back the way we'd come to see the moor and sky rearing up behind us like a dark wave. Rock and heather and bracken trembled, and then the wave broke, everything dissolving into itself. The earth shrieked as boulders wrenched free from their lodgings; they span through the air, light as dust, and then the hillside was gone, and a great torrent of mud and water was sliding directly towards us. Nancy had Anne in her arms now.

Sarah pushed me forwards and then my feet broke into a run as she propelled me through a gateway and towards an abandoned barn on the far side of the field, that vast gathering roar behind me. When we were almost at the doorway of the barn, I turned again, saw the mud-water crash towards the foot of the moor, high as a wall, wide as a valley. Then we were safe inside gaps of sky through the roof, damp cold of the walls, Nancy blocking my view. She moved aside just for a moment as the torrent seemed to hesitate in its path then pushed on through a drystone wall. Upended bushes, roots, virgin earth, black as night, the wind howling and then dropping almost instantly as the wave came to a treacly halt in the middle of a cornfield. I saw a familiar figure coming up the road from the direction of Ponden Hall and thought how funny it was to see Papa running, his legs as long a stork's.

When we were safely home again, he told us that he'd glanced out the study window to see the sky so dark that he'd come looking for us. 'What you witnessed today, children,' he said, stirring his tea with such energy that it spilt into the saucer, 'was an earthquake.' He wrote one of his letters to the paper telling the story of what had happened, and in his Sunday sermon he said it was a warning to sinners, but later we found out that it was not an earthquake after all. The rain had been falling on the heath all week and the peaty soil had absorbed it like a great sponge, grown heavier and heavier, the ground swelling to accommodate the moisture. It bore down on itself, started to liquefy with the pressure, and then, deep in the unstable darkness at the heart of Crow Hill, currents began to move. Still the rain kept falling and when the ground could contain no more, it burst in a great deluge. It was this and not a punishment for sinners that we had seen from the doorway of that ruined barn, and it was magnificent.

I left the window now and returned to my desk, intending to work on a poem about Alfred Sidonia, a Gondal nobleman who had been charged with conspiracy. I'd made a start on it long ago, just before I'd begun teaching at Law Hill, but never found the time to complete the final stanzas. For half an hour or so, I worked on the poem in a desultory manner, then pushed the verses away and picked up my German grammar instead. I'd only just begun this new language when we had to come home for Aunt's funeral, was anxious not to forget the verbs that I'd learned. Outside, lightning fired up the heavens again. When the first crash of thunder came it felt catastrophic, an immense axe striking the earth. Keeper opened an eye yet did not budge from his favourite sleeping spot. Returning to the window, I watched as the rain finally came, great billowing sheets driving across the graveyard.

Another flash of lightning came, and then thunder, full-throated. The storm must have turned up the memory of the peat burst, still so vivid in my mind. Or was it Charlotte and her desperate need to rearrange the world into a different shape? I took a notebook from the bookshelf, recently purchased, not yet used. The first page was blank and beguiling. Lightning flashed through the room, illuminating the solid sleeping figure of Keeper. He whimpered to himself, resettled. My hands twitched. I went back to the table and reached for my pen again. There was a strange feeling in my fingertips and in my chest. Words that had been waiting all these years, an ancient language tamped down since I was a small child: Cowan Bridge, Roe Head, Law Hill, Brussels. Words heaped on words, the pressure growing. When I looked up next, the storm was almost overhead. The wind shrieked around the eaves, and the words that had spilled over the pages of my notebook had nothing to do with Gondal. Rain was driving sideways through the window. A little pool had gathered on floor. By the time the clock in the stairwell struck midnight the storm was subsiding, the earth had contained it. Unpinned from the past, I lay my head down on the table and slept till dawn.

For the first time since I was a child, I could be at home without the uneasy feeling that I was failing everyone. I was busy every day with my new writing and happy as I'd ever been, knowing that at some stage my sisters would return, and we would try with our school again. But then the doctor came to see Papa and insisted on speaking to me afterwards. The reason Papa's vision was failing, he explained, was due to cataracts. They would grow worse as time passed. Eventually he would lose his sight completely.

'Both eyes?' I asked, fear overcoming my usual reluctance to speak. Though Papa had never relied on a script to deliver his sermons, I did not see how he could bear the loss of his books, or the ability to walk for miles whenever the mood took him. In the corner of the study, or sometimes in the umbrella stand in the hallway, was the staff he'd owned since he was a young man, always at hand for an impromptu outing.

Autumn was nearly over now. The hills had turned brown, and the fallen leaves softened and collapsed into the earth. As the days grew shorter and the light dimmed, Papa could make out still less, though he tried his best to go on as if nothing had changed, using the magnifying glass the doctor had recommended. Now that he actually needed his staff, it became an irritation to him. To prove it a mere accessory, an affectation, he would set off at a great pace, outstripping anyone hoping to accompany him. Even in the best of health, he'd appeared uncomfortable in his tall frame, was given to clumsiness and sudden movements that gave the impression he was not in control of his own person. For safety's sake, an observer might think, he ought to exist closer to the ground. This inherent ungainliness, coupled with his new sense of urgency, saw him slipping on the village's steep, cobbled lanes, or tripping over his own feet as he hurried down Main Street, staff sweeping aside the air, or any small child who happened to get in his way. Hurrying to the church one morning, he caught his staff on the boot scraper outside the front door. I heard his shout, ran down the hallway to find that he'd fallen face down in a thorn bush to one side of the steps. He looked so ridiculous, flailing around in the flowerbed as he tried to right himself, that at first, I wanted to laugh. Once I'd managed to get him upright again and seen the scratches to his hands, I had to stop myself from scolding him like a small child. I was used to his natural impatience, the fits of temper over small matters, but now he grew peevish and more easily disheartened. He missed Aunt's company more than ever, particularly in the evenings when his work was done. I did my best to distract him by re-lating passages from Charlotte and Anne's letters—Branwell wrote infrequently—reading out loud or playing some new piece on the piano. Still, his spirits were very low. On one such night, when the horror of perpetual darkness had slunk into the room uninvited and could not be banished by happy mu-sic or light-hearted stories, Charlotte arrived home. She'd sent no warning, stood exhausted and frozen by the range while I hurried to make her a hot drink. She looked tinier than ever, shrunken into herself, and her face was tinged green as though the effects of the North Sea had pursued her on to land. She had left Brussels, she told me, for good.

'Nothing was the same anymore,' she explained, as she sipped the steaming coffee I'd put in front of her. Her plate of bread and butter remained untouched. 'I started to believe I would vanish altogether if I stayed.' Her eyes were red-rimmed and dull with tiredness. 'I wonder if I'll ever be so happy as those first months we shared at the *Pensionnat.*'

'You need a good night's sleep in your own bed.' I pushed the plate towards her. 'Tomorrow you can start thinking about this school of yours.'

'Of ours,' she corrected, voice devoid of all emotion.

The next morning she stayed in bed, complaining of a headache. I took her tea and some dry toast to quell the nausea that always came with these attacks, found her curled in upon herself, barely able to open her eyes or speak, except to beg me not to open the shutters. When I next looked in, she was lying on her back with her arms flung out to either side, like an object dropped from a height. Except for the weight of her coiled hair on the pillow, she resembled a small, sickly child. She stayed in bed all the next day too, but early the following morning, long before it was light, I found her at the table in the dining room, a poor excuse for a fire in the hearth. Dressed in her wrapper and slippers and her hair unbrushed, she was busy writing a letter.

'To Monsieur,' she said, barely glancing up at me as I stoked the fire, then added some more coal. 'Some questions of grammar I need him to answer.' As if I had challenged her, she added: 'I'm used to being tutored now. Can't be expected to work everything out for myself.'

Later, she wanted to come with me when I took Keeper for his walk. I avoided the path that led towards Top Withens and then wondered why when there was nothing tangible to hide. It was not as if Charlotte could see into my soul. We walked for miles, but she did not complain of exhaustion, seemed too lost in her thoughts to register fatigue. By the time we dropped down the hillside towards the village, it was almost dark.

I stopped at a stand of trees and pointed to a jumble of boulders beneath.

'Remember when I persuaded you to climb up there?' I

smiled as Keeper nosed around the base of the mound. 'You only agreed because I said I'd hidden your Duke of Wellington soldier in that hole. You put your hand all the way inside.'

'And then you told me weasels were nesting there.' She gave a little laugh and then shuddered. 'Horrible girl.' How glassy her eyes looked, as if she had not slept for days. Beneath us, a dense fog rose from the valley, pawing at the village. The air smelt of woodsmoke, damp moss.

'We must live in the loneliest place on earth,' she said.

A letter arrived from Brussels. Charlotte snatched it from Martha's hand and then rushed up to her bedroom to read it. Within ten minutes, she was back downstairs and taking out her writing desk. In the days that followed, she walked round in an inward daze, not seeing what was in front of her, unable to settle to anything. Happy as I was to have my sister home, I felt my equilibrium disturbed. I yearned sometimes for the quiet solitude of previous months, when all the energy in the house had belonged to me. I wondered again what, if anything, had taken place between her and Monsieur *Héger*.

I was just starting to rearrange myself around Charlotte's restless presence, when Anne came home, bringing with her all her belongings and a little soft-eared spaniel named Flossy, a gift from the Robinsons. Charlotte pressed her for information, but she would say only that the situation no longer suited her. A letter came from one of her former charges, and for several days afterwards she was melancholy, distracted, her needle hovering in mid-air as she worked. I reread her last letter from Thorp Green, looking for a sign.

I have tried to finish my story, but I cannot seem to find our Gondals and Gaaldines when I am here. I pray they are not lost to me—they have been our companions for so many years! There is little time to write at all—Lydia will need help with some simple

*arithmetic problem, Elizabeth and Mary quarrel often which
vexes their mother, so I must broker peace between them, or Mr.
Robinson will decide upon a family walk that must include me.*

I knew from my own experience how devastating it was to
lose sight of Gondal but I felt sure she would rediscover that
world now that she was home. Charlotte thought she must simply have grown tired of occupying the lonely space allotted to
a governess—never quite part of the family, held at a distance
by the other servants who imagined condescension. 'There's no
occupation more designed to sap the life from a soul,' she said,
her voice flat. 'At least, one with any kind of sensibility.'

She herself spent most of her time waiting for the letters that
came less and less frequently now, or else taking up her own
pen in the hope of spurring a reply. Occasionally she'd pick up
a book, hold it just inches from her nose, and then drop it in her
lap with a mournful sigh, convinced that she'd inherited Papa's
disability and would probably go blind before he did. I was
tempted to agree, if only to jolt her out of her self-absorption—
she was so entirely lost in her own misery that she barely seemed
to notice Papa's daily struggles and frustrations. Her eyes were
good enough to reread all her old letters from Brussels, and I
came into the dining room one morning to find her with our old
childhood atlas open on the table before her. She was staring
intently at the map of Belgium and its surrounding countries,
trying, it appeared, to transport herself there by the power of
concentration. I said nothing but took it as a lesson to myself.
Now, whenever we walked in the direction of Top Withens, I
made myself look straight past, ignored the pull of that dark,
lonely farmhouse. The weeks went on and Charlotte grew taut
and perilous, like a violin string that had been over-tightened.
Eventually she broke and I found her in a storm of tears, head
down on the dining room table.

'He says I must only write every six months.' She held out a letter to me, her tiny hand trembling. I read it. The letter was terse affair, urging Charlotte to apply herself to her studies and to her plans for a school and ending with the instruction to write less often. The only indication of friendship was a post-script to say the *Hégers* might send their youngest, Louise, to board at any school we established. I pictured Monsieur at his desk, Madame overseeing the writing of this letter. I suspected the postscript was added later, when he was alone again, an act of kindness rather than anything more. For all his intel-lect, it was clear that Monsieur *Héger* did not know what to do with my sister's passion for him, regardless of what might have passed between them before. Every line of the letter suggested a man at the end of his resources.

'He's the only person who's ever listened to me, who actually wanted to hear what I have to say,' she sobbed. 'And just as I've grown brave, dared to speak what I truly feel, he orders me to be silent again. It is too cruel!' I thought of Miss Wooler, Ellen, Mary Taylor, all of whom had valued Charlotte's opinions over the years. Me. We did not matter. She took the letter from me and flung it across the table, then covered her face with her hands, shutting out the unjust world. 'Oh Emily, how am I to go on without him?'

'What is it?' Anne came in from the yard to find Charlotte and I listening at the kitchen doorway. She'd been to visit Tabby Aykroyd, now retired, taking some of the sweet buns I'd made for her. How pretty she looked in her lilac dress, with her bas-ket on her arm. She was beyond girlhood now, but everything about her was still finely made, a delicate line drawing, the soft shades of a watercolour.

'Sssh,' said Charlotte, gesturing down the hallway. 'It's Branwell.' Our brother was home for a short holiday before joining the Robinson family for their annual trip to Scarborough.

'Papa was shouting,' I said. 'He's stopped now though.'

The study door opened and then slammed shut. We retreated from the doorway, listening to Branwell's quick footsteps in the hall and on the stairs. They were followed by another slam—his bedroom door this time.

Anne dropped down at the kitchen table. 'He's been dismissed.'

'What?' Charlotte glared at her.

'Or he's had the good sense to resign. I wish that were the case, but I don't think so. Not if they're arguing.'

'What are you talking about?' said Charlotte. Her voice was choked. 'Explain!'

'Stop hectoring, Charlotte.' I sat down opposite Anne.

'I don't know when it started. Not exactly,' she said. 'I had an idea, a sense . . . but one day last month, just before I resigned, I saw Branwell coming out of Mrs. Robinson's bedroom.'

'Mr. Robinson was at home?' I asked.

'He might have been in the room with them,' Charlotte said. 'Perhaps he and Mrs. Robinson wanted to discuss something with . . .'

'In a *bedroom*?' I looked at her.

'Mr. Robinson had been in London for three days and wasn't expected home until the weekend. Mrs. Robinson was standing in the doorway so I could see her clearly. She wasn't fully dressed.' Anne's tone was quiet but certain. It left no room for doubt.

'Did you speak to Branwell?' asked Charlotte.

'I couldn't bring myself to ask him outright. I made a remark about her familiar manner with him, but he carried on as though he hadn't heard me.'

'Why didn't you tell us? We might have been able to do something.'

'I don't think anyone can stop Branwell when he makes up his mind. I hoped . . . I thought it might have happened just the once and that they would think better of themselves. Or I thought she might tire of him—' Anne's violet eyes filled with tears and my heart almost burst in the cage of my chest, her pain being mine. 'About a week later, while Mr. Robinson was in the garden talking to the groundsman, I heard . . . noises from that room and I couldn't stay any longer, not once I was sure. I told everyone that I was sick with longing for home, which was partly true.'

'You ought to have spoken to him again,' said Charlotte. 'Given him the opportunity to think about what he was do-ing or,' she pondered for a moment. 'To be more discreet. This could bring shame on all of us.'

'Anne's not accountable for Branwell's behaviour,' I said.

'I can't believe he'd do such a thing. That he would be so stupid as to be discovered! Oh, we have no luck in this world, no matter what we do.' Charlotte slumped into a chair, the fire leaving her quite suddenly. The study door opened. A fast, shuffling noise came from the hallway, followed by the creak of the front door. I flew to rescue Papa from the possibility of another fall.

Branwell showed no contrition. 'I don't expect you to un-derstand,' he told us. 'None of you have been in love, so you can't imagine what Lydia means to me. I'd do anything to be with her.'

'You cost Anne her position as well as your own,' I said, glancing at my sister. She did not look up from her work, a pencil sketch of Flossy. I'd worried that Keeper wouldn't take to another dog in the house, but he seemed to regard the little spaniel less a rival than another species.

'I'm sorry about that, of course. But you'll find something else, Anne. And you can't pretend that you were happy there. Not in the way that I was.' He smiled to himself in wonder.

'As happy as I could ever be away from home,' said Anne in a low voice. She put down her pencil and looked at him for the first time. 'You must see that what you did was wrong. I've prayed for you every night, but it's no good if you don't ask forgiveness for yourself.'

'Don't be so pious, Anne! Or naïve.' Branwell pulled a face, indicating her stupidity. 'Even you must know that kind of nonsense is just a means of controlling people. Everyone toiling away as if Heaven is to be earned by a lifetime of misery and self-sacrifice. If there really is a Heaven, it's right here on earth, and the only Hell is every day that I am forced to be apart from Lydia. I belong with her, as she does with me. We will find a means.'

'And yet she keeps you at a distance?' I said. 'She must know by now that her husband's written to Papa to dismiss you.'

Branwell batted away the idea with his hand. 'Only until she's settled matters with *him*. She's doesn't love him, never has, and he long since gave up paying her the attention she deserves. I've explained everything to Papa, it's only matter of time before we are together again.'

'Then you're very foolish,' I said, getting up from my chair by the fire. 'You've nothing to offer a woman of her standing. No income, no property.'

'Have you not a jot of romance in your soul, Emily?' Branwell rolled his eyes towards the ceiling. 'If you must talk of practicalities, I intend to write again. I've time now and more experience. And the old man would not dare leave Lydia or the children penniless.'

Charlotte had sat in silence till now.

'We *toil away*, as you so kindly pointed out, because we have no other choice. Do you have any conception of that?' She slammed shut her volume of Tennyson. 'You may try your hand at anything which takes your fancy—artist, romantic hero, *railway man*—' her voice was acid with contempt. 'And then abandon it at a moment's notice.' She held up her hand to prevent him from interrupting. 'The world will always forgive a personable young man his wrong turns and misdemeanours, but I don't suppose you've thought for a second about the trouble you could bring upon us. What should happen if word gets out among the parishioners? I wonder how your toiling sisters will earn their livings if you become known as an untrustworthy reprobate? No parent is likely to send their daughter to our little school *then*. You may not care about destroying your own future, Branwell, but this is our one chance of independence!'

Charlotte's extremes had, as usual, a cooling effect on me. 'It's not so desperate yet. I don't suppose the news will travel, though you might want to think of us before you actually run off with your Mrs. Robinson. And consider Papa. You can see for yourself how frail he is—don't go sharing your views of Heaven and Hell with him.'

'I lost my faith long ago. Why shouldn't I be honest about that?'

'Your beliefs are your own affair. You're not a child in need of validation for every thought. There's no reason to worry him about your troubles with Mrs. Robinson either.' Knowing my brother, I felt sure that this latest passion would die as quickly as it had started.

'Lydia is no trouble to me. She's an angel, my life.'

He smiled beatifically and it struck me that there was something wrong with all of us. Life was not as we'd imagined it to be when we were children, our minds pulsing like summer wildfires. Had we really believed the world to be peopled with kindred spirits, sympathetic to our desires? Even now, when it had repeatedly been proved otherwise, we persisted, trying to make it so by the power of our imaginations, refused to accept the true story of our lives—that the world valued us at nought. At least that was the case for my sisters and me. We could not adjust to the world; it would not adapt to us. And I was as foolish as Charlotte, disappointed as Anne, deluded like Branwell, with my lost words and wild thoughts, my ungovernable feet, forever carrying me towards the shadow of a stranger.

I was folding collars in my little bedroom over the stairs when Charlotte knocked. She took a deep breath as she entered, then steadied herself against the door frame. At first I thought it was a letter she was holding to her breast—a long-awaited reply from Brussels or an invitation from Ellen Nussey perhaps. It was not a letter. It was a notebook with the initials E.J.B. written on the cover. Beneath, and also written in my own hand, was the word *Poems*. Just last month I'd copied the poem I'd written about the peat burst on Crow Hill into this new book, along with a number of others I'd written since that stormy night.

'What are you doing with that?' I slammed shut the top drawer of the chest and reached for my notebook. 'Give it to me!' She did so immediately, darting back like one expecting a blow. Could I have dropped it somewhere around the house? Not possible. That notebook never left its place at the bottom of my writing desk, beneath all my Gondal papers. 'You've not opened it? You would not dare.' I threw it down onto the bed, out of her reach.

'I ran out of nibs last night and knew that you'd bought some last week.' Charlotte folded her hands together which might have given her an air of resolution, except that they were visibly shaking.

'Then you should have asked! You know better than to go through someone else's belongings.' I was tempted to suggest she was writing too many letters to Brussels if she went through so many nibs, but my mind was already racing ahead. There was only one reason Charlotte would dare come to me with my notebook right there in her hands, instead of putting it back where it belonged. The scale of her crime made my ears ring.

'I've read your poems, Emily. All of them,' she confirmed. I watched her make a visible effort to steel herself. 'They're extraordinary.'

My fists were clenched. I had never hurt another being in my life but just then I could have happily boxed my sister's ears. 'Those,' I said, my teeth clamped together so hard that it was difficult to speak, 'are private. If I had wanted you, or anyone else, to know of them, I would have invited you to a reading.'

'I can't explain,' said Charlotte. She retreated still further, onto the landing, but her eyes were still fixed on the notebook, framed now by a slab of innocent autumn sunshine falling across the counterpane. 'I know I should be sorry, but I'm not. You never said you were writing anything except your Gondal stories.'

'You wish me to report to you?' I stared at her.

'Anyway, I read your poems all last night, after everyone had gone to bed, and then again this morning. I couldn't speak about it at breakfast, not in front of the others, but I came as soon as I could.' With an air of generosity, she gestured to herself: here I am.

'I thought you'd given up confessing your sins. Don't think I'll absolve you like some foolish priest, Charlotte, because I can't. I won't.' The enormity of what she'd done engulfed me once again. 'I shall never forgive you!'

'They are extraordinary,' she repeated. 'My own verses are passable, but yours . . . No-one has written in such a way.'

'Your opinion means nothing,' I said, straightening my hairbrush and comb on the chest, though they were already neat. 'I didn't seek it. I do not value it.'

'I spent half the night in Papa's study, going through his

books for names and addresses of publishers. I was in a fever by then, couldn't rest for imagining and then reimagining. It was dawn before I could calm myself enough to sleep.' She pressed her fingers into her temples, pushing scalp-deep into her hair.

'Get out,' I slammed the bedroom door shut.

For the rest of the day, I couldn't bring myself to speak to her. It would have been bad enough if she'd read my Gondal papers without first asking permission, but this new notebook contained thoughts and feelings entirely personal to me. After all these years, she still felt she had the right to interfere, to play God with my life. I felt spied upon, exposed, didn't know what I might do if she were to quote a line or expression that had been dislodged from the deepest part of me. I spent the morning giving the fireplaces a vicious cleaning and then went out alone as soon as dinner was over. The sunlight was viscous, honeyed by the ageing year, and the sight of Keeper bounding through the tawny bracken soothed me. By the time we joined Papa for prayers that evening, I'd almost resolved to let the matter pass, on the understanding that we never spoke of it again. Still, I avoided Charlotte by staying in the study to work on a piece by Beethoven. Keeper drowsed at my feet, and the pools of golden candlelight, the familiar give of the keys beneath my fingers made me almost peaceful.

I was just about to get into bed when Charlotte came knocking again.

'You'll wake Papa,' I told her.

'Let me come in then.'

'I've nothing to say to you.' I extinguished my candle and waited for my eyes adjust to the darkness. She remained in the doorway, ghostly in her nightgown. There was a gust of wind outside, the tap of the cherry tree against the windowpane. I sensed her edging towards me, the creep of small feet.

'Hate me if you want to. Never speak to me again, but you can't hide your poems from the world.'

'Or my own sister. Why must you annoy me?'

She dared to sit on the very edge of my bed.

'What if we were to send our work to a publisher? Together. Southey said I showed promise, and I've definitely read worse things in print than my own verses.'

'He told you to give it up.'

Charlotte wriggled back on her bottom until she was leaning against the window frame, her still-stockinged feet pointing towards the ceiling. 'At least we'd know for certain if we have talent. I *know* that you do, Emily. Your poems are wild and strange—'

'Like me,' I warned. 'You should be more careful.'

'There's a peculiar music to them; they are *you*. Imagine what—'

'I told you before,' I said, sitting up abruptly. 'I have no interest in anyone else's opinion. I wrote those poems for myself. And if you honestly believe some publisher from London would have the faintest interest in anything . . . I am starting to think you lost your mind completely in Brussels—'

I stopped. Even in the darkness, my eye caught movement, the presence of another.

From the doorway came a soft voice, almost inaudible. 'I have some poems too.'

A nne's cheeks were flushed as a linnet's breast as she placed a bundle of papers on the dining room table. 'Please don't read them until I've gone.' She already had on her boots and grey winter cloak and little Flossy waited at her feet in anticipation. She lost courage then, mumbled something about running an errand for Martha and hurried out. From the window I watched her leave, bonnet bobbing down the lane towards the village.

Half an hour passed. 'They're actually well-constructed,' said Charlotte. She turned over a sheet of paper, read it again.

Anne's poems surprised me for a different reason. I'd expected to find at least one or two of the characters that she and I had invented over the years but, like my own poems, there was barely a trace of Gondal to be found in these verses.

'There's sincerity in the way she expresses herself. An Anne-ish sort of purity too.' Charlotte gathered up the papers. 'And they're a contrast to our own work which might appeal to a publisher.'

I heard footsteps and Flossy scrabbling back along the gravel path outside. I hurried to the front door. Anne had her head down, a parcel under her arm. I put her out of her suffering.

'They're good.' Around her boots were the bright, decaying leaves of the cherry tree, spatter of fruit, long since fallen. 'You should be proud.' She fiddled with the string on the butcher's parcel, tending to nothing. Blood was already seeping through the paper. In the distance, I could hear the thud, thud of the cleaver.

'Not good enough to send out though?'

'That's not what I meant.' For a moment I could not locate myself. Ever since Brussels I'd lived exactly as I wished and now Charlotte wanted to change things. Charlotte always wanted to change things. 'But think of some *person* in London judging our work, passing it around to others.' It occurred to me only now that Southey's letter must have left a barb in me all those years ago, though he knew nothing of my own work. I glanced behind me. Charlotte was standing in the hallway, Anne's poems still bundled in her hand. 'Nothing could induce me to do it.'

They came to me in the back kitchen, where I'd just finished scrubbing the potatoes for dinner with unnecessary violence. 'Aunt's legacy can't last forever,' said Charlotte.

'I do well enough budgeting for the house.' I took up my knife and potato peel began falling in practised curls. 'I need almost nothing for myself. And Branwell's sure to find something else, so that will be one less person to feed.'

'What about Papa?' said Charlotte. She started taking tea-towels from the drying rack, folded them with quick little movements. 'I was shocked to see how bad his eyes were when I came home, much worse than before. Mr. Nicholls seems to be covering most of his duties and I see you write all his letters for him now.' There she went, chipping away at me in that timid, persistent way of hers, seeking out weak points.

'Isn't that the point of a curate? To help?' I thought of Mr. Nicholls guiding Papa to the pulpit every Sunday, then glanced at Anne who was listening in silence. Was it possible that she could have given up on Gondal without telling me? My knife slammed against the board as I chopped the potatoes into rough chunks. I threw the peel into the scrap bucket. 'I've plenty of time to read to him or whatever else he needs. Dr. Wheelhouse thinks an operation might even be possible.'

'He's nearly seventy, Emily.'

He might not survive the operation was what she meant.

And even if it proved a success, he would still die, perhaps one day soon, and we would be left homeless, this house returning to the Church governors as we had always known it must.

I went through to the main kitchen, carrying the potatoes with me. When the two of them followed me, I put down the bowl and went to the dresser. Opening the drawer, I took out the school cards and dropped them in front of Charlotte. 'Your last plan.'

'We've asked everyone we know,' she said, pushed aside the stack which was already beginning to yellow.

'Then what was the point of Brussels?' I made a start on the onions, knowing they would make Charlotte sneeze. 'That was all part of the plan, you said. Or did you drag me halfway across Europe for nothing?'

'Brussels was for the right reasons, Emily! You know that.' Charlotte's voice rising. 'I'm forever telling people about our school, our qualifications. I can't force them to enrol their daughters with us.' She shook her head violently. 'Why is it always down to me to rescue us?'

'You like it that way. Telling everyone what they must do. And I don't see how this latest scheme of yours will help anything.'

'You live in your own little world, Emily. Always have done. You never listen to a word anyone tells you!'

'Because I have a mind of my own, am not some puppet for you to play with.'

'This has nothing to do with our poems,' said Anne quietly. 'I see no reason why we shouldn't send them out to see if people think we have something worth saying. As Charlotte says, Aunt's money will only last so long. And we can still advertise for our school, either here or elsewhere.'

'It's a ridiculous idea, Anne. *You* must know that. I don't see how—look, Branwell has a poem in the paper every five minutes and has never once been paid for them.'

'But a proper publisher,' said Charlotte, blinking rapidly.

Any moment now she would start crying and blame the onions. 'I still think Branwell will do something remarkable one day.'

'We won't make a penny.'

'How will we know unless we try?'

'We're perfectly happy as we are.'

Charlotte squeezed her eyes shut and became still. 'Do as you wish, Emily, but if our school doesn't work, and I cannot go back to—' She came to a halt, biting down on her lip.

'Where?' Daring her to speak of Brussels, of Monsieur. It was cruel of me, but I was past caring.

'If you're saying I'm to be nothing but a governess for the rest of my life. Or a teacher in some miserable school.' She opened her eyes and looked directly at me, her gaze unwavering. 'I'll take that knife from your hand and plunge it down my own throat.'

I've a condition.' Thud of the dough on the floured board. I pushed with the heel of my hand, gave the dough a quarter-turn and pushed again. Within the hour it would be nudging the cloth into a mound, trying to steal over the sides of the bowl, pale doughy fingers feeling their way out into the world. I would not be surprised to find it missing altogether one day, escaped from its confines like Frankenstein's monster. I looked forward to the daily ritual of push, turn, push, turn, the soft rub of flour through my fingers. Secretly I thought this domestic miracle as wondrous as anything a man could create: a bridge slung across a river, a cathedral straining towards the heavens.

'Anything,' said Charlotte. She threw open her arms in a rare, unselfconscious moment. Most of the time she inhabited her body with an air of grievance, huddled down inside her tiny stature, appalled by her own appearance. How often had I witnessed her disappearing in the presence of beauty, the intellect of which she was so proud suddenly counting for nothing? What I was about to stipulate had come to me last night while I lay in my little room over the stairs unable to sleep. Our poetry would never make money—I'd not changed my mind about that—but despite everything I'd said, I knew that a spark of ambition had been ignited in me. I was still furious with Charlotte for spying on me, recoiled from the idea of strangers judging my work, and yet another part of me yearned to know if it had any worth. I'd lain awake for a long time, trying to put my thoughts into some sort of order, listening to the hoot of a Tawny owl from the lane, its mate responding at each cue. Their last set of off-spring had been so tame that they would follow me around the graveyard where I liked to wander sometimes, imagining the lives once lived. I asked myself if the thought of sending out my work had already been in my mind before Charlotte discovered it for herself. After all, I had deliberately separated those poems from my other stories and verses, copied them carefully into a different notebook. Gondal would always be for me and Anne alone, but what of those other words that had seemed to flow straight from my veins and onto the page? I had thought them beautiful and true, but once Charlotte started shunting me in all directions, it was difficult to remember what I'd wanted for my-self. I'd drifted into sleep eventually, then found myself crawl-ing through the Fairy Cave until I reached the middle point. I felt safe there, buried inside the rock, never wanted to leave. When I woke there was no sign of dawn, but my agitation had gone. I lay in the peaceful darkness and thought of all the things that belonged to me—the slow drip, drip of time, blackening gritstone, lichened slate, creep of moss on drystone wall, on headstones, echoes of generations along Haworth's dark-setted streets, the chack, chack of jackdaws in the churchyard, break-ing the fragile air.

'Firstly, we have to continue advertising for the school. There must be people we've overlooked. Also, if you insist on sending our work to London, you can't mention my name.'

Charlotte stared at me without comprehension. 'I don't un-derstand. How am I to explain our poems to anyone . . . to a publisher?'

'You and Anne don't have to—,' I hesitated. 'No, that won't work. We all have to disguise ourselves.' Light had been seep-ing into the world when, finally, I'd happened on this solution. The dough was beginning to lose its tackiness now, became smoother and more malleable. Back and forth I pushed it, the calm, repetitive rhythm freeing my thoughts.

'But people will think it extraordinary—'

'Plenty of writers use pseudonyms.'

'You said nobody would take any notice of our work.'

'I wouldn't care about my name,' said Anne. 'If only my work could encourage or comfort someone, even in some small way.'

The dough was blood-warm, moved of its own accord now—retreating from the stretch, gathering itself in again. I set it in a deep bowl and covered it with a damp cloth, then rubbed the drying mixture from my fingers.

'You've settled on a name?' said Charlotte, with a sigh.

'Ellis.' A grave I'd seen at the far edge of the churchyard, the ground collapsing in on itself, headstone sloping, lichen-scarred. Time's fingers had smudged the epitaph, only these letters and the remains of a date '-01.'

'As a surname?' said Anne.

It had been impossible to tell on the gravestone. 'Christian.'

'Ellis what, then?' said Charlotte with an edge to her voice. 'Assuming Brontë is unacceptable to you.'

She caught me off guard. I'd been so pleased with those five letters—E L L I S—standing like monoliths between me and the world, that I hadn't thought any further. In the hallway I could hear Papa, the shuffle of his feet as he made his way to the door, then the sound of Mr. Nicholls—the Irish bear as Charlotte had taken to calling him—wishing him good morning. Despite his failing eyesight, Papa still insisted on being taken to visit parishioners. He was busy too trying to make peace between the church governors and the local dissenters who objected to paying church rates; to do something about the village's water supply. A few days after his curate had arrived in the parish, a letter had come, addressed to *Mr. Arthur Bell Nicholls c/o The Parsonage, Haworth.*

'Bell,' I said, setting the mixing bowl near the warmth of the range. Later I would hold the newly baked loaf to my ear so that I could hear the tiny crackles of life, feel the yeasty breath on my cheek. Already I liked the clear ring of the word. 'Ellis Bell.'

By the end of the morning, we had settled upon Currer, Ellis and Acton Bell as the names we would use, the initials of each Christian name being the only clue to our respective identities. 'CURRER BELL. I think it suits me!' Charlotte said, cheerful again. 'And everyone will assume we are men, which should work in our favour. When is Branwell home?'

'Tomorrow,' I said, setting down my copy of *Don Juan*. I took the list of publishers from her. Our brother had spent the last week on holiday in Liverpool with his old friend, John Brown. We were optimistic that he would return cured of his current obsession.

'I'm worried he'll object to a pseudonym. You know how he loves the glory.'

'He's used one before,' I said. 'Just as well.' Recently he'd had a number of poems published in the newspaper, thinly-disguised odes to Lydia Robinson. 'The important thing is, can we trust him not to shout about this to everyone?'

Charlotte tipped her head to one side and then back the other way, weighing up the matter. 'Well we can't exclude him. And it might be exactly the right kind of distraction he needs.'

'We'll wait then.' I felt accommodating, easy in myself now that I'd prevailed about names.

'No.' The fender crashed to the hearth, buttons scattering in all directions as Anne's work bag tumbled from her lap. She steadied herself against the mantelpiece. 'I know it's wrong—I struggle with myself every day—but I can't forgive him for spoiling everything at Thorp Green, just when the girls had started to pay attention.' She took a breath, unused to speaking so emphatically. The fine skin over her collarbone was blotched with pink. 'I'll have no part in this plan if Charlotte tells Branwell about it.'

'Why not Emily too?' said Charlotte. 'I'm the only one incapable of keeping a secret?'

'He probably wouldn't be interested anyway,' I said. 'Not at the moment. When he's feeling less agitated . . .'

Anne shook her head in distress. 'I don't like to ask for anything.'

'But we've always shared our work with him,' said Charlotte. 'At least I have. I don't see how we're to—'

'I'm sorry but that,' Anne held fast to the mantelpiece, her fingernails white, 'is *my* condition.'

For the rest of the morning, Charlotte wrote and then rewrote an increasingly florid cover letter. Eventually we persuaded her to reduce it to a few brief lines, and then we packed our manuscripts into a parcel and addressed it to the first publisher on her list. It looked slight, inconsequential, even in Charlotte's small hands. We went to the Post Office together, hardly noticed the rain lashing the shop fronts on Main Street, tearing down the steep gutters in dirty streams. The parcel was damp by the time we arrived, but I imagined the postmaster's fingers burning as he took it from us.

'We won't hear anything for ages,' said Charlotte who knew as much about publishing as anyone else, on the way back to the house.

The following morning, I found her waiting by the door for the postboy, for a miracle of time. But nothing came, of course, and there was no post at all for us over the next few weeks, only a series of letters for Branwell, who had now returned from his holiday. He scribbled his replies, and then we watched him bounding down the hallway like a faun, energy springing from his limbs, waited for the slam of the front door behind him.

'For *her*,' said Charlotte. 'Apparently, he addresses his letters to Mrs. Robinson's coachman, who passes them to her when her husband is out.'

I left off sweeping the flagstones. 'Has he said anything about looking for a new position?'

'Not to me, but he told Papa he's working on a novel.' She gave a terse laugh. 'Apparently, that will secure an income until Mr. Robinson has the courtesy to die.'

'You've not mentioned anything about us?'

'I gave my word, didn't I? Though it still feels wrong to exclude him. I'm hoping Anne will change her mind. Anyway, he's too caught up in his own affairs to notice what anyone else is doing.'

'Perhaps Mrs. Robinson really does love him. She risks losing everything by keeping on like this.'

'She's flattered by his attentions,' said Charlotte with an air of certainty. 'I know Anne said she's very handsome, but a woman of her age can't rely on her appearance for much longer. What sort of woman seduces a young man when there is a husband and children to think of? If only Branwell could just *restrain* himself.'

Later, when I went into the dining room with a stack of newly ironed napkins and tablecloths in my arms, I found her at her writing desk, head bent low, hand whipping back and forth. I did not need to look at the envelope to know that it was addressed to the *Pensionnat Héger*, Brussels.

A parcel arrived, addressed for Currer Bell, c/o Miss Brontë, The Parsonage, Haworth. Charlotte ran into the kitchen, ripped open the paper with a knife, and pulled out the manuscripts we'd sent, together with a short letter.

Please to be informed that we are not seeking material of this nature at present

'Oh,' was all she could say. We looked at our returned manuscripts, back on the kitchen table. I felt a thump of disappointment in my stomach.

'We didn't expect to succeed immediately,' said Anne, casting down her eyes.

After a few days, the blow seemed less catastrophic. The very act of sending the parcel to the second publisher on Charlotte's list had the effect of cancelling out that first failure, and we were buoyant again. This time a whole month passed till we received a reply.

While certain verses therein are of merit, we are not, at present, able to offer publication

'There's encouragement, I suppose,' said Charlotte. She squinted with her left eye, the line between her brows deepening. Within the hour she'd given in to a headache, closing the bedroom shutters against the jabbing sunlight. If this second rejection proved that I was right, that no-one would pay a penny for our work, I did not feel like celebrating my prescience. The outrage I'd felt when Charlotte discovered my work had been replaced by some nascent hope that she did, after all, know better. It was the nudge-nudging I objected to, Charlotte sniffing me out like a tiny mouse and me resisting, retreating, trying to heed my own voice instead, the endless push-pull of us.

I grew used to the sight of Charlotte and Branwell pacing up and down the hallway every morning, hovering by the door for the postboy to come. Letters arrived for Branwell but it was another five weeks until a parcel arrived for Miss Brontë. Our poems had been returned to us again, this time without an accompanying note.

'I'm not sure they've even read them!' Charlotte gazed in despair at the suspiciously neat stack of papers in her hands. 'And now it's Christmas and no-one will want to be bothered with new work.' The manuscripts thudded onto the kitchen table. Charlotte went to the dresser drawer and took out the school cards. She stared down at them as if they were a heavenly judgement. As agreed, we'd sent more of the cards to Papa's clergy friends and asked the Heatons at Ponden Hall to distribute them to any family they thought suitable, but still not a single enquiry. Charlotte's left eye, I noticed, was starting to flicker.

Anne suffered in a different way. Not given to extremes of emotion, it was easy to miss the days when her voice dropped to a whisper, and she gave up smiling. The prayers at bedtime became too fervent and went on long past the hour when the rest of us had made our peace with the world. One evening I caught her gazing at a profile of William Weightman that she'd sketched when life had coursed through him like a sparkling beck. She'd captured his beauty, but also that genial nature, delighted with the world. It was hard to believe three years had passed since her dreams for the future had been buried with him, though she'd never once complained. My sister, I believed, was a creature of unqualified goodness, the only one of us who had swallowed Papa's teaching whole, lived it in concentrated form. But she could not see it in herself, would be struggling with her conscience, punishing herself day and night because we'd excluded Branwell from our plans.

We did not speak of any of it, but she sought out my company more than ever, bringing the lace collar she was working on to the kitchen where I was busy making a pie. Loops of shiny, green peel lay on the table and the bare, white, bumpy apples were ready for coring and quartering now. I'd propped my German grammar against the bowl where the pastry rested.

'It is from Aylott and Jones,' said Charlotte, bursting into the room and making Anne prick her finger. Flapping a letter wildly in my face.

'Who?' I didn't recognise the handwriting and the flapping was irritating.

'The publisher in London!' She held up the pages. 'They thank us for sending our poems, want to make us an offer!' Her eyes glowed with excitement and her cheeks were scarlet.

'What else?' I urged, seeing that the letter was considerably longer than this. Anne said nothing but left her stool by the range.

'They want us to pay the cost of publication,' said Charlotte, reading on. She looked at us in dismay.

'Aren't they supposed to pay us?'

'It says they can't afford to because we are entirely unknown. *However, we believe the work is of sufficient quality to appeal to the discerning reader . . . if reviewed it might reach a wider audience.* Oh, what shall we do?' Charlotte collapsed into a chair. 'We can't afford to spend any money, but we might never receive another offer.'

'Find out how much they want.'

Charlotte stared as if she did not recognise me. 'We've Aunt's money,' I reminded her.

'I'm not sure she'd have approved,' says Anne, bending like a wilting flower over the letter.

'She's not here to give an opinion. We must decide for ourselves.'

'I didn't think it mattered to you,' said Charlotte. 'It's not that I'm faint-hearted, Emily, but what would Papa say? And you've had your doubts all along.'

I swept the peelings into the slop bucket, then took the rolling pin from the hook where it hung by a blue ribbon. Mamma had brought it with her from Cornwall. It was decorated with delicate forget-me-knots the colour of the sea. 'We should finish what we've started.'

Later that day, Branwell showed us the advertisement he'd placed in the *Halifax Guardian* for a tutoring position abroad.

'It's exactly what I need,' he said. 'It's no use sitting around here waiting for things to change, it's a waste of time. This place is so oppressive.' He pressed his palms against his temples to demonstrate and then snatched up the newspaper again, giving it a triumphant shake. 'A less resourceful man might've gone mad.'

'It still feels wrong,' said Charlotte when he'd gone, glancing at the letter from Aylott & Jones tucked beneath my grammar book. 'Though he'd probably laugh at the idea of paying for publication.'

'We agreed,' I reminded her. 'I don't suppose he'll ever find out.'

Yet there was a feeling of hope, the promise of spring after a hard winter. Aylott & Jones wrote back asking for a little over £30, which was almost as much as Anne's annual salary at Thorp Green, but we had made up our minds by then, immediately arranged for the money, which was enough to print a thousand copies of our poems, to be sent. Charlotte was invited to stay with Ellen and left in high spirits. A week after her departure, she wrote home to report a conversation with Ellen's cousin, who was a doctor, about Papa's eye condition. I ran to the study to read to Papa:

Dr. Carr says there is now an operation which can be undertaken once the cataracts have hardened sufficiently. He says that most patients have their sight entirely restored and recommends a surgeon in Manchester for when the time comes.

Papa laid down his magnifying glass and looked up at me through clouded eyes. 'Oh my dear,' he said.

Anne's mood lifted too. She even suggested that the two of us should take a holiday when Charlotte returned.

'Bridlington would be beautiful in summertime,' she said, sniffling a little because of a light but persistent cold. 'We might meet families who'd be interested in our school.' I smiled at the idea of us mixing with others. 'I long to see York again too.'

The summer before, we'd taken the train to that city and spent two days quite by ourselves, exploring the grand shopping streets and the little ginnels that threaded between ancient buildings, come upon York Minster quite suddenly, when we least expected it, a wall of stone rearing up and blocking the sky at the end of some narrow, twisting lane. We'd spent many hours exploring the cathedral, Anne in a trance that could not be broken. She whispered to herself the epitaphs on the marble tombs which lined the Quire aisles, gazed up at the Great East Window, which was an immense Gothic arch.

'The bottom third of the window depicts scenes from the Apocalypse,' she'd read from the leaflet we'd bought at the cathedral entrance. 'While the upper sections contain scenes from the Old Testament. The tracery depicts the heavenly realm, with God the Father at the apex.'

She stared in dread at the monstrous beasts of the Apocalypse, until I suggested we find the Chapter House. According to the leaflet, its acoustics allowed those seated on the stone benches around the octagonal space to hear one another perfectly clearly. Anne was keen to test this, speaking in her softest voice from the opposite side of the room, was so delighted when I repeated her words back to her that it made me smile. The Chapter House would make a splendid meeting place for the Gondals, I decided, while the nave would be perfect for a coronation. I'd been busy with my new poems by then, but still found time to think about the islanders, and Augusta in particular. I'd wondered if she might uncover the shepherd prince's identity next, so that they could marry legitimately, had quickly abandoned the idea because it seemed like the end of an adventure. I'd attempted to sketch the shepherd boy several times, seeking the shape of him on the page, but his face wouldn't come right, no matter how often I tried. His features were suitably aristocratic, reflecting his heritage, but the expression was too unyielding, kept melding with that of the farmer from Top Withins as he'd watched me from the side of the path that day. Eventually I abandoned the sketches and made numerous close studies of forearms and hands instead, my pencil flying over the page, my breath audible in the quiet of my little bedroom. Hands were easier I decided, no matter what other artists said. Hook of a thumb, knucklebones, the hard swell of a fist. They could belong to anyone.

Charlotte unpacked the box from London, her fingers made clumsy by haste. She held up the first copy of our book like a prize. It had a cream cover and an unremarkable typeface.

Poems, Currer, Ellis and Acton Bell

She laughed in delight and clutched it to her chest, and then she and Anne began turning the pages, Charlotte giving little cries of joy and recognition and Anne's cheeks growing pink.

'It's a pity Southey is dead,' was all I could bring myself to say. 'We might have sent him a copy.'

But later, when I was alone in my room, I traced the letters on the front of the copy I'd taken for myself. *Ellis Bell.* Firm, anonymous. I opened the cover, made myself turn the pages and begin to read. At first it was hard to focus, but gradually my vision steadied, anchored by sense and rhythm. Strings of letters became words; words turned into phrases. I lit upon one or two ill-expressed ideas, inexact reflections of the thought that had produced them, but the shock of exposure I'd anticipated did not come. Those five letters E L L I S stood between me and the world. I could conceal myself behind any one of them. A different feeling came, something expanding and lifting within my ribcage, like the balloon we'd seen when we were children, with the celebrated Mr. Green a small stick person hanging beneath. I felt as light as a bird, as powerful as wings beating against a winter sky. Here, at last, were my own words and they had liberated me from the earth.

I n May, when the cherry blossoms were whirls of pink confectionery against the bright blue sky, Branwell received a letter from the Robinsons' physician.

'The old man's weakening,' he said flying into the kitchen. 'He won't last much longer!'

Anne bit her lip, in a low voice said: 'You mustn't rejoice, Branwell. It's too wicked.'

'Why should I care? He's made poor Lydia miserable for years.'

'You might think of the children.'

For the next few days, Branwell was half-crazed with excitement; could not sleep, barely ate. With a new idea for Gondal forming in my mind—an invasion of barbarians from the north—I did my best to ignore his agitation, though I couldn't help wondering why the Robinsons' family surgeon should be in contact with a disgraced tutor. Another letter came, written in the same hand. Branwell snatched it from the postboy and then dropped to his knees in the hallway. Mr. Robinson was dead.

A week passed without further communication from Thorp Green. We wondered if grief had brought Mrs. Robinson to her senses; if Branwell had started to have second thoughts about pursuing a woman newly-widowed. I was out in the yard one morning, tending to the geese, when young Joe from the Black Bull Inn came through the gate.

'There's a man wanting to speak to Master Branwell, Pa says. I forgot his name.'

He stared at his feet in discomfort, but I could see him edging towards the snowy geese, wanting to take a better look. Victoria and Adelaide had pure white plumage, pristine against the clear morning light. I liked to watch them move around the yard in tandem, a stately dancing pair, talked to them in my own way. I knew that Joe was fond of animals, so I handed the bowl of vegetable peelings to him, then spread my palms, indicating that more information was needed. 'A coachman, I reckon. He says to come quickly.' He threw a great handful of the peelings, just missing Adelaide's head. With a degree of reluctance, I went inside to relay the message. Branwell tore out of the house without a word, but within the hour he was back, half-carried into the back kitchen by John Brown. The commotion drew the rest of the household, including Papa who immediately began trying to heave a stupefied Branwell from his chair.

'We'll manage,' I said, signalling to the sexton for help. Branwell was lightly built but neither Papa nor my sisters had the strength to move him in this drunken state. Between the two us, John Brown and I managed to get Branwell out into the hallway. As we began climbing the stairs, his feet slithered from underneath him, banging against the stone. We released him only when we reached his room and could drop him onto the bed. He lay stiffly at first, with his arms above his head like a man on the rack. In a moment of tenderness at odds with his rough exterior, John Brown removed his shoes for him and placed them neatly by the wardrobe. Branwell gave an anguished moan, then curled in on himself and began to sob.

'Branwell!' I shook him to restore some sense. He flinched and withdrew to the far corner of the bed, turning away from me.

'I'd leave him be,' said John Brown. 'For now.'

Anne, Charlotte and Papa were waiting in the hallway—three white faces, Papa's eyes like frozen milk.

'What on earth now?' said Charlotte. 'Come into the kitchen, Mr. Brown.'

Planting himself by the range, though Anne urged him to sit, John Brown told us all he knew. Mrs. Robinson had dispatched her coachman to share the contents of her late husband's Will, which had been rewritten at the beginning of the year. In this new version, Mr. Robinson no longer provided for one of his daughters, who had married unwisely and against his wishes. This new Will also stated that if Mrs. Robinson chose to re-marry after her husband's death, she would forfeit all rights to her income.

'The fellow said the lady's right upset, talks of entering a nunnery.' John's face twisted into a grimace. 'But maybe she's not so keen on the lad, now her old man's gone, and she can do as she pleases.' He motioned to the ceiling with fingers knotted from years of labour. It was strange to see him inside the house like this. I couldn't remember the last time he'd come past the front door. It struck me what an odd friendship they had, he and Branwell. John was many years older, lived such a different life. But Branwell could make a friend of anyone, was easy to love when he was at his best, with his endless chatter and laughter, his enthusiasms. 'You can't tell that to the boy though,' John said. 'He's taken it hard enough already.'

'Thank you for bringing him home.' Papa held out his hand.

'How cruel to break the news to him so publicly,' said Charlotte afterwards, when Papa had shuffled upstairs to check on Branwell. 'She must have planned it that way, but why? At least this will be an end to it now. He will know that it's over; that there is no hope.' She winced and then changed the subject. 'If only Aylott & Jones would write with news. I wake up with knots in my stomach every morning, thinking about our little book being read by strangers.' We'd asked our publisher to send copies to all our favourite authors, as well as newspapers and literary journals. 'It's like waiting for execution.' She closed her eyes and held her hand over her heart. Melodrama usually brought out the stoic in me, but for once I knew exactly how she felt.

At last, we heard from London. Reviews were always a challenge, the publisher wrote, especially when the authors were unknown in literary circles; when they did not even live in, or write about, the capital. To date, *Poems, Currer, Ellis and Acton Bell* had sold two copies.

'What does it matter?' I said, when Charlotte fell into instant despair, certain that she must become a governess again. The rain was rattling against the window, driven by a pettish wind, and the garden and churchyard were a grey-green blur. Hearing Branwell outside the door, I dropped my voice. 'Our poems are published. They can't be erased now.'

Branwell did nothing without conviction. In the days following the coachman's visit to Haworth, he paced around the house in a restless fever, his eyes as unseeing as a sleepwalker's. None of us knew what Papa had said when he called Branwell to his study after breakfast one morning—I imagined it to be the sort of frank talk men had among themselves—but the whole house heard Branwell flying into a fit of rage. I ran downstairs from making the beds to find him on his knees in the hallway, collapsed in agony so extreme that it seemed to emanate from some animal part of him. Saliva stretched from his mouth and mucus dripped from his nose as he howled and rocked, cursing the late Mr. Robinson for ruining his life. When I tried to lift him to his feet, he wrestled free and began dashing his forehead against the flagstones. Keeper, thinking me in trouble, launched himself down the hallway, knocking Papa off his feet and sending Mamma's little sea-green vase crashing from the hall table to the floor. I dragged him into the back kitchen, fetched a broom to sweep up the shards of china which would never fit back together again, then washed away the blood. The collapse was followed by complete apathy. For the next few days, Branwell lay in bed, refusing food or comfort.

'I'm starting to wish he'd stay there,' said Charlotte when we heard him moving overhead once. 'I should be writing again, but it's impossible to concentrate with all this . . . *tragedy* going on.' By the next morning she'd forgiven him, taking a plate of food and the newspaper up to his room, and in the afternoon, he managed to get himself out of bed and downstairs, though he wasn't properly dressed. He spent the next day or so marching in and out of rooms, wanting to air his latest theory on Mrs. Robinson's predicament to anyone unlucky enough to encounter him. Charlotte was at one moment sympathetic to his plight, convinced he'd been cruelly manipulated by his lover, then enraged by the storms of tears that erupted at the very mention of her:

'Imagine if one of us were to indulge in such behaviour!' she complained to me. 'Everyone would say we were weak and womanish, while a man is admired for his delicacy of feeling, his ability to name his suffering. I don't understand it.'

My own sense was that the storm must be allowed to rage until it blew itself out. When a friend from Halifax invited Branwell to stay, a sculptor by the name of Leyland, his spirits lifted immediately. Watching him prepare for the trip, it seemed to me that this latest fixation had already begun to wane, and that it would soon go the way of all his past passions.

The day after he set off, we received a short note from Aylott & Jones with two cuttings enclosed.

'"Here,"' read Charlotte, white with excitement, '"we have good, wholesome, refreshing, vigorous poetry—no sickly affectations, no namby-pamby, no tedious imitations of familiar strains—"'

'I should think not,' I said.

'"... original thoughts, expressed in the true language of po-etry ..."' Charlotte's eyes moved down the column, '"We see, for instance, here and there traces of an admirer of Wordsworth, and perhaps of Tennyson; but for the most part the three poets are themselves alone."' She stopped to breathe.

'And the other?' said Anne. The second review began in a more restrained fashion, seeking to differentiate between the merits of each of writer and finding 'Acton Bell's' work the least successful.

'Then they've no ear for nuance,' I said, seeing Anne flush. 'We should pity them.' It was time to sweep the hearths, to get on with the rest of the morning's chores.

'But look what they say about you, Emily!,' said Anne, read-ing over Charlotte's shoulder.

'"A fine quaint spirit has the latter, which may have things to speak that men will be glad to hear."' Charlotte's voice was rising in pitch. '"And an evident power of wing that may reach heights not here attempted."' She shook the review at me. 'Didn't I tell you? Was I not right?'

'We had to pay to be published,' I reminded her, affecting only now to notice a scuff on the wall that Keeper had made yesterday. I rubbed it with my apron, magicked it away.

Our brother returned from Halifax determined to resume the old plan of travelling.

'I thought you'd given up on your Grand Tour,' said Charlotte, a bite of sarcasm in her voice, but when he fetched the atlas, she couldn't help being drawn in. Ever since we were chil-dren, sketching outlines of Ashantee, of Gondal and Gaaldine, maps had been the beginning of a story. I waited for Charlotte to make some comment about the cost of the proposed journey or ask when Branwell would get round to looking for new em-ployment, but for once she kept her thoughts to herself.

'Branwell thinks novels are the only way to make money

from writing,' she said, coming through to the kitchen a little later. I'd just finished preparing stock from leftover beef bones and vegetable peelings and was now scouring the table. 'I've not said a word,' she added, seeing the look I gave her. 'He was talking about himself.' Despite our agreement, it was a small miracle she'd resisted sharing the news of our recent publication. The real battle would come, I knew, if our poems sold, or received any more favourable reviews.

'I've actually made a start on something,' said Anne. She was kneeling beside the range, stroking Flossy's stomach. He lay with his legs up in the air and did not care how foolish he looked.

'A novel?' said Charlotte. 'You've never mentioned it before.'

'I've only an outline so far, but I've been thinking about it for a while. Even before I came home from Thorp Green.' She stood, then began smoothing down her dress self-consciously. 'It's about a plain, quiet girl who is eventually rewarded for resilience and virtue, a governess, in fact.'

Not a Gondal tale then.

'Didn't we read that that publishers like stories in the same vein as established works, to be sure of sales?' said Charlotte. 'I don't recall ever reading a servant's story.'

'Then nothing original would ever see the light of day,' I said. On the range, the stock was bubbling too fiercely. I moved it to a cooler spot.

'I've always thought I could write a novel with popular appeal,' said Charlotte with a sigh. 'I've read enough of them to know how they work. I just need to settle on the right story.'

I felt her looking at me out of the corner of her eye. It was the old game, played at least with a modicum of subtlety now. For once, I didn't bother to resist.

'I have hundreds of stories,' I said.

A letter came for Branwell from Lydia Robinson. He replied immediately, and then wrote again the following day. Within the week, there was no more talk of Europe or seeking a new position. Francis Grundy was in town, a friend from his time on the railways, and the two of them spent most of that visit in the Black Bull Inn.

'I'll fetch him myself!' said Papa in a sudden temper, when Branwell had been late for prayers on three consecutive evenings. Always punctual himself, Papa hated even the smallest disruption to his routine—a meal delayed, a visitor arriving late. It set him out of countenance for days to come. He fumbled for his staff in the corner of the study where he'd left it earlier, and then waved it in the air, seemingly intent on driving Branwell home. There was a crash—the sound of the back kitchen door being flung back—followed by smothered laughter.

'Mr. Grundy goes back soon,' said Anne, staying Papa with a gentle touch to his shoulder. Papa nodded, his colour returning to normal.

'You test our patience, boy,' was all he said when Branwell entered, carrying himself rigidly, the caramel smell of rum on his breath.

Several days after Francis had gone home, Joe from the Black Bull arrived in the yard again.

'Someone's to come for Master Branwell,' he said, his eyes already drifting to Adelaide and Victoria. 'Pa's busy.'

I hurried out of the yard and down the lane to the inn. As I arrived, Branwell was being shouldered to the door.

'You'll manage?' said the landlord, looking doubtfully at me. He held on to Branwell as he attempted the first of the steps. My brother's shirt was hanging half loose from his trousers. One sleeve of his coat hung empty.

'Put your arm around me,' I said.

'S'not necessary.' He drew himself up, immediately lost his balance and then stumbled down the remaining steps. Grasping him round the waist, I managed to turn him in the right direction, and then we tacked our way up Parsonage Lane, a small unshipshape vessel bound for home. When we reached the hallway, my sisters stood aside, heeding my command, but Papa could not be deterred from helping, so I found myself supporting two grown men up the stairs, one half-blind, the other incapable. Somehow, we got Branwell to his room and onto the bed. In the time it took me to pull a blanket over him and fetch a pitcher of water, he had already fallen asleep, breath coming thickly from his throat.

'What must people think?' said Charlotte, finding me in the back kitchen the next morning. Sometime during the night, Branwell had been sick on his bedside rug. I'd opened the window to let out the cloying, acrid smell and then dragged the rug down here for cleaning.

'I didn't have you marked as one who would care,' I said, bringing a can of water from the stove, and then looking around for the scrubbing brush. 'Branwell's never lived gently.'

'I don't mind for myself, but I'm thankful we've no interest in our school at the moment. Imagine!' I said nothing, began with the soap and brush. 'You might at least let him clean up after himself.' Her voice was as sour as an underripe plum.

I had hundreds of stories and none of them would do. While Anne sat opposite me, attempting the first chapters of her novel, I went through my Gondal papers. Beside her, Charlotte scribbled notes, and then just as quickly tossed them into the fire. I'd been sure that Augusta Almeda would be the place to start. Her story was certainly dramatic enough—vengeful plots, lovers aplenty, lifelong feuds—and I was happy for the most part with her portrayal *here*, in these papers that went back so many years, but for some reason I could see no way to extract her. Every time I tried, she stayed flat on the page, would not inhabit her own body in the way I wanted. I needed her to be a wayward soul, driven by passion, but she had always refused to show human weakness, was too perfectly in control of her own flesh, even when it came to her shepherd prince. She had devised numerous ways to be alone with him, but every time I tried to consummate their relationship, I did not know how to write it and the two of them faded from sight. The most reckless of Augusta's actions appeared staid when there was nothing at stake; she could lose everything yet never be destroyed. Some of her earlier stories, and even a few of the more recent ones, struck me as childish. I turned to her father instead, began pulling out various episodes of Julius Brenzaida's stormy life. Once again, the stories stretched back forever. Countless times, I'd added new chapters, subplots, or rewritten an entire section. I considered something from the point of view of one of Julius's wives, but the idea bored me before I'd even started. I was puzzled and then impatient with myself, started to wonder if all the trouble with Branwell was affecting my brain.

'It will pass,' I'd assured Papa. His face had been stricken, grey with the effort of manhandling his son up the stairs.

I pushed aside my papers now and went to the window. The clouds were low this evening, blanking out the village and the hills beyond. A feeling of panic rose in my throat. My imagination had rarely failed me, yet now, when I tried to summon inspiration, I was unmoved. Worse still, I had started to doubt my past creations. I left my sisters to their work and went to bed early.

Branwell fell outside the Fleece Inn, twisting his ankle. John Brown delivered him home, this time endured a telling-off from Charlotte for his pains.

'Nowt I can do, Miss Brontë,' said John, undaunted. 'He'd find his way there wi' or without me.' When the ankle swelled, I bandaged it and Charlotte spoke to the apothecary, who recommended laudanum. The worst of the bruising was gone after a week. Still, Branwell sent for more.

'It takes the pain quite away!' he told me, smiling and dreamy-eyed from his bed one morning. 'Open the window, won't you? I'd like to feel the air on my skin for a change.'

'Open it yourself. You're not an invalid.'

'I think I'll go Bridlington when I'm better.' His face was smooth and pain-free. He might have been fifteen years old again. 'The sea restores everything to its rightful place. How strange, that one form of pain should obliterate another.'

'How many holidays does one man need?' said Charlotte, later.

There was shouting from upstairs while I was in the middle of checking the butcher's delivery. Last week's bacon order had been under. I wiped my hands and went out into the hallway to see Martha coming downstairs with her hands to her face.

'What's the matter?'

'I was supposed to stop for Master Branwell's medicine, but it went out of my head.' Being a sensible girl, she was already scrubbing her eyes dry on her apron and attempting a smile. 'He's never spoken that way to me before now.'

I took the stairs two at a time. Entering Branwell's room, I found him dressed but in a haphazard way, with his shirt half-fastened and his hair unkempt. I could see the line of his scalp where his hair had parted above one ear, from lying in one position for hours.

'Don't ask Martha to fetch laudanum for you. Go yourself if you need it so badly.'

'Of course, she came complaining.' He ran his hands through his hair. It sprang back again, needing the firmness of a brush to hold it in place. 'She was already going out, so it wasn't as if I sent her especially.' The edges of his words were beginning to fray.

'She's enough to do.' I could feel my temper rising.

'Why can't we employ a servant with a fucking brain for once? I don't see why we should have to take in the village idiot.'

'Have you told John Brown your opinion of his daughter? He won't be so keen to carry you home next time you fall down in a stupor.' I crossed my arms in an attempt to contain myself. It was not that his language shocked me—I heard worse among the millhands on their way to and from work or the draymen unloading at the inn—but that he dared to use it inside this house, against one of our own. In front of *me*. 'Would you speak that way about Tabby Aykroyd?'

'Tabby's different.' He brushed my words away with a sweep of his arm. The movement was clumsy. I saw that he was not quite in control of his limbs.

'What would Aunt say if she could hear you now?'

'Do not speak about her!' Branwell shrieked. He clutched

himself around the middle and then doubled over as if I'd plunged a sword into his abdomen. He pointed a finger at me, the beginning of an accusation, but then changed his mind and allowed his hand to drop. It landed against his thigh with a useless thud, appeared almost transparent against the dark material of his trousers. 'You weren't here, Emily. Laudanum was the only thing that gave her any blessed relief. There was no rest for her without it, for any of us. If you'd ever watched someone dying . . . Everyone leaves me,' he said with a miserable smile. 'And I am lonelier than I can stand.' He dropped onto the bed and began to sob, his mouth twisting with the unfettered grief of a small child. I laid a hand on his shoulder until the crying became less jagged. When it settled into a rhythm, I went downstairs to fetch my bonnet.

By the time I returned, Branwell was sitting in the kitchen and properly dressed. In front of him was a plate of bread and butter, half-eaten. There was no sign of Martha or my sisters.

'Throw it away,' he said, motioning to the paper bag I set down on the table. 'I'll not take any more of it. And I've made up my mind not to drink anymore. It numbs me for a few hours but the pain is tenfold afterwards.'

I was tempted to point out that there was no growth poisoning his blood or seeping into his vital organs, no obstruction twisting his bowels in agony like Aunt's. Always pale, my brother looked no worse than any other young man after a night of excess. He could decide that he was done with suffering and recover in an instant, just as Charlotte could choose not to be in love with Monsieur *Héger* any longer. It ought to be easy when the body is in no danger, but then I remembered the bottomless black hole I'd poured myself into at Roe Head, and again when I was a teacher at Law Hill, suffering no malady that a doctor could pinpoint, just my mind working against me, punishing my own flesh. And what of feet squelching through peat, pushing aside the heather that turned dark as a bruise in winter, the stems coppery, roots like ash, exposed by the constant wind that blew across the tops? Whenever I escaped the trouble with Branwell, I set off with all sorts of directions in mind, yet time and again I found myself drawn to Top Withens, could no more help myself than Branwell or Charlotte, than a fledgling when it falls from the nest. I saw no-one except the old woman who fed the chickens or scrubbed the doorstep, but it made no difference. I had no idea what I would do if the farmer were ever to walk out of the front gate towards me. What reason would I give for my presence when I could not explain it to myself? There was no story on my tongue, nothing in my mind, but my body ached in memory of the darkest hours of the night, and I could not stay away.

For the rest of the day, Branwell was studiedly cheerful and active, even offered to accompany Papa to visit the Cartwright widower in Stanbury, whose seventh child was soon to be added to the list of his siblings on the family headstone. On his return, he went straight to the dining room, saying that he had a poem in mind. He was still there at tea-time, bothered by my need to clear the table, then restless throughout the meal. He ate little, tapping his knife against his plate until Charlotte begged him stop for the sake of her nerves. Afterwards, while I was wiping away crumbs, he began pacing up and down the room.

'I might go out.' He went to the window and wrenched up the sash. 'You should have seen Cartwright's place today, Emily. Such a dank, foul little hole though he tries his best, I suppose. Hard to believe there was once nine of them packed in there. I'm surprised people don't give up sooner when their lives are never going to get better, and yet we expect them to believe that God cares more for them than those who live in ease and luxury, that He will reward them in some notional Heaven. What a terrible lie.'

'You were supposed to be offering cheer.'

'They live like rats in those cottages, scrambling over one

another for the next scrap. If there is a God, we must all seem so, just that some of us live in bigger nests. He must wonder why He bothered.'

'You should walk,' I said. 'It will improve your mood.'

'You're as bad as Papa.' He slammed the sash window shut again. 'Thinking a walk the cure for all ills.' He raised a finger to his temple and tapped it. 'Some people are more finely calibrated.'

'Make up your mind,' I said, turning my back on him. 'We were all rodents just a second ago.'

When he had not returned for supper or prayers, I told Papa to go to bed. He agreed only after I'd promised multiple times to lock up for the night, and then I went out in search of Branwell. At first, I thought that someone had thrown a bundle of rags into Parsonage Lane. Then I recognised my brother's grey coat. He was unconscious, lying face down next to some discarded potato peelings, with his feet at an awkward angle. Somehow I dragged him from the ground and got him to move. When we were almost home, he wrenched himself away from my grip and then vomited into the gutter. The local strays appeared out of nowhere for a rare, semi-digested meal.

'Which one are you?' he said when he was upright again. His eyes were unfocused slits. He steadied himself and then peered at me as if through deepest night, though the sun had not long dropped over the hills. 'You're all indistinguishable.' He dismissed me with an ill-judged wave of the hand that caught me on the cheek.

'Don't touch me!' My blood rose despite myself, and it was lucky for Branwell that I'd left Keeper asleep by the fire or he might have found himself savaged. I seized his arm. 'Now walk!'

'Bitch,' he muttered to himself.

'He's fine,' I snapped, when Papa and Anne came fussing on the landing—Charlotte had retired earlier, with her cheek swollen from toothache. 'Go to bed.' I waited up for another hour, checked on Branwell twice during that time because I always feared that he might choke. His breathing was still clear when I went in a third time, to reassure myself before bed, but it was obvious that he had soiled himself. I closed my eyes. Then I opened them and began stripping his wet, stinking, sticking clothes from his body. I bundled everything into a clean sheet and went downstairs. Unlocking the back door, I threw the bundle out into the yard. Then I went back upstairs and began the task of cleaning him, sending up a prayer of gratitude that he remained unconscious and quite unaware, as I rolled and lifted and scrubbed his deadweight, that he was lying in his own filth. I forced myself to think of him as an injured, begrimed animal and not my own brother. I was not entirely ignorant of the male body, had seen pictures in a book of anatomy, but here was the reality of a naked man: buttocks smaller and firmer than a woman's, the red hair flaring from his crotch, fox-bright against his pale belly, and the part that made him male lying slack and shrivelled across one thigh like a wormcast. There was something pathetic about it, not at all what I'd imagined when I was lying in the heather with the damp scent of the earth in my nostrils. I had not thought the source of procreation could look so defeated.

'What are we going to do about him?' My shadow fell across Charlotte, blocking the sunshine. She was leaning with her back to the garden wall, reading a book.

She frowned up at me. 'How should I know? He's impossible.' The wind blew softly across the lawn, bending each shining blade of grass. Briefly, I told her what had happened the night before. 'That's disgusting!' she cried, dropping her book into her lap. 'How could you stand to do it?' I spread my palms to signify that I'd had no choice. Charlotte cupped her sore cheek, and then flinched. 'Papa keeps saying he should see a doctor, and yet the next minute he makes excuses for him.' She gave a tight little laugh. 'Apparently, lots of young men have no control over themselves at this age and then turn out perfectly well.'

I knelt in front of her. '*You* have to speak to him. I can give him practical help, but he cares for your opinion more than anyone else's. You avoid him though.'

'I don't! And you overestimate my influence—Branwell thinks me just a silly girl who couldn't possibly understand.' Something closer to the truth was welling up inside her. I waited as she drew her knees up to her chest and then stared down at the sprigged blue cotton of her dress for a minute, as though she was trying to memorise the pattern. Then: 'I don't want to, Emily. His weakness repulses me, I feel as if I might be infected by it! Do you know, I used to think we were twins when we were children, that it had been kept a secret from us. I really believed thoughts could pass between us without either of us saying a word, that we could feel one another's pain.' She smiled at the memory. 'I thought it was a magical gift, that others would envy us. Now though . . .' She looked up at me, the smile gone, her face a picture of despair. 'I still don't know where he ends and I begin, but I've only just recovered from Brussels. I didn't tell you everything, I couldn't, but there were times when I honestly thought I would lose my mind. When Branwell's at his worst, his most selfish, I start to panic, fearing I'll be dragged down again.' She looked at the grass around her feet, searching for a better comparison. 'Sometimes I think there's only so much air and he's taken all of it for himself. I can only breathe easily when he's out of the house altogether.' She gave another joyless laugh. 'Or unconscious.'

Branwell had his hand in the tin where I kept the house-keeping money. Without thinking, I reached for a pan and threw it at him. It caught the side of his head, felled him. By the time Charlotte had run into the kitchen to see what was happening, he had staggered to his feet, clutching his bleeding brow bone.

'You might have killed him!' she said, holding a cloth to the wound. I could not speak, knowing something had come loose in me. I prided myself on running our household on the tight-est of budgets, had learned where economies could be made and where a little luxury could be afforded, but none of it was worth injuring my own brother.

'I was only borrowing,' Branwell muttered. He stared at me in disbelief. 'You know Lydia sends money when she can.'

Hot with shame, I called for Keeper and hurried out of the house. Most of the time I gave only half an ear to Charlotte's catastrophic predictions for the future, but no matter how fast I walked today, they pursued me all the way across Haworth Moor. *Aunt's legacy cannot last forever.* By laying out our fi-nances so carefully I'd felt that I was exerting control, playing my part, but now, in one movement, Branwell had whipped the tablecloth away and sent everything tumbling. Our poems were of no interest to anyone, a waste of time and of Aunt's money; for all my years of writing, my boasting to Charlotte, I had not one single story to tell that might earn us a penny or two. I marched on until Top Withins came into sight, its deep, narrow windows like a medieval castle, the boundary trees flattened by the bullying wind today. I smelt peat-smoke and beasts. A movement caught my eye. The man I'd met on the path that day was standing by a small outbuilding that sat just outside a new section of boundary wall. I took hold of Keeper's collar and then dropped down into the heather before the man could see me. The wind was tugging at his hair. It flattened his clothes to his body. I saw that something—not me—had caught his attention. Words carried on the wind, and then a girl with long fair hair, of my age or thereabouts, came into sight. She was leading a rough-maned pony, which she tied up against a post at the entrance to the farm before approaching the man. A little dog ran around her feet while they talked, jumped up at her until she made him sit. I began edging closer, towards a small rise in the land. The voices grew louder and I saw the farmer seize the girl by the hand. I felt as sure as if I'd been in her place that she would resist, but she stayed her dog and let the man lead her into the outbuilding. I bade Keeper to stay as well and crept nearer, making sure to keep low in the undergrowth. I was too close now. Anyone looking in this direction might easily have spotted me. Still my feet moved forwards. When a noise came from inside that building, I dropped to the ground and crawled forwards on my belly, elbows and knees sinking into the water-logged ground and my hand just missing a fat, black slug. Its antennae waved blindly at me like an inchoate warning. I was so close now that I could see the building was partly in ruins, light spilling both through the roof and one half of the far wall. Then I jolted back. The man was right there, just inside the doorway. My first feeling was relief that he had his back to me and then I saw that his breeches were pulled half-down. Shock of bare skin, unearthed, and then an animal noise coming from inside the building, female, feral. I saw a pair of stockinged legs around the farmer's waist, a hand clawing his hair, another on his buttock. There was some piece of farm machinery behind the two of them, brutal prongs gleaming in the semi-darkness. The girl was still wearing her boots. My eyes pulled back to the hard grind of hips, the dark hair where the man's thighs began. I felt myself flushing all the way down my body, ears ringing in alarm, shame, and my hand already up beneath my skirts. As the noise from inside the building intensified, I pushed two fingers, wet and muddy from the boggy ground, hard inside myself, could not stop myself from crying out. A moment later I returned to my senses and wriggled back through the heather as fast as I could until I reached the spot where I'd left Keeper. My breath began to quieten. I wiped the smell of myself from my fingers. The couple were emerging from the doorway now, the girl repinning her pretty hair and smoothing down the bosom of her dress as the two of them walked to the post where she'd tethered her pony. She put up her face to kiss her lover, but then something changed between them and there was a sudden, angry exchange. She pushed him away with surprising force for one so slight, and then mounted the pony. More angry words. Her little dog jumped at the man's legs and barked, wanting to protect its mistress. Without looking down, he swung back his foot and launched the creature across the ground. It gave a screaming whimper and then slunk away down the hillside. The girl shouted something and lifted her riding crop high against the scudding clouds, brought it down hard across the man's cheek. Then she dug her heels into the pony's flanks, and it cantered off in the direction of Stanbury, the little dog scampering behind.

I slept fitfully that night, sliding in and out of dreams which twined and slithered, eel-like, through my waking moments too. I thought I heard the clatter of people arriving at the front door, children's footsteps scampering over the flagstones in the hallway. I remembered that Papa was dead, and I was not supposed to be in this house anymore, must think of a way to explain my presence.

'I'm the housekeeper,' I said, going down the stairs.

A small boy stared at my bare breasts: 'We don't need you.' He pointed to the front door, where a line of uniformed servants streamed through the entrance. I woke in terror, damp sheets and my dreams clinging to me.

The following evening, Branwell went out in a cheerful frame of mind. He'd received both a letter and some money from Mrs. Robinson which meant at least an hour or two of peace before someone brought him home or came to fetch me. I went into the dining room where Charlotte and Anne were already settled for the evening.

'I'm going to write about a family living up on our own moors. Something like the tales Tabby used to tell us when we were small.'

Charlotte pulled a face. She set down her pen. 'Wouldn't you be better with a more civilised setting, more *known*? I can't imagine anyone wanting to read about our part of the world.'

'It has to be here.' I went to sit down and then decided against it. I walked around the table, trying to order my burgeoning thoughts. 'I want characters who've grown out of the land; have been formed from heath and rock and icy water.'

'A love story, though?' Anne had already decided that her fictional governess would be rewarded by a happy marriage to a curate.

I nodded. The outline of the story had come to me on the walk home and, in flashes, during the night, but the detail was forming only now, as I paced around the room. 'But so passionate that it destroys the lovers and everyone close to them. A jealous, selfish, unthinking love, wicked even. But it will endure beyond death, like bedrock beneath the flimsiness of existence.'

'You'll want selfless characters too.' Charlotte frowned. 'For balance.'

'No-one shall be without fault. I want to show what lies beneath the veneer of civility.'

'You think good breeding and manners count for nothing? That true virtue is only to be found in the peasant or a savage?' Despite herself, Charlotte was interested.

'Manners may be a manifestation of a good and virtuous soul, or a pretty disguise. There's no inherent virtue in poverty, of course, just less time and energy to conceal one's true nature.'

'Your people half-frighten me, Emily,' said Anne. 'Is there to be no happy resolution? No redemption? I wonder who would dare read a story of such wickedness.'

'I think there will be. I haven't settled on it yet. It will have to be hard-won though, and all the more delightful for that. Like the first of our spring picnics after a long winter.' I paused. Doubt was setting in now I had emptied myself of words. 'It's all I have.'

'You'll find my story rather dull then,' said Charlotte, with a laugh. 'My narrator is a man, as usual.' She glanced down at her notebook. 'After a bitter family dispute, he travels to Europe to teach, where he becomes beguiled by the mistress of the neighbouring girls' school. She turns out be an unscrupulous, conniving woman, lacking in morals, and he falls in love with one of the virtuous young pupils at the school . . .' She flushed slightly, keeping her eyes on the page. 'I haven't worked out the detail yet.'

It was midnight when I lay down my pen, the first pages of my novel complete. As I prepared myself for bed, I no longer felt afraid of the future. Those fresh, newly inked words felt like a leap across shifting sands, firmer ground beneath my feet now. I slept deeply and easily and then awoke with a start, unsure, at first, what had pulled me to the surface.

'Emily!'

A white angel burst through my doorway: Charlotte dressed only in her nightgown. I smelled burning, was fully awake and out of bed in a second. Stumbling out onto the landing I realised that the darkness was opaque, with no nuance of light coming from the window on the stairway. The air tasted thick, acrid in the back of my throat. Then Anne appeared and Charlotte grasped me by the arm, began pulling me towards Branwell's bedroom, his door already half-open.

'I can't wake him! I tried!'

I saw a flickering from behind the doorway, heard a hissing sound, and then I was inside, my eyes taking in everything at once, too slowly: the candlestick tipped over on the bedside table; the flaring tumble of the blanket, half off the bed; a pool of darkness on the floor where someone—Charlotte?—had thrown water from the pitcher but missed the target. Branwell was on his back, fully dressed, with his arms stretched into a crucifix. Discarded beside him was an opium bottle. The glass looked black in this light, but I knew it was really dark green. For a moment, I could not move. Then I heard Papa's voice on the landing. Pulling my nightgown tight around me, I seized the edge of the burning blanket and whipped it away from the bed in an attempt to prevent the sheets from catching. The flames roared in protest. Keeper was behind me, tugging at my hem.

'Branwell!' I lifted my hand and slapped him across the face, hard. Again. Heat came from the burning blanket nearby. I slid my arms around his torso, just beneath his outstretched arms, and tried to drag him from the bed. Though he'd grown thin in recent times, he was still a dead weight, entirely unresponsive to my efforts. Someone was beside me now, and then I heard Anne's voice rising above the sound of the fire, loud and firm for once.

'Leave it to Emily, Papa!'

I glanced back to see her and Charlotte pulling Papa back to the safety of the doorway. Cold air on my cheek. The bedroom window was wide open, the draught goading the flames towards the edge of the rug. Using every bit of my strength, I finally managed to get Branwell clear. At the foot of the bed, I saw the twisted weight of the counterpane. He must have kicked it off while he slept. I let him go, gathered up those heavy folds and ran to the blazing blanket. Wrenching the counterpane from Keeper's jaws—he was under the impression it was attacking me—I smothered the fire, stamped down with my bare feet. There was silence, then a groan from Branwell, still supine. Papa and Anne had managed to get him halfway towards the door. I could hear my breath coming hard. My hands were only now beginning to shake. Keeper panted beside me.

'Are you hurt, Emily?' cried Papa. He was down on his knees, patting his hands over an unscathed Branwell.

'I am not,' I said. My hands and the soles of my feet felt hot, the skin tightening, but it was nothing to the pain of a hot iron pressed into a raw wound.

Charlotte was at the door with another pitcher of water. With no more use for it, she upended it over Branwell's head.

He was to sleep in Papa's room from now on, agreed to it the morning after the fire, while still in an opium fog. There was an argument that evening, when he realised that Martha and I had actually moved his bed.

'I won't have my things meddled with!' he said, flying downstairs and into the dining room. 'I want my bed back immediately.'

'Then move it.' I put down my pen. Charlotte and Anne kept their heads low over their work. I knew Branwell would struggle to shift the heavy bedstead without help.

'Papa will be in bed any minute now. Where am I to work?' he said, his voice rising. I smiled to myself at that. Only a fool would believe that anything so productive as work took place in his room these days. He caught the smile and lost his temper.

'What a foul old maid you are these days, Emily! I've not taken a drop of drink these past few days, must have knocked that candle over in my sleep. You've become a sort of dictator since Aunt died!'

The study door flew open. Papa strode across the hallway and into the drawing room with the sudden vigour of youth. Somehow, in his half-blindness, he found Branwell and seized him by the arm.

'You will do as *I* say while you live in this household. I can't stop you from sending yourself into a stupor every night, my boy, but I won't have you endangering the entire family while we sleep! I hope you understand me?'

He'd drawn himself up to full height and his eyes were blank and wild. All of us knew that Papa had been terrified of fire since he was a small boy in Ireland, when he'd witnessed bodies carried like charred logs from the smoking remains of the neighbouring cottage.

'I want to work.' Branwell's voice was almost inaudible. 'That's all.' A tremor ran through him; his hands began to shake. 'None of you understands how much I loathe myself. I would die if I could.'

There were dark hollows beneath Papa's cheekbones. In the last few months his hair had turned from grey to white, fine and soft as an infant's, matching the snowy cravat he wore to keep the cold from his chest, even in summer. 'My poor, dearest boy,' he said. His hand scrabbled, claw-like, for Branwell's shoulder.

The next morning Branwell rose early and headed off in the direction of Penistone Hill. When he hadn't returned by tea-time, Charlotte became agitated, wanted me to come with her to search for him.

'What if something's happened?' Fear was sharp in her eyes. 'I'm scared that he . . . You heard what he said.'

But I thought him unlikely drowned in the beck, that time beneath the skies might bring him to his senses. He arrived home before prayers, undamaged except that the wind had flayed his pale flesh pink and tender. He ought to have been exhausted but when the three of us took out our writing things, in hope of an undisturbed evening, we could still hear him pacing around upstairs, muttering against the night.

'At least he's not drunk,' said Charlotte. The acrid smell of burning was still catching in our throats.

'Thank goodness you're so strong, Emily,' said Anne with a shudder.

S he *spits* at him?' Charlotte interrupted me reading out loud from my manuscript. 'What sort of love story begins in that way?'

'They're still children,' I explained. 'And she's disappointed, because her father had promised to bring home a riding crop for her, not some strange orphan boy. It is exactly what *he* would do if the tables were turned. They are wild creatures, you see, both formed from the same material.'

'But they'll improve, as they grow up?'

'They'll assume the trappings of civilisation but if anything they grow worse, caring only for their own needs, wreaking damage on one another and themselves in the process. I have to write the truth, Charlotte. Not some polite, drawing room drama.'

'But why should anyone care for your characters if they've no redeeming features? It seems to me that you're taking a great risk. A gentle reader mightn't be able to stomach your creations.'

'And not every human being is wild at heart,' said Anne, laying down her pen. 'Some live quietly and that is just as much the truth.'

'Yes, but these are moor folk.' I began pacing around the table again, needing the motion to bring the words the surface. Every hour of the day, the story roiled in the darkness of my brain, figures emerging from the shadows, narrative forming without conscious effort. My thoughts were like a cauldron coming to a simmer, energy waiting to spill over. 'They've grown up in a household mired in superstition, are hard and desperate and godless. There *will* be gentler souls, but most of them will be battered by the winds, uprooted too soon.' How often in springtime had I come across a raw-skinned fledgling, its chest fluttering, beak flapping at the air, its parent nowhere to be seen, or the remains of a tiny rabbit or stoat, its flesh torn away by a raptor?

'No redemption then,' said Charlotte. 'For anyone?'

'Not until the love story has played itself out.' I thought of the day when the earth had exploded on Crow Hill. All these years later, the boulders that had followed in its wake were still strewn down the fellside. 'Destroying everything in its pathway.'

'I still don't understand how you will hold the reader's attention. They might leave off in disgust, seeking a moral and finding none, unable to find a character for whom they care.'

I stopped by the window and stared out across the garden for a minute, at the graveyard.

'Remember when we read *Paradise Lost* for the first time? How compelling we found Satan, though we knew we shouldn't. We fought among ourselves to read those passages! I've always believed that Satan must have set out to be a good angel but could not help himself, it was not in his nature. I want *my* hero to be just as bad and compelling. If he cannot have what he wants, then the whole world must pay for his suffering, his pain.'

'He was mistreated as a child, you said,' Anne joined me at the window. She slipped her hand into mine. Her palm was cool and soft, as soothing as balm. 'That might account for his rage.'

'Only in the sense of making him more himself. Both lovers care only for their own wants. You would no more expect a rock or a tree to show empathy or gratitude. They love each other because they are one and the same. Look.' I left the window and went across the hallway to the study. I returned to the dining room with our worn copy of *Paradise Lost*. 'Book 6.' I ran my finger down the page, seeking the line. 'Abdiel says that Satan is "to thy self enthrall'd." So shall be my Heathcliff, my Cathy. They cannot help themselves.'

Charlotte raised her eyebrows. 'It sounds a most peculiar story, Emily. I hope you know what you're doing.'

About Branwell, we stuck to exchanges of fact now: he had written another letter to Mrs. Robinson; Papa wanted him to try for another position on the railway; one or other of us had tried to reason with him about his behaviour, his health, but got nowhere; yesterday was difficult. As we entered the middle stages of our novels, we stopped reading passages aloud to one another and wrote feverishly, each locked into our own kind of sickness that could only be cured by the scratching of a nib on paper, by the push towards the final paragraphs. Branwell had released an anxiety in each of us, a need for progress, completion. We pinned down our stories like butterflies on paper as if they were the means to exert control over our brother, to salvage him from himself, or else we were trying to rescue ourselves, afraid that something of Branwell's capacity for self-ruination lay in all of us. I watched Charlotte's dark head bob as her hand moved furiously across the page, listened to Anne's soft breathing. Ever since we were children, we'd thought our brother so full of promise that he was sure to succeed in some field, would one day be able to help support his three sisters and an elderly father. I did not think we believed that now.

On a day when the rosebuds were about to burst, and the daisies on the lawn were lifting their open faces to the sky, I read aloud a scene between my wayward heroine and Nelly, her old nursemaid and one of my two narrators:

'If I were in heaven, Nelly, I should be extremely miserable.'

'Because you are not fit to go there,' I answered. 'All sinners would be miserable in heaven.'

'But it is not for that. I dreamt once that I was there.'

'I tell you I won't hearken to your dreams, Miss Catherine! I'll go to bed,' I interrupted again.

She laughed, and held me down; for I made a motion to leave my chair.

'This is nothing,' cried she: 'I was only going to say that heaven did not seem to be my home; and I broke my heart with weeping to come back to earth; and the angels were so angry that they flung me out into the middle of the heath on the top of Wuthering Heights; where I woke sobbing for joy.

I saw Anne look anxiously from our spot on the lawn towards the study window. Papa's eyesight worsened by the day, but there was nothing wrong with his ears. In a hushed voice, she said, 'Do you really believe Heaven will be intolerable?'

It was so unlike her to ask such a direct question, that I hesitated before answering. I thought of the last letter she'd sent home before leaving Thorp Green:

The girls are good-natured at heart, and it is wrong to complain, only I long for a little time to myself. The fault lies in me of course, some ingratitude for my good fortune. I resolve to follow the Sunday sermon more closely in future, to think less of my own needs. My soul troubles me sometimes, Emily. When I was a child, I was quite certain of redemption but now there are times when I cannot sleep for worrying. I wonder if you ever feel so? I cannot imagine it. The contents of that letter had come as no surprise, though it was unlike Anne to be so open. All I knew was that these agonies of belief came down on her as regularly as Charlotte's headaches, made her melancholy and then as fearful as a child when the bedtime candle was snuffed and darkness engulfed her.

I modulated my voice. 'Cathy's thoughts are her own, but I've always thought the Heaven we learned about as children sounded . . . sterile, blank almost, those hordes of angels an oppressive image.' Seeing that this troubled her, I tried to explain better. 'Too much dazzling light and brightness, I mean, no shadows or nuance. I think I would tire of the perpetual singing and praising too.'

'Then what *do* you believe?' Charlotte set down her own work on the blanket, though it was her turn to read. She half-whispered: 'You're surely not an atheist, Emily?'

'Never!' I said. 'But I can't imagine a Heaven without . . . heather and harebells. Rocks, trees. Nor do I think it can be contained within the walls of a church or described in the pages of a book.' My thoughts, till now unspoken, began to order themselves. 'Oh, I often doubt God when I am taking tea with the Sunday School teachers or wasting a fine day in some stiff drawing room, but He is everywhere.' I gestured to the hills that cupped the valley on all sides. 'I believe Heaven is personal to each of us.' I came to a halt, having surprised myself by speaking for so long and with such passion.

'Then mine will be a seat on a cliff looking out to sea.' Anne smiled inwardly and I knew she was remembering a trip to Scarborough with the Robinson family. She had written with unusual spirit of the vastness of the horizons and the rush of the waves on the shoreline.

'And mine would be a never-ending journey to new cities and realms,' said Charlotte. 'For some reason I'm less fearful when I am cast into unfamiliar situations.' She stared across the valley. The day had started out fine, but now clouds were building above the hilltop, and a rogue wind had come to shake the cherry leaves. Soon the rain would arrive in fine, soaking billows. She laughed. 'I believe I should grow quite brave.'

I was reading over my manuscript one evening, when there was a knock at the front door. I'd been looking over the scenes that involved the first of my two narrators, a city-type with a high opinion of himself, and resented the interruption. What fun I'd had, throwing him out of doors in the most ferocious weather, casting him into the company of the moor's inhabitants, where he supposed himself welcomed even in the face of open contempt. By turns, he shuddered and fawned in their presence, a feeble flicker of light in the blaze of their suns.

I heard voices and went out to the hallway to see Martha showing a woman into the study. For a moment I wondered if she might be Lydia Robinson, then realised that this could not be so. The woman's face was veiled but I felt sure she could be no more than thirty years of age, and the children who clung to her, looked around the hallway with big, scared eyes, were far too young to belong to Branwell's beloved. From the study I heard soft crying, Papa's steady voice, but it was not until the next day that we learned the lady's identity. She was a Mrs. Collins, wife of one of Papa's former curates. Her husband had turned out to be a gambler and a drunkard, entirely neglectful of his wife and children.

'A man's allowed one or two vices, I suppose,' said Branwell, pushing fruit cake into his mouth. After a rare day without drinking, he'd gained a sudden appetite. 'He'll grow tired of himself eventually.'

'Mrs. Collins wears a veil for a reason,' said Papa sombrely. 'Her doctor tells me she's lucky not to have sustained permanent injury. Or worse.'

'You'll speak to the husband, won't you?' said Charlotte. 'He'll listen to you.'

'Those poor children must be terrified,' said Anne with a shudder. It occurred to me that if William had lived, she might have been a mother herself by now, the only one of us truly suited to that role. I felt sudden rage that my sister's capacity for tenderness and love could go to waste, that the world could find no other way to accommodate her.

Papa shook his head. 'The man is beyond help, Charlotte. I've advised Mrs. Collins to go back to her family in Ireland.' There was silence. None of us had expected that. 'For good,' he confirmed, answering the unspoken question.

'But no-one is irredeemable?' There was a look of terror on

Anne's face. She gazed at Papa. 'God will forgive us even at our final hour.'

'I chose my words badly.' Papa nodded to himself, as was his habit when he was thinking through an argument. 'But I couldn't live with my conscience if I were to send a helpless woman and children back to that household.'

'But how *can* she leave him? Marriage is sanctified by God.'

'What would you have me do, Anne? Some matters require our own judgement.' He stood in a temper, shook out his napkin. 'God will understand my intentions well enough.'

Used to his crotchety ways, I thought little more on the matter, but Anne was silent for the rest of the evening. When I passed her room at bedtime, I saw her down on her knees by the window, rocking backwards and forwards in anguish, whispering to her unheeding God.

'It's the best thing I've ever written,' said Charlotte as she finished wrapping our completed manuscripts. 'Whatever happens, at least I can say that.' We walked down to the village together, superstitious enough to think it mattered. Each of us placed a silent kiss on that plain brown parcel and then it was gone, to the first publisher of fiction on our new list.

'We'll be more patient this time,' Anne said, as we turned for home.

Have you ever waited for judgment to fall on something that matters a great deal to you? A creation born from a part of you that is intrinsic to your very functioning, as vital for survival as your lungs or liver? Or so it feels. There is not a writer, artist or composer, I believe, however humble and self-effacing, who does not believe a flicker of genius burns in his insignificant body. We keep on in the face of all discouragement, every failure, driven only by the hope that someone might recognise our innermost thoughts and feelings; that one soul might chime with another, if only for a moment, distance and the dark turn of the centuries meaning nothing, and existence would feel less lonely. Why else would we spend years trying to forge the chaos of our minds into something tangible, immutable, other than the hope that some essence of ourselves might live on long after the flesh has fallen from our bones? It is this hope that sustains us through every disappointment, each show of indifference. It sustains us and then destroys us every time our efforts are overlooked, unrecognised; when the world sends us message after message telling us that no one is listening, and we do not matter. We believe those judgements entirely, writhe in agony at every blow, yet within a day, a week we are on our feet again, wounded, hopeful.

Within the month our parcel came back to us. We sent it out again. It was returned.

'Perhaps it was a mistake to leave out Aylott & Jones,' fretted Charlotte. We'd agreed not to approach the publisher of our poems, because of the paltry sales. She fetched her list and her writing things. 'Who next?'

It was the same hope over experience that kept Branwell writing to Mrs. Robinson, believing that the money she sent only occasionally now, the letters that grew shorter, less frequent, were a sign that she still loved him, that the universe would find a way to bring them together.

'I can't go on this way,' he said eventually, dropping down on the stairs one morning after the postboy had left only a letter for Papa. In the last month, every one of his letters had gone unanswered. He went up to his room, then came down properly dressed and settled himself with a book. At midday, he ate a full meal and talked of taking a walk later. By evening, agitation had set in, his fingers drumming, face tightening as we fetched the things for tea. Every movement was an irritation to him; Martha's voice was too shrill to be borne, Anne's too soft to be heard. He was hungry but there was nothing he could stand to eat. After supper, while I played a new piece for Papa, I could hear Branwell complaining about the noise. How could anyone be expected to concentrate through such a racket? Had I not thought to shut the door? Next, he was in the room, whispering into Papa's ear, holding out his hand for money.

'For a debt,' Papa explained, after he'd handed over a sovereign. We heard the crash of the front door and there was Branwell passing the window, on his way to the Black Bull, or one of the other inns. 'I keep hoping he will grow tired of it, Emily. If only I could see properly, I might . . .' His hands waved helplessly through the air. Papa did not know what he might do, felt only sorrow and shame for his own actions. But each of us had given money to Branwell on occasion, knowing exactly what he intended to do with it, though he lied and lied to cover his tracks. The fact was that a wondrous peace settled over the house whenever the door slammed behind him, all the more precious because when he came stumbling back down the pathway later, cursing to himself, there might be a long night ahead.

As Papa's cataracts worsened, he grew depressed, his predictions favouring catastrophe. Charlotte's eyesight was sure to go the same way as his; Anne's asthma was worse than it had ever been. His conversation returned to Aunt's final weeks and the horror of her suffering. When they'd both been in good health, they often used to quarrel. She'd thought him too pleased with his own opinions, his behaviour plain odd at times. Her forthrightness had bruised his finer sensibilities, but it was clear that he missed his companion of so many years now. With his nights so often disturbed by Branwell, he would sometimes fall asleep at the table, dropping off mid-sentence. One morning I found him at his desk with his head in his hands and his mail unopened before him. When I spoke to him, he hardly seemed to know my voice. I went to find my sisters.

'What happens when he can't work anymore?' We looked at each other in silence. For all his years of work, Papa was of no use to the church trustees if he couldn't tend to his parish. We'd earned no money from our book of poems and none of us had a paid position or any prospect of one, our school being an impossible idea all the time Branwell was living at home.

'I'm going to talk to that surgeon in Manchester,' said Charlotte. 'His eyes are surely bad enough to be operated on now.'

'Emily can go with you,' said Anne, nodding. Seeing me look doubtful, she added, 'Branwell's going to stay with that Leyland man. I can take care of Papa for a few days.'

We travelled the next day but might just as well have written. Arriving in Manchester after a tiresome journey, we learned that the surgeon was unable to make a decision until he'd examined his patient.

'Bring your father to see me,' he said, seeing us out of his pristine offices onto the grimy street below. 'If the operation proves viable, he'll need one of you to stay with him for a month while he recuperates.' Perhaps he noticed our despair, some mark of poverty upon us, because his voice lost its clinical impartiality and became human. 'I can arrange very reasonable lodgings if that would be helpful.'

On the train home, we agreed that Charlotte would accompany Papa—the house would not run without me, and I was the only one who could deal with Branwell on his worst days. We expected resistance from Papa at first, some argument about the weight of work that would fall on Mr. Nicholl's shoulders in his absence, but he was as compliant as a child, wanted only to hear the arrangements again, to be clear in his mind what was to happen. The following week, Charlotte wrote from Manchester to say that the operation had taken place.

I was horrified to learn that no anaesthetic would be administered, but Papa was remarkably brave and managed to ask questions of the surgeon throughout the procedure, which took around fifteen minutes to perform and required the application of belladonna to dilate the pupils. You'll be relieved to know that Dr. Wilson thinks the operation a success, but to allow proper healing, Papa's eyes will remain bandaged for the next month and he must lie completely in the dark. The guesthouse is empty, other than us, but with the landlady away, I am having to manage the domestic tasks I'm least fitted to! Still, it was kind of Dr. Wilson to arrange everything for us and I'm thankful for the nurse he sent, who applied leeches to Papa's poor eyes, and takes care of all his needs. I'm glad to hear Anne's new story is progressing. I don't know where she finds the resilience when you say our parcel has been returned yet again. The days are endless, and the rain never seems to stop in this city. Writing might pass the time, I suppose.

On Christmas Day, Papa's voice rung out from the pulpit with new vigour, and he shook the hand of every parishioner as they left the church. 'Quite remarkable,' I heard him saying, time and again, gesturing to his newly restored eyes. Branwell attended all the Christmas services and made no fuss about the absence of wine at dinner. In the New Year, he started joining us in the dining room, sometimes sitting by the fire with a book, at other times taking out his writing desk. Once the driving force behind all our creative ideas, I am ashamed to say that his presence now constrained us. We passed rejection letters between us in silence, adding them to the growing pile in Charlotte's desk. Anne was making good progress on a new story, but with our brother in the room, she could no longer read passages out loud to us. The fire crackled, while outside nature perished in the bitter January wind. I could hear Papa moving around across the hallway, his footsteps no longer tentative. Peace held but it was as fragile as newly formed ice, a word, a hasty movement could break it.

Early summer. The swallows were back and waiting now for their first broods. I came in from feeding the chickens and the geese one morning to find Charlotte in the kitchen, an opened package on the table, knew right away that our manuscripts had been returned once more. We'd hoped that our volume of poems would lend us some credibility in the world of publishing, but time and again our words had come back to us, unwanted.

'Thomas Newby offers to publish your book, and Anne's. We'd have to pay the expenses.'

I put down my basket of eggs with more care than usual, hardly trusting myself not to damage them.

'What about yours? The package on the table was too big to contain only a letter.

'They don't want it.'

She nodded towards the parcel, the letter lying beside it, and then chopped her hand through the air, a desperate, truncated little movement.

'You'll send it out again, of course?' I said, forcing my mind to narrow upon this question, ignoring the excitement that threatened to explode inside my chest.

'I'm running out of publishers.' She laughed without joy.

'You have to carry on. Keep writing too.'

'I've nothing more to say.' She shrugged, tried to smile. 'I'm not surprised your book has found a home.' Her voice rose with the lie. 'It's such a rare and strange creation, but I'd thought my little story as good as Anne's, if not better. You mustn't tell her I said so.'

I longed, suddenly, to run and find Anne, to tell her the news, but Charlotte could not be left alone with her returned manuscript. 'There's truth in Anne's story,' I said. 'I can see why a publisher would put his name to it, but it's nonsense to say you've no more stories. You've been writing them all your life.'

'The world does not want my stories, Emily.' She sat down with a heaviness that belied her stature, with the weight of finality. 'I've always written for myself, and it's made every day delightful, the hardest of times bearable, but all these rejections have tainted everything. I'd actually started something new while I was in Manchester for Papa's operation, just because I was feeling so desolate and alone, but *now* . . . I won't be able to sit at my desk without sensing the entire publishing world peering over my shoulder, eyeing my poor words. I should hear them talking among themselves, wondering where I find the audacity to keep on presenting my inferior work to them.' She wrapped her arms tightly around herself. 'It's a punishment for judging myself too highly. Ever since I can remember, I've dreamed of great achievements, of making my voice heard in the world, Heaven knows why.' She gestured to herself with a mixture of mockery and self-loathing. 'For some reason, I never quite believed that God truly meant me to be a governess all my life, thought it just a test.' With a brave little smile, she handed me the letter from Thomas Newby. 'You should find Anne.' She gathered her rejected manuscript to her breast.

After two days in bed with a severe cold, she came downstairs pale and resolute. I was in the hallway with Don Juan, our newly adopted stray cat, who was trying to cough up a fur ball.

'I'm going to try with the school again, Emily. I've thought about it. If I reduce the fees, aim for just one or two girls in the beginning, then word will spread. Goodness knows, I'm well enough qualified and I can't bear to go away just yet.' She looked through the half-open door into the dining room, where Anne was immersed in her writing. She took a deep breath. 'I can teach by myself if need be, could employ another mistress later. Who knows, Branwell might even make himself useful. He's not exactly under-educated, and he's vowed he won't touch opium again; that he's going to drink less from now on.'

Only yesterday, another debt-collector had come to the door, wanting payment for old bills that Branwell and his friends had run up in Halifax. I'd tried to take the matter outside, to persuade him to seek out my brother for himself, but Papa had rushed out of his study and started pushing notes into his hand. The man had left, clearly disappointed not to be accompanying Branwell to the debtor's prison in York.

'I won't have such a man here, at the parsonage,' said Papa, opening his empty palms to me afterwards. He'd sighed and I could hear his chest rattling.

'Anyway, we can't just give up on him,' Charlotte said now.

'It's hardly giving up!' How many times had I heaved Branwell's drink-sodden, protesting body up the stairs and into his bed, tolerated the stream of foul abuse, the stench of soiled sheets and clothing that could not wait till wash day. It would be a grim matter if I allowed myself to dwell on it and I wondered sometimes what Aunt would say if she could see me scraping and scrubbing and soaking in the back kitchen with my face averted. 'But he might as well be a child for all the help we can expect from him.'

A flash of pain on her face. I should have kept my thoughts to myself. Charlotte was still too wounded by her rejected manuscript to withstand another body blow, least of all about the bright, capricious brother she professed to despise.

'What *am* I to do then?' Her voice rose tearfully. Her hands flopped at her side. She was lost as an orphan, standing in the hallway. 'I can't carry on sending out the same novel. It's destroying me.'

'Write something new then,' I said, picking up the stray in my arms. For the first time in my life, I felt in a position to offer her advice. It came to me, only as I spoke, that Charlotte's novel had failed because she'd held back her true nature, her own voice. Where was her rage, the sense of injustice she felt at being constantly overlooked, that small fist shaking at the indifferent world, insisting on itself? 'We have to write what we really feel, regardless of what anyone expects. Nothing else will do.'

'I'm not sure I have the courage.'

'You're the most courageous person I know.'

She looked around her, seeking inspiration in that plain, homely hallway. 'I suppose I could look at some old work. And there's the thing I started in Manchester I mentioned before. It's a miserable little tale—I was feeling sorry for myself—but I could try to go on with that if you really think it's worthwhile. All I need is to earn enough to live on.'

She'd misunderstood me. I'd meant that writing was the only salve, the one medicine guaranteed to pull her back from the edge of despair. Charlotte knew as well as I that all our literary efforts to date had actually cost us money; an unkind observer might have described them as acts of vanity. I said nothing to contradict her though. More than once recently, I'd had the strange sensation of reminding myself *not* to speak.

That evening, after he'd carped about every aggravation from the quality of conversation to the infernal rustling of the newspaper, Branwell took himself off to bed at an early hour, preferred to be asleep than in our wretched company. I thought Charlotte calmer, looking through her old papers and scribbling the occasional note to herself. We went to bed in peace, but in the early hours I was woken by shrieks coming from Papa's room. I found him half-risen from his bed, still dazed by sleep, and Branwell huddled in the corner of the room. When I approached my brother, he began rocking violently, muttering to himself.

'A demon,' he cried out. 'Sitting on my chest!'

'There is none,' I crouched down beside him. 'It's just the opium.' He began to tremble and his eyes darted around the room. I needed him to look at me, to understand the truth, but his gaze slid past me to the doorway, and he screamed in terror: 'Black-eyed angels!' He turned and started scrabbling at the wall. 'I won't go with them!'

'It's Charlotte and Anne,' I told him, grasping him by his shoulders. 'Your own sisters.'

He howled again and when Papa tried to lay a hand on his head, began to kick and flail, lashing out in all directions.

'Help me!' I shouted, astonished by the strength that emanated from his wiry frame. Keeper's great paws landed on Branwell's shoulders, knocked him flat. As he fell, his fist flew backwards and caught Anne in the face. Papa gave up praying then and between the four of us we managed to hold him down until, finally, his eyes cleared.

'I was so frightened,' he said, his breath coming in small gasps. Anne was crouched behind him with her hand to her mouth. Already, her top lip had begun to swell. Branwell clutched my arm. 'Thank you.' At last, his breathing quietened. Tears slid into his hair which was the colour of beech leaves in autumn.

Anne and I were waiting for the final proofs of our novels, when Charlotte's first manuscript arrived back once again—it seemed that she'd found the courage to carry on sending it out after all, though she'd made no mention of doing so. Like every other organisation she'd approached, the company named Smith, Elder & Co. did not want to publish the novel, but their letter was not without encouragement.

'They say there's something in my writing and want me to

submit something else.' Charlotte was pink from the neck upwards. 'Emily, if I really work at it, I can get something to them very soon!' She dropped the letter and seized me by the hands. 'I carried on with that story I told you about. I haven't shared it with you yet because it felt like a solitary project. I reread the early chapters the other day and I thought them good; closer to my own experience of life than the other story.' She laughed—a rare thing these days. 'Of course, I can't stick to reality for long, you know how it is with me—there *must* be mysteries and terrors and great passions. I think my little novel lies somewhere between yours and Anne's, so perhaps it will appeal to some poor reader in want of distraction!'

After that, Charlotte was a woman a dream. She gave up all other occupation in order to write, refused to take fresh air though the weather was still fine, with only a hint of the coming autumn. White-faced and distracted, she wrote on until Branwell came crashing through the door, the clink of the opium bottle in his pocket. A stranger might have thought her on the verge of breaking down, but happiness showed itself in my sister in strange ways. By the time our proofs finally arrived, she had completed her new manuscript.

We knew only the outline of Charlotte's new novel. I'd assumed this was because she'd started writing it while alone, was superstitious about sharing in our usual way until it was complete. Even now, when Anne asked her to read aloud to us, she seemed uncharacteristically reluctant. It wasn't until she reached the point in the story where her young, orphaned protagonist was sent away to a charity school that I began to understand.

'You must read the rest for yourselves,' she said, coming to sudden halt. She thrust the remaining pages across the table in no-one's direction. They landed somewhere between Anne and me. 'Don't look at me like that!' she said, meeting my eye for a brief moment.

'It sounds just like—'

'Well it's not! Not really. Anyway, you won't find a trace of yourself in my story, if that's what you're worried about.'

'I wasn't. Not till a moment ago.' I looked at her in wonder, horror. 'I never dreamed you'd write about that time.'

'Won't you carry on reading to us?' said Anne.

'You told me to write the truth. That nothing else would do.'

'I didn't mean about us.'

'You think I should just forget about what happened?'

'I should like to hear,' said Anne.

'No.' I shook my head. 'But you could choose not to think about it. It's different.'

'But what good does that do?' Charlotte opened her palms, inviting enlightenment. 'Ignoring bad things doesn't make them go away.'

'It keeps them . . .' I was struggling for words. 'Safe.'

She looked at me. 'Nobody listened to me then and there's every chance that no-one will pay any attention to me now.' She gave the manuscript an angry nudge. 'Read it if you want, or don't. Both of you. But I refuse to keep quiet, Emily. Not until the day I die.' She gave a sob and then hurried from the room. Anne and I sat in silence, listened to the tick of the clock from the stairwell, Charlotte's abandoned manuscript lying between us on the table. Eventually, Anne stood.

'I shall read it after you.' Her voice was steady. She stopped at the doorway and looked over her shoulder. 'Nobody ever told me what happened.'

T he clock kept on ticking, though time seemed to re-
verse as I read those pages.

'Yes,' I said, in response to the question in Anne's eyes
when she eventually came back in the room. I handed her the
manuscript. The heroine of Charlotte's novel was recognis-
ably her own small self, enraged by the injustice and suffering
she'd endured as a child. There was a persecuted schoolgirl
too, older than her protagonist and bearing a strong resem-
blance to our eldest sister, though I didn't recall Maria being
so saintly. As Charlotte had promised, there was no trace of
me in those pages, nor of Elizabeth. 'But it's not the way I
remember it.'

Anne pulled up a chair and read quickly, pushed aside each
sheet as she finished with it. They formed a growing stack on the
table beside her. I waited in silence. In her haste, she knocked
the pile with her elbow. I crouched to retrieve two of the sheets
that had fallen to the floor. When I stood again, it was clear that
she had finished the part of the narrative that mattered most.
When she looked at me I felt the old urge to lie down on the
floor and close my eyes. I left her, went upstairs and curled up
on my bed. I stared at the blank wall, listened to the ticking
of the clock in the stairwell. Feeling a little calmer, I opened
the drawer where I kept my sketches, thinking I might distract
myself by making some alterations. As I went to take them out
my fingers touched something solid. Beneath the drawings and
wrapped in a chemise, I'd concealed my copy of our *Poems*. I

pushed aside the sketches and pulled the book free, then turned the pages until I found what I was looking for.

> Cold in the earth–and the deep snow piled above thee,
> Far, far, removed, cold in the dreary grave!
> Have I forgot, my only Love, to love thee,
> Severed at last by Time's all-severing wave?

I'd written the poem some time before the ones in the notebook that Charlotte had found. It had been a Gondal poem at first, an elegy for Julius Brenzaida—for poetic purposes I'd killed him off well in advance of his own death—in the voice of Rosina Alcona, his first love. The passage of time had assuaged the worst of her pain, but she would always stay true to his memory.

> Cold in the earth—and fifteen wild Decembers,
> From those brown hills, have melted into spring:
> Faithful, indeed, is the spirit that remembers
> After such years of change and suffering!

I'd removed all references to Gondal, then named the poem *Remembrance* before including it with our submission to Aylott & Jones. With Rosina and Julius erased, I could now see what had been true all along: the poem was as much about Maria and Elizabeth as any fictional character.

When I went back downstairs there was no sign of Charlotte. Anne was where I had left her, the manuscript still stacked in front of her.

'I don't remember Maria dying,' she said, looking up at me. 'Not properly. Only Branwell crying because Papa had made him look at her in the coffin. I do remember when Elizabeth came home because I asked Aunt if she was going to die too. Aunt said I had to pray very hard for her.'

'I should have listened to Charlotte,' I said. 'She begged me to make Papa take us all home from school. I shouldn't have ignored her.' Shouldn't have made Maria climb the fell when she was already sick; shouldn't have left Elizabeth all alone just because I wanted to see an ocean for the first time. Into the dark well of my mind, the facts fell like stone.

'You were so young,' said Anne. 'No-one could have expected you to understand.'

'Charlotte did.'

'Not really.' Anne shook her head. 'She was just an unhappy little girl, wanting to feel better. You can't be sure Papa would have agreed, even if you'd done as she wished.'

I said nothing but Anne's clear-eyed judgement fell on me like a cooling rain. I felt a shifting sensation beneath my surface, a cloud rolled back and that long-ago past was exposed for what it was: a series of events over which I'd had no control. I wondered if Charlotte had felt the same way when she'd emerged from the *Cathédrale St. Gudule* into the dazzling sunlight after her impromptu confession.

'Besides, you can't shoulder all of the blame,' said Anne. She smiled sadly as she tidied Charlotte's already-neat manuscript. 'I always thought Elizabeth's death was my fault. I felt sure I hadn't prayed hard enough, that my voice was too quiet for God to hear.'

Charlotte looked up from her writing desk one morning and nodded to the opened letter on the table. 'They'll pay £100 for this novel, plus right of refusal on two more works,'

'100 *pounds*!' Anne came hurrying down the stairs and into the dining room. She put her arms around Charlotte from behind. 'Show me the letter! I can hardly believe it.'

'You'll accept, of course?' Her reply, I noticed, already stretched to several pages.

'I've told—' Charlotte checked the name at the top of first

page. 'Mr. George Smith, that it's not enough. It sounds a huge sum but what of the cost to me? New books come out every five minutes and the world begins to think writing them easy, a delightful pastime. Perhaps it is for some, but I must cut myself open every time.'

'It's what you love most,' I reminded her. 'And they want to pay you.'

'Oh, I'm accepting.' She was about to sign the letter when she checked herself after the first *C* and wrote *Currer Bell* instead. 'Only they must promise to pay more if the book should sell.'

Smith, Elder & Co. wrote back immediately, accepting her terms. In turn, Charlotte accepted an invitation to stay with Ellen Nussey.

'Promise me you'll send the proofs on,' she said, as she climbed up into the coach at Keighley.

'Can't they wait until you're back?' I asked, suddenly afraid that Charlotte would not be able to resist sharing her news with her oldest friend. If Currer Bell was discovered, so too were Ellis and Acton. Ellen was one of the few people outside of my family that I loved and trusted, but I could not have her peering into my soul.

'Don't fret,' laughed Charlotte, leaning down to me. 'They're used to my strange ways at Brookroyd. The family won't think twice if I take myself off for a few hours when visitors arrive.' The horses started and Charlotte gave a swirl of her hand, perched on her seat like a little queen.

She returned later in the month in high spirits, bringing presents from Ellen—a crab apple cheese for Anne to help her recover from her cold, apples and a pretty collar wrapped in soft blue paper for me. No-one, she assured me, as we helped her unpack, had taken the least bit of interest while she worked on her proofs. She'd completed them and sent them back to Smith, Elder & Co. before her return home.

'I can hardly wait for *our* books now,' said Anne, when we took a walk later that day. It was weeks since we'd corrected our own proofs, yet we'd heard nothing more from Thomas Newby about a publication date. I stopped to move a snail in danger of being crushed underfoot. With a sudden fervour, she said: 'I always think my life is so small and how little I matter. It's different for you, and Charlotte *makes* the world take notice of her, but if I could help another person in the right direction with my work, give hope in some way . . .' She stroked Flossy's ears and looked up to the hills that surrounded Haworth on all sides.

'You matter to us,' I said, my hand firm over hers. 'It won't be much longer now.'

But it was December before the parcel we'd been waiting for arrived. We hurried upstairs to find Charlotte. Her own novel had arrived a full two months earlier, in October, though it had been submitted so much later than ours. During those first weeks of publication, she'd been bright-eyed and the blood had seemed to thrum just beneath the surface of her skin. But then she'd received a couple of reviews which she pronounced 'lacklustre' and immediately put them away out of sight. She spent three days in bed suffering from a vague, enervating illness she felt certain was a prelude to death, but by some miracle recovered as soon as a cheerful letter from Mary Taylor arrived.

'Your Mr. Newby doesn't like to hurry himself for anyone,' said the experienced author as we tore open our own parcel. But she took over all the morning chores, so that Anne and I could savour our books in peace. We shut ourselves away in my little bedroom until dinner time, delighting in the sensation of finding ourselves published novelists, though every one of the meticulous corrections we'd sent to Thomas Newby had been ignored.

I was cutting lengths of ivy on Parsonage Lane for our Christmas mantelpiece when Charlotte came flying with a letter in her hand.

'From Thackeray,' she gasped, her breath coming like steam from a small engine. She was dressed only in a wrapper and the frost had already melted on the toes of her slippers, turned the flimsy material dark. '*W. M.* Thackeray!' As if I didn't already know the author of *Vanity Fair.* 'Mr. Smith enclosed it with a letter of his own. Can you believe it?' She widened her eyes, looked, for a moment, like a little girl again. 'He asks all sorts of wonderful questions about my book, says how much he admires it!' She seized my hand so hard I almost dropped the scissors. '*Thackeray!* And Mr. Smith says all the literary people in London are wild to know about Currer Bell. There are more reviews too, Mr. Smith sent them in the same letter, but I had to find you first—he says they'll have to think about reprinting because the books are—'

'Come inside before you die of cold,' I laughed, gathering up my greenery. I took her by the arm and marched her back down the lane. 'Anne needs to hear everything too.' Martha was busy in the dining room, so I took Charlotte into the study— Papa was out at Governors' meeting—and made her sit by the fire, while I fetched Anne. Charlotte's whole body trembled as she read aloud a snippet that proclaimed her book

Decidedly the best novel of the season

Another critic wrote: *All the serious novel writers of the day lose in comparison with Currer Bell.*

We stared at each other in disbelief. The heap of ivy I'd cut lay abandoned on Papa's desk. Anne wanted to see Mr. Thackeray's letter for herself, to run her fingers over that venerated man's handwriting.

'Mr. Smith really wants to reprint?' I said.

'Read what he says!' The pages fell into my lap. The demand was overwhelming, her publisher had written, word-of-mouth having spread news of Charlotte's novel across the capital. There was immense speculation about the identity of the author too. All agreed that the book had been written under a pseudonym, yet no-one could connect the style or content to a known author. Some thought the book must have been written by a man, while others deemed that impossible: no male could write about a poor, plain governess with such power and empathy.

'I'll do nothing to enlighten the world, Emily,' cried Charlotte, seeing my expression. 'I could die right now and be perfectly happy with my life exactly as it is!' She went to the window and stared out across the bare, frost-damaged garden, squinting as the low winter sunshine caught her. 'Though it still feels wretched, hiding all this from Branwell.' By mid-morning, the letter had brought on the severest of headaches. When I checked on her, she was lying in bed with a damp cloth over her eyes, a little smile still on her lips.

While Anne's novel received barely a comment in the press, my own was judged more harshly. According to one reviewer, it was a *strange book*, inhabited by *savages ruder than those who lived before the days of Homer*. Another reader found himself *shocked, disgusted, almost sickened by details of cruelty, inhumanity*. The next review mourned the lack of *a single character which is not utterly hateful or thoroughly contemptible*.

'Oh, Emily,' said Charlotte breaking off in the middle of one particularly excoriating article. 'Don't make me go on. You're entirely misunderstood and misjudged! If these . . . *people* only knew you as we do, if they could see where we live . . .' She threw down the article and swept her hand in a vague arc, indicating not the parsonage itself, I assumed, but this little piece of earth in West Yorkshire.

I picked up the flimsy cutting and read the words for myself. 'I agree with them,' I said when I'd finished. 'Well, most of it.'

'You don't mean that.' Anne was close to tears. 'Pay no mind, Emily. Remember how your poems were received.'

'Perhaps I should take one or two of these *men* up on the moors in the middle of a storm.' I smiled to myself and glanced towards the window, which was a block of grey, midwinter light. 'As punishment. I'd like to see how long it would take until they threw off their sensibilities. Listen, the band is starting up.' But Charlotte would not be distracted by the Christmas concert on Main Street, needed me to make her feel better about the criticism. 'Look, there are enough writers turning out well-mannered novels, but I can't do it. I shall not!' I swept up the reviews and put them out of sight, at the bottom of my writing desk. To cheer her up I said: 'Remember when Keeper took a dislike to those two ridiculous curates who came over after the harvest supper in the schoolhouse?' Charlotte covered her mouth with her hand, laughing. 'They were all politeness and piety until Keeper leapt at their throats and chased them up the stairs,' I explained to Anne, who'd been away from home at the time. 'They tried to get into my room, but you know how stiff that door can be, so they started thrusting one another back down the stairs into his jaws, each trying to save their own skin by sacrificing the other! That's what I mean about writing the truth about people. I can't stop. I won't.'

Charlotte looked at me as if I were mad but knew better than to argue.

'You won't give up then?' Anne said later, when we took Flossy and Keeper for an evening walk. The hills turned black early at this time of year. In the valley, a thick tail of fog drifted along the river. 'It's strange, but I mind less about my first story being overlooked now that I'm writing again. It's almost as if another author produced those pages. I think this new story of mine might offend, but you've made me braver about speaking up.'

That night, when Charlotte and Anne fetched their books and papers and took their usual places at the dining room table,

I sat on the sofa and watched the coals throbbing in the fire. There was a warm, citrus smell in the air, from the cloved oranges Anne had placed on the bookshelves. Keeper was snoring by the hearth, while beside him Flossy stretched prettily to absorb as much warmth as possible. The holly on the mantelpiece shone in the candlelight, its berries gleaming like jewels. I listened to the well-mannered tick of the clock in the stairwell, and to the chime as it marked out the hour. Outside, the wind howled across the church yard. I heard the rattle of fine hail against the window and remembered a line from *King Lear* that had always stayed with me:

unaccommodated man is no more but such a poor, bare, forked animal

Poor Tom, lost on the desolate heath, the madman who spoke the truth. I sat for a little longer on the sofa and then I fetched my things and joined my sisters at the table. At the top of a blank page, I wrote *Ellis Bell*. The curl of the letters contained and liberated me at the same time. I smiled to myself, dipped the nib back into the ink.

Y ou should tell Papa,' I said to Charlotte as we returned
from the Post Office with another parcel of books
sent for her enjoyment by Smith, Elder & Co. Her
own novel had sold out in three months and was about to be
reprinted.

'I daren't. Not after he warned me not to spend all my time
writing.'

'He'll forgive you once he hears how much you're earning,' I
smiled and then glanced towards the Black Bull Inn. 'He needs
distracting.'

'It *is* extraordinary, isn't it?' she said, once we had turned
onto Parsonage Lane. The wind caught her bonnet, too loosely
tied, threatened to tear it off. 'I can hardly believe it myself
sometimes. People talking about the book in London was wonderful, but now that news has made its way north . . . Did Anne
tell you that she heard Mr. Greenwood discussing it with a cus-
tomer the other day? She was tempted to tap the man on the
shoulder and tell him that Currer Bell lived just down the lane,
was at that moment polishing the silverware. I *would* love to tell
Papa, so that he knows I've made something of myself at last. I
think he would be proud. But then he'd be sure to tell Branwell
and imagine what he'd have to say.'

I shrugged. 'You've always been in competition with one another. I can imagine him rushing to take up his pen again, even
now.'

'He'd never forgive me. I really believe he'll go on like this forever now. He's lost all self-respect, doesn't once think about the rest of us.' She tied her bonnet more tightly. 'I will tell Papa, but only if you do the same.'

'There's nothing to tell, except that Anne and I paid for our own books to be published instead of getting on with proper work. It's worse than nothing. But to know that all of London is wild for your book, that Mr. Thackeray keeps up a correspondence with you, that's another matter.'

It was worse than nothing and yet the success of Charlotte's novel had awakened the flame of ambition in all three of us. The criticism of my own book took a different turn. Thomas Newby sent me the cuttings.

Fascinated by strange magic we read what we dislike, we become interested in characters which are most revolting to our feelings, and we are made subject to the immense power of the book . . . we are spell-bound, we cannot choose but read.

a strange sort of book—baffling all regular criticism; yet, it is impossible to begin and not finish it; and quite impossible to lay it aside afterwards and say nothing about it . . . We strongly recommend all our readers who love novelty to get this story, for we can promise them that they have never read anything like it before.

The world steadied beneath my feet. With several different ideas for a new novel, I exchanged letters with Thomas Newby and was pleased when he encouraged me to write just as I chose. At about the same time, Anne asked if she might read us some chapters from her new novel. At the close, Charlotte fell silent and even I was shocked that my gentle sister could produce something so brutally honest: the story of a woman escaping her violent, alcoholic husband for the sake of her little boy.

'It's powerful, of course,' said Charlotte with the air of sagacity she'd adopted since becoming a successful author. 'And quite unlike your first. I worry that people will be put off by the subject matter though. You might want to edit some of the more brutal scenes.'

Before I could jump to her defence, Anne answered for herself.

'No. If just one person hears what I have to say and benefits from it, then I'll be satisfied.'

As we readied ourselves for bed that night, it came to me how happy we were, each of us doing what she loved most; the three of us together taking up new space. Until recently we'd believed that Branwell had the power to destroy our futures, but now, and entirely by our own efforts, we had contained his suffering, assimilated all that pain. I felt sure that Papa sensed the change too, though he had taken the news of Charlotte's success quietly at first, not understanding, until she'd explained properly, that his own daughter was the author of the most talked-about novel of the season. We'd agreed that she would make no mention of the books published by her literary 'brothers,' and Papa had not read any reviews that might lead him to make the connection for himself.

'Remarkable,' he kept saying. 'Quite remarkable.' How disappointed he'd been when she'd insisted that he maintain her anonymity; that in his current condition even Branwell could not be trusted with the secret.

'Just for now,' she comforted him and then signalled an apology to me.

For once I didn't mind. For the rest of that day, Papa had a smile on his face, and I heard him whistling to himself as he locked up for the night.

Anne and I had argued, and I could not concentrate on preparing dinner. Or rather, we'd had a difference of opinion which was as painful to me as a violent battle with any other person. I could not remember a time when the two of us did not agree. I would have talked to Charlotte about this distressing development except that she and Anne were busy packing bags, and I was not speaking to her either.

Ever since the delay in publishing our books, Charlotte had maintained that our Mr. Newby was unreliable, not the same calibre of publisher as her own Smith, Elder & Co. I'd paid little attention, but now that Anne's new novel had been sent out for reviews, Mr. Newby had given Charlotte further cause to think him inferior, by putting it about in American publishing circles that Currer, Ellis and Acton Bell were one and the same person; that the same hand that wrote Currer Bell's hugely successful story was also responsible for this new novel. Learning of this, Charlotte's Mr. Smith had written to Currer Bell in unhappy terms, wishing to know if 'he' was, in fact, producing work for two different publishing houses.

'We'll have to go to London,' Charlotte had said, as she pushed the letter into my hands.

'Why?'

'Because I can't have Mr. Smith thinking Currer Bell is a charlatan! It will ruin everything I've worked for. I must explain to him myself.'

'You don't need to go to see him. Just write to say that Mr. Newby is mistaken.'

'Read the letter, Emily! Mr. George Smith is entirely a gentleman, but you can't mistake his anger! I need to tell him the truth.'

'That we are three brothers?'

'How can I maintain that if I go in person?'

'Which is why you can't go. Write to your Mr. Smith, and Anne and I will write to Mr. Newby to tell him to stop spreading misinformation.'

'Charlotte's name could be tarnished,' said Anne. Her volume of George Herbert's poems lay abandoned in her lap. 'Mr. Smith and his colleagues might refuse future manuscripts.'

'And risk losing their most successful author? Even if they

were so foolish, I'm sure Mr. Newby would be happy to consider anything Smith, Elder & Co. reject!'

Charlotte had been pacing up and down the dining room. She came to a halt, halfway up the room and turned to me.

'I have to go. Please try to understand.'

'Currer Bell must do as he wishes.' I struggled to keep my voice steady. 'Always does. But I forbid you to disclose *my* name to anyone. I will never forgive you for it.'

'Charlotte is entirely right,' said Anne. She pushed her chair into place beneath the table, then put her volume of poems back on the shelf, maintaining order even in a crisis. 'And I'm going with her.'

The two of them left for London that afternoon. I broke a vase, trying to clean it, burnt my hand on the range, spilled ashes all over the kitchen floor, nearly knocked Branwell's portrait of us from the wall while dusting. I straightened it out of habit but would have preferred to turn it around or throw it in the cellar. I wished I could paint myself out of it, just as Branwell had done shortly after he'd completed it, replacing himself with a vague pillar shape. I'd only ever liked one picture of me and that was by my own hand—a quick sketch I'd drawn for the diary papers that Anne and I wrote, when we remembered, on our birthdays. It showed the two of us busy at work in the dining room, Anne on the far side of table, nearest the hearth, and me with my back to the viewer.

I gave up on chores, put on my cloak and bonnet and called for Keeper. It was summer but you would not have known it. The wind blustered and a rumble of thunder rolled through the valley beneath us. A cold rain began to fall. Ahead of us on Haworth moor, I could not see another living creature, only the bog grass bending to the wind, flickers of lightning. I wondered if Anne and Charlotte were at Keighley yet. I pictured them boarding the train at Leeds, figures so tiny and neat that you would not think them capable of damage; thought of those rails slicing the countryside in two, wheels destroying the distance between Haworth and London.

London. From the day that Charlotte received her first glowing review of *Jane Eyre*, I'd known this moment would come. Mr. Newby's behaviour had only brought forward the inevitable. For all her terror of strangers, Charlotte could not resist courting attention, was driven, always, by the need to prove her small, plain person exceptional. I knew she could only bear to stand in the shadow of Currer Bell for so long, and not receive the accolades for herself. I understood, but I'd spent too many years being dragged along in Charlotte's wake to sympathise. Just days ago, she'd persuaded Anne and me to tell Papa about our own books. I'd been relieved when Papa took the news quietly, asked only if he might yet tell Branwell—we both said no— but now I felt doubly exposed. I could not stop that train to London, had no way of influencing what might follow, but from now on I must take control of my own words, let Charlotte and even Anne, go their own ways. For a moment, I was desolate, sensing an empty space on either side of me, then I pulled up the peat-stained hem of my dress and broke into a run. Keeper barked with excitement and plunged into the heather, tearing ahead. The wind swirled around me. It shrieked in my ears and then the rain came harder, flaying my skin and finding its way beneath my collar. I ran until my breath was gone, then tore off my bonnet and lifted my chin to the sky. My hair had come loose. Dark, dripping hanks hung on my shoulders and down my back. The sky pulsed with light and I was a wild creature, uncontained. I opened my mouth and let the rain pool there, swallowed it down.

Anne and Charlotte brought the east wind home with them, as well as many assurances from Mr. George Smith of Smith, Elder & Co.

'He promised never to reveal your name to another soul,' said Charlotte, eyes wild with excitement and exhaustion, words spilling out of her even before she'd removed her bonnet: Mr. Smith's shock on learning of our true identities, his kindness to them, how he implored them to stay at his home as honoured guests . . . They'd declined, preferred to remain at the Chapter Coffee House where Charlotte and I had stayed before Brussels, but could not refuse a visit to see *The Barber of Seville* at Covent Garden.

'He simply arrived at our doorstep that evening and swept us up! Imagine how shabby we looked with everyone else in the party in evening dress! You needn't worry, we passed ourselves off as Mr. Smith's cousins from the country and were barely questioned after that.'

I said little, relieved that my anonymity was almost intact; yet to be convinced that Charlotte would be satisfied with this halfway arrangement for long.

'But the music, Emily!' said Anne, her eyes shining. She had been silent till now. 'How you would have loved the music.'

The east wind went away and then abruptly returned, bringing with it the usual coughs and colds. By now we were used to Branwell's periods of agitation or apathy, the occasional outbursts of passion for Lydia Robinson, or rage towards her late husband, the hallucinatory dreams that made him scream in terror in the middle of the night. The washing had become a matter of routine for me, Anne and Charlotte helping with some of the other chores on the bad days. He rarely ate a proper meal now and was a shrunken version of his old self, but we comforted ourselves with the fact that he no longer walked for miles, so needed less sustenance than before. Even on his better days, he was withdrawn, had almost nothing to say on any subject, though all of us did our best to draw him out. Still, we expected him to rally at some point, for the old Branwell to spring up like a jack-in-a-box, brimming over with opinions and schemes. When he told us he was to take a trip, a gentler version of the Grand Tour he'd once envisaged, we were relieved. Papa had a clergy contact in Rome apparently, and another in Naples, had promised to write to both on Branwell's behalf.

'*O for a beaker full of the warm South,*' he quoted, a blissful smile on his face. In Italy, he said, oranges hung heavy on the trees and flowers perfumed the air even in the winter months. In that pure light, and with the mild lull of the Mediterranean Sea, he could return to the novel he'd been planning to write. There were plenty of English families scattered around the country in need of a good tutor too. It would be the best place for him to convalesce, to begin again. Even now, his excitement was infectious. If Anne had been out of earshot, Charlotte would almost certainly have burst out the news of her own novel.

We returned from church one Sunday to hear from Martha that he had taken to his bed with a fresh bottle of laudanum. Anne suspected that he'd spied the letter she'd received from Mrs. Robinson's middle daughter the day before. The letter had contained the usual flurry of complaints, gossip and nothing. Only towards the end came the news that her mother was soon to marry again, to Sir Edward Dolman Scott, Baronet.

'So much for the clause in Mr. Robinson's Will,' said Charlotte. 'I knew that was nonsense.'

'I don't like to think so,' says Anne. 'I suppose Sir Edward is rich enough for the stipulation not to matter.'

A few days later, Branwell was brought home by Mr. Driver, the grocer, who had found him crumpled on the ground in an alleyway off Changegate. I could smell no alcohol on him and wondered if the collapse might be a long-term effect of the laudanum.

At the darkest point of the night, Papa woke me.

'He's very bad,' he whispered as I pulled on a dressing gown.

In Papa's room, I found Branwell up on all fours on the bed, like a boy waiting to be punished. His legs protruded from beneath his nightgown—white, finely-haired. I knew he'd lost weight in recent months but still it was a shock to see how wasted they looked, incapable of holding the weight of a grown man. He lifted his head as I approached and then started to cough with such violence that I almost recoiled. The sound of flesh tearing in deep, dark places. Finally, he collapsed onto his side, sweat and tears glowing in the candlelight. His eyes glittered, ice blue. His cheeks were scarlet against the pallor of the rest of his complexion and the white sheet. A cold feeling crept over me. I had seen that look before.

'I'll fetch the doctor.'

'I'll go,' said Papa. 'Charlotte can sit with you.'

I pulled up a chair next to Branwell's bed. 'Let her rest for now.'

But dawn had long since seeped over the hills, orange streaked with red, by the time Dr. Wheelhouse arrived. He'd spent all night assisting a difficult birth in Oxenhope. He examined Branwell and then bled him.

'Has he been exposed to bad air?' he asked, as he stepped out onto the landing where Papa and I were waiting. 'Trips to low parts of a city, for instance.'

'He's been home for months,' said Papa.

The doctor looked grave. 'He mustn't exert himself on any account, Reverend Brontë. There's an infection of the lungs, exacerbated by his weakened condition. I'll come to bleed him again tomorrow.'

From the bedroom came the sound of that awful, wrenching cough.

'I can't see what good it does,' I said after that second bleeding. Branwell had been lying on his back with his arms thrown open. From the landing I'd seen the flash of the scalpel, thick dark blood running into the shiny bowl beneath. He had turned onto his side now, appeared to be asleep, but the coughing went on, his ribs bunched like a concertina beneath his nightgown and his eyelids flickering. I thought of Maria and Elizabeth, neither of whom could be saved, Aunt's suffering. As a child, Branwell had wept on this very spot, prevented from seeing Mamma whose agony only the Great Healer could alleviate. 'His sheets need changing,' I said, seeing flecks of bright blood on the pillow.

'There will be other treatments,' said Papa.

I held his gaze though it hurt me to do so. Papa had spent his life attending sick beds, must have recognised the signs by now. I'd known even before Branwell began drifting in and out of consciousness with none of the restfulness of sleep. His breathing had become laboured now, and in his few moments of lucidity, he struggled to recognise any of us. The doctor must have known too.

'Oh, my darling boy!' Papa dropped to his knees. Behind us, in the doorway of the bedroom, Anne gave a little moan and started to cry.

Papa refused to leave Branwell's side, even though sharing a room with him these last months had exhausted him profoundly. The three of us begged him to rest—feared he might drive himself to collapse—but he took little notice, gazing down at his only son as he slept. Branwell was barely ever conscious now, except for the coughing fits that took hold of him like the jaws of an invisible, thrashing beast. They left him gasping for breath, eyes wide open with terror when he caught sight of blood on his pillow. His own lungs were tearing themselves to shreds. I dreaded the moment when Papa stopped whispering beneath his breath and began to pray out loud. It *would* come and he must be allowed to do it, but I was afraid that Branwell would reject him, that even as he fought for his final breaths, he might dredge up the words to banish Papa's God from this room.

'He can't go on like this.' Charlotte had come to relieve me so that I could prepare some food for us. Did she mean Branwell or Papa? I couldn't be sure. It surprised me how hungry we remained, that we must still sleep, visit the privy, our bodies insisting on their crude, domestic needs even as we waited for the unthinkable to come to pass. I'd propped Branwell up with extra pillows, hoping to ease his coughing. His mouth was half open, his breath viscous, bubbling in the back of his throat. A trail of yellowish saliva slid from the side of his mouth. I dampened a cloth, wiped the trail away, and then opened the window to let in some clean air. Everything in this room was the opposite of health.

'It will be a blessing when it comes,' said Charlotte, staring down at him.

He grew restless, moaned to himself and shrunk from things we couldn't see.

'Fetch Anne,' said Papa, with sudden authority. Charlotte was already seated on the opposite side of the bed, her hands folded in her lap. Anne was asleep but fully clothed, having sat with Branwell during the latter part of the night. She woke with a start and needed no explanation. In the bedroom, Papa put down his Bible and got to his feet. Laying his hand on Branwell's forehead, he began:

The Lord is my light and my salvation; whom then shall I fear?

We bowed our heads. The grey light of morning was a winding-sheet. My only prayer was that Branwell, who in his short life had given Papa such agonies, should allow him his only comfort.

*I believe that I shall see the goodness of the Lord
in the land of the living.
Wait for the Lord;
be strong and he shall comfort your heart;
wait patiently for the Lord.*

Branwell flinched at Papa's touch. His chest heaved. Then his fingers flickered with life. Who could tell what effort it took to lift that wasted hand from the bed, to reach up blindly towards Papa? I could not tear my eyes from either one of them, dreading that Branwell might find some last ounce of strength to push Papa's hand from his forehead.

Our Father who art in Heaven

Their fingers met. The room disappeared from me, then came into view again. Branwell's fingers had closed around Papa's.

hallowed be Thy name,

Thy kingdom come

Branwell's mouth quivered. No sound came but his white lips worked to form the shapes we had known since childhood.

Thy will be done,
on earth as it is in Heaven.

For the very last time, we were a chorus:

Give us this day our daily bread.
And forgive us our trespasses
as we forgive those who trespass against us.

Charlotte's voice came loud and high, asserting her strength over something we could not see, and which threatened to overcome her tiny frame.

Lead us not into temptation
but deliver us from evil.
For Thine is—

'Father!' cried Branwell, opening his eyes. He shot up from the bed and into Papa's arms. We heard a rushing noise, an immense and final exhalation and then he was gone.

Charlotte broke down at his passing, sank to the floor and sobbed with such animal anguish that I wondered for her sanity. I got her to her feet, held her steady until her eyes focused and she could breathe again. She left the funeral arrangements to the rest of us, for the next few days went about her normal business as hard and cold as a statue. Branwell had long ago ceded to her as an opponent, even without knowing that the famous author Currer Bell was his own sister. To whom would Charlotte direct her scorn now? Even in death, Branwell had disappointed her.

We buried him in the family vault. It was hard to believe that small, cold space could contain one who'd burned so brightly. I wondered what the days would hold without my brother to exasperate me, to exhaust me with his needs. The sheer messiness of him had spilled into all our lives. I did not understand how the world that had spun around Branwell could go on without him. I glanced along the pew at my sisters. Charlotte sat quite still, her expression frozen as she gazed straight ahead. With a gloved hand, Anne wiped silent tears from her cheeks. Ever since we were children, we'd behaved as though Branwell was the most important member of the family, but what if the three of us had taken all the air in the house for ourselves? Might we have saved him if we'd invited him to share in our plans for publication? Instead, we'd excluded him, left him to his fate. I'd lied outright too, told him that Charlotte and Anne had been invited to Ellen's house, when they'd gone to London to see George Smith. I pushed these thoughts away, reminded myself that I'd barely slept these last few days, that each of us had done our best for Branwell, who had been his own worst enemy, yet as we made our way to the schoolhouse for the wake, the idea still hovered like a bird of prey at the edge of my vision.

Despite some unkind reviews, Anne's new book sold sufficient copies for a second edition to be printed. In the preface of this new edition, she addressed the critics who'd taken offence at her subject matter.

I wished to tell the truth, for truth always conveys its own moral to those who are able to receive it. But as the priceless treasure too frequently hides at the bottom of a well, it needs some courage to dive for it, especially as he that does so will be likely to incur more scorn and obloquy for the mud and water into which he has ventured to plunge, than thanks for the jewel he procures.

She and Charlotte tried to hide from me an American review of my own book, thinking it too soon after Branwell's death. I snatched if from Anne's hands and read it for myself.

Acton [he had managed to confuse me with my sister], *when left altogether to his own imaginations, seems to take a morose satisfaction in developing a full and complete science of human brutality . . . has succeeded in reaching the summit of this laudable ambition. He appears to think that spiritual wickedness is a combination of animal ferocities, and has accordingly made a compendium of the most striking qualities of tiger, wolf, cur, and wild-cat, in the hope of framing out of such elements a suitable brute-demon to serve as the hero of his novel.*

For the sake of my sisters, I had always braved criticism, yet there had been nights when those brute male voices had come to haunt me. In the darkness of my little room their authority would become omnipotent, the judgements coming not from the mouths of over-refined individuals whose boots had never stepped in the mud, but as if from on High. When morning came, I could return them to the miry part of my mind where I stored unpleasantness and sickness and death, and they would lose their power over me. Now, with Branwell gone, the unkind review did not even touch the surface of me. I went to bed that night untroubled by a single word, rose in the morning knowing I would go on writing exactly as I pleased.

Y ou're very thin,' said Charlotte, eyeing me at breakfast one morning. 'And pale.' It was November, a month since Branwell had died. A fog had been hanging over the house for days. It wiped out the hills and dripped softly from the eaves. Anne's asthma was always bad at this time of year and Charlotte and Papa were little better—the weather settled on their lungs as soon as the wind came from the east. 'You need some beef tea. Or I could order some mutton for a stew?'

Keeper clipped into the room, threw himself against my thigh, a slab of warm flesh. I reached down, both to nuzzle his damp, leathery nose and to hide my smile. Charlotte hated cooking and this antipathy found its way into any dish she attempted. Cakes stayed resolutely flat, pastry was overworked and hard, gravy full of lumps. 'I'm dreading Christmas,' she went on. 'It feels wrong to celebrate with Branwell only just—' Her eyes swum with sudden tears. She blinked, annoyed with herself for giving way.

Both she and Anne had finished their breakfasts. I tried to do the same with mine, if only to stop Charlotte from commenting, but the porridge was a beige unnavigable sea on my plate, each spoonful seeming to thicken and stick in my throat. Recently, I'd noticed my bowels cramping painfully as soon I started eating, had put it down to an excess of nervous energy since Branwell had died.

'The preparations will do us good,' I said. 'Even if we can't be merry.'

'I'm worried for Papa,' said Charlotte. 'He takes on so much, will make himself really ill if he doesn't take more care.' In the last month, I'd noticed the colour seeping out of our father, his skin and hair now gradations of grey and white. It was hard, at first glance, to tell where the dividing line sat.

'Work's a comfort to him.' Sensing Anne watching me too, I forced down the last few mouthfuls of porridge, then scraped the remains from the pan into the dogs' bowls.

As soon as the fog lifted, I took Keeper and Flossy for a proper walk. Freed from the weight of condensation, the moor relished itself, an exuberant wind charging through the purple-brown heather and flattening the bracken which had been turned crisp by the autumn frosts and was now dampening towards decay. I threw a stick and the dogs raced after it, Flossy's enthusiasm never waning, even if Keeper always won the race. I'd planned to walk to the Meeting of the Waters—I wanted to see the waterfall in full spate—but long before we reached that secret valley, I found myself tiring. I turned for home, the dogs still bounding with energy. By evening I had a pain in my side which distracted me from writing. I moved to the sofa just to change position, thinking that I must have twisted something while throwing the stick earlier.

'Anne and I think you should see a doctor. You've been coughing for weeks now.'

'We are all coughing,' I said shortly, measuring flour by eye as I scooped it into the mixing bowl. When Charlotte co-opted Anne into an argument it was because she expected resistance. I would not disappoint her.

'I don't mean Dr. Wheelhouse,' she said. I used my hand to stir in the warm, yeast-frothed liquid. 'I know you don't have much faith in him since . . . But Mr. Smith recommended an excellent homeopath. Of course, you won't go to London, but apparently he is happy to dispense . . .'

'Mr. George Smith, you mean?' Charlotte kept up a regular correspondence with her publisher, savouring his interest in her, and also the gossip from London literary circles, a world removed from her life here in Haworth. Recently, she'd talked of going to stay with him and his mother, though she maintained she'd be too nervous to meet the great Thackeray in person. I'd witnessed her ordeals in public too many times to doubt her—was equally sure that she yearned for the very thing that paralysed her. Curiosity about the true identity of Currer Bell showed no sign of waning, either in London or here, in our own part of Yorkshire—the who and what and where. She'd started exchanging letters with other authors now: G. H. Lewes, Julia Kavanagh. Names we'd only read in newspapers. It was easy to forget that she was tiny and plain when you'd witnessed the ambition that drove her over and over into an until-now indifferent world. How long could she bear to hide behind her pseudonym? I did not think it would take much to persuade Anne to put her name to her own novels now that she'd raised her voice enough to be heard. Some hope then, of Ellis Bell remaining a mystery to the world. 'Why are you speaking about me to a man I've never met?' I asked. 'And have no intention of meeting.'

It occurred to me that Charlotte might invite her Mr. Smith here now that Branwell was gone. No matter how affable a man he might be—and Charlotte was evangelical on this point—I could only think of such a visit with horror.

'I understand why you'd be reluctant, Emily, but you're ill. Even Papa has noticed, and he can think of nothing but Branwell. You're exhausted, I know—Anne and I ought to have helped more in those last few months with—'

'I'm perfectly well,' I said, flouring the table and then tipping the dough from the bowl. 'Except for this cold on my chest. And I certainly don't need a diagnosis from Mr. Smith.' I began to knead, my body swaying with the motion, my hands, as ever, firm. 'Or his poisoning doctor.'

Blood came before Advent, red as holly berries. In the back kitchen, I rinsed my handkerchief under the pump and carried on blacking the fire grates. At night, Keeper shifted and turned on the rug beside my bed, unable to settle until I slept. The ache in my side insisted on itself. When the coughing would not stop, he clambered up beside me and I buried my face in his fur to stifle the noise. Charlotte was at my door now, with a jug of fresh water, a mouth full of words she was desperate to speak. I drank the water and sent her away. When we gathered in the dining room at night, I kept my head down over my work but the room was too quiet, waiting for my coughing to fill it. A feeling of intense irritation came over me one evening, a desire to sweep everything from the table, to smash this eggshell silence. I could not stand to be watched every minute of the day like some . . . *invalid*, my sisters' concerns so tangible that they might as well be daubed on the dining room walls. The pain in my side was a dagger wound. I pushed my hand into my mouth to suppress a cry and stared down at the page. There was my sloping handwriting, the neat curl of the letters, but I could make no sense of the words. Eyes on me still as I gathered up all the pages and put them aside. I went to the window and cupped my hands to blinker the light from the room behind me. The wind had eased, was moaning gently through Papa's cherry tree, and the fog had not returned. I strained my eyes, but the stars were out of reach, high above the churchyard, and the moon would not speak to me. It hung like a blank eye socket in the night-sky, just a lump of inert rock, stealing light from another source. Grief collided with me so forcefully that I had to grip the sash to prevent myself from falling though I did know where it came from, to whom or what it pertained.

The remains of half my family lay in the church, *Mamma*, *Maria*, *Elizabeth*, *Aunt*, *Branwell* and the graveyard was full of bones, but I had never been melancholy by nature, saw it only as a place of beauty and life: the sunlit green of the mosses, their spongy filaments softening the stone, frescoed lichen, the flick of a squirrel's tail, the glint of his dark eye as he searched for his cache of nuts among the gravestones. *Mamma, Maria, Elizabeth, Aunt, Branwell*—a soothing repetitive litany in my mind. For a moment I saw my eldest sister catching her breath in the dusk, with her hand pressed to her side and the green-black fellside rising like a monument behind her. Elizabeth too, asleep on the little sofa in this very room, her face white against the dark fabric, soft brown hair spilling over the cushion, her neck a stalk that might break at any moment.

My sisters gave up offering to help, but one or another of them was always there first. Charlotte, who hated rising in winter, now insisted that setting fires was just the kind of task to take her mind off the dark mornings and the trouble of thinking up the next bit of plot for her novel. I came down to the kitchen before daybreak to find that Anne had already fed the dogs and made a start on breakfast, had also been out to the icy yard to feed the geese and the hens. I kept my patience until I found Charlotte and Martha in the storeroom trying to work out the butcher's order between the two of them.

'Don't treat me like a child!' I said, snatching the order from Charlotte's hand and finding that they had forgotten the extra bones for Keeper and Flossy. I might have gone on, but I could feel a cough rising. I hurried out into the yard and slammed the door behind me, my chest about to explode. The cough bent me double, was both wet and dry at the same time. I put my hands to my mouth to contain it. Phlegm hit my palms, warm and viscous. A stab of pain in my side. I'd spent too much time in the house when Branwell was ill, I told myself, or around the village where the unhealthy air rose from the valley at this time of year, got into everyone's lungs. As soon as my legs were back to strength, I'd let Anne and Charlotte have their way with the chores and take Keeper out for the whole day. We'd climb the lane where the birds searched for winter food in the stark haw-thorn, the rowan, carry on until we were high up on the moors, where the good, clean air stung your cheeks and sliced cleanly across the tops. There would be little sign of life, but Keeper would bound after the odd grouse, barking with excitement, and the call of the wind would be enough.

In December, Charlotte wanted to know when we should order the meat for Christmas.

'I've already done it,' I said. I turned away, leaving these words unspoken: *I will not be here*. The knowledge did not seem new, yet I reeled from it. By Christmas I would not *be*. I'd understood for weeks, ever since the first spatter of blood on the blank canvas of my handkerchief, but only in a closed-off room of my mind. My heart had denied the truth, carried on beating like an arrogant drum, and death had remained incom-prehensible. Yet in recent days I'd sensed that organ slowing, forgetting its purpose once or twice. When did a heart start to function, I wondered now? It felt important to know. I imag-ined a ripple in the crimson darkness of the womb, like a fish rising to the surface of a pool, and then that tiny knot of flesh contracting for the first time as it began to beat out its lifelong rhythm. How many beats? How many hours, months, years till silence fell and the darkness returned? There wasn't a doctor in the land who could say. Perhaps the heart knew better, under-stood its own capacity, the chain of days allocated, right from the beginning. I opened my palms, examined them as if I were the fortune-teller who came each year to Haworth Fair. The skin on the inside of my wrists was fine-grained, so delicate that the blue-green veins seemed to stand proud. How perilous, how

vulnerable was life, and yet this body of mine had functioned almost faultlessly till now, every intricate, complex system working in unison with the whole. Even my monthly bleeding had
caused me little bother, while others curled up in agony, turned
white and sickened. Half my family were dead. *Mamma, Maria,
Elizabeth, Aunt, Branwell.* Still, I struggled to conceive of a
world in which I no longer existed, every thought and feeling
inside this me-shaped container of flesh and bones, gone. Life
could end with the snap of a bone, one misfire of a heart, and
yet mine had seemed unending, unbreakable. I pushed back
my right sleeve to examine the triangular scar on my forearm.
The skin was dented and ugly, forever altered by the hiss of a
hot iron. The wound had healed though, never shown any sign
of infection. All my life I'd withstood any damage inflicted on
me, even by my own hand, felt sure that I would always recover.

That night, the weight of Keeper was almost too much to
bear. He muscled down next to me and lay his nose against my
outstretched hand, his huge paws sticking out over the edge of
the bed. His head was bone-hard, and he smelt of woodsmoke,
animal, clean air. A wholesome warmth rose from him, like a
loaf straight from the oven.

'Don't worry, darling,' I whispered, when one of my wrenching fits of coughing made him whimper. 'Hush now.'

I was not scared to die, but I was afraid of mental weakness,
and the failing of the flesh was more humiliating that I could
have imagined—the run to the privy as soon as I ate, gasping for
breath halfway up the stairs while the clock in the alcove ticked
on. My eyesight was dimming. When I tried to read, I had to hold
the book as close as Charlotte did, whose own short-sightedness
did not prevent her from noticing this new development. The
terror of doubt gripped me then. How would I bear it when the
light was gone, when I could no longer see dearest, exasperat-
ing Charlotte, Anne's sweet, grave face? Now I understood why

Papa's spirits had almost failed him when his cataracts were at their worst. It was hard to believe in anything when the light was fading. Perhaps there *was* no other light than that of this world, eternal darkness looming from the moment we were born.

Twilight came early at this time of year. One afternoon in the week before Christmas, I took the pages of my new novel from my writing desk and folded them into an old tin box from the cellar, once used for storing nails. Then I carried the box outside, taking with me a trowel I'd found hanging on the cellar wall. When I could be certain that no-one was nearby, not even in the shadows, I went into the churchyard and made my way past the sloping headstones towards the far corner, a place where the top section of the wall had tumbled inwards and was yet to be repaired. Already, a tangle of bilberry was starting to creep in from the moor. With my trowel, I sliced through the grass and then dug a hole in the rich, black earth. By the time I had finished, my breath was coming fast and hard and the light was almost gone. I lowered the tin into the hole, backfilled it, and then covered the little mound with dried leaves and some thorny strands of bramble.

The following morning, my comb fell from my hand and clattered into the fire grate. Martha rescued it before the flames could take proper hold, knew better than to say anything. I came down to find that the bread dough had risen in a half-hearted way, had swollen to little more than its original size, which meant the loaf would be leaden. I had never failed at bread-making since Tabby Aykroyd had stood over me as a girl, giving me instructions, the rocking motion as natural to me now as walking. The east wind must have chilled the dough to recalcitrance. It soured my temper too.

'I'll take the dogs out this afternoon.' Anne and Charlotte glanced at one another over their breakfasts. 'Please don't try to stop me. Have they had the scraps?'

'I fed them first thing,' said Anne. 'Keeper always wants more.'

I rubbed his jowls, loose and warm beneath my hand. He pushed his nose into my palm. 'Come on, boy!' I carried my breakfast plate out into the hallway, where the dogs' bowls were lined up next to the pantry. In his eagerness, Keeper pushed past me. I stumbled and felt my shoulder hit the wall. In the blackness I heard the smash of a plate, barking.

I used to think of angels as Titans, their wings like the sweep of great forests, brows as immense as the horizon. This angel was small and white: Charlotte in her dressing gown. A candle burned on the chest by my bed. She was curled up on a chair that did not belong here, feet tucked in and her eyes closed.

'The doctor's been, dearest,' she said, waking. 'You said we might call him. He bled you, which is why your arm is sore, and will come again tomorrow.' I tried to focus on her, but my vision began to skew, and my thoughts were flying. I was crossing the frost-covered fields at Cowan Bridge. The church steeple pierced the sky and little Jane Sykes walked ahead of me, her thick red plait fresh with dirt. I heard a voice which I knew to be Mamma's, felt arms drawing me onto a soft lap. There was no fire, but I was burning. Someone—Anne, I thought—put a cool cloth on my forehead, soothed me, as ever, without a word. I knew it was daytime.

'I've brought you something.' Charlotte was gentler than she'd ever been. She lay something on my pillow. 'Oh, she cannot see it!' I heard the break in her voice.

I sensed Papa's presence then—could feel his height; the gravity that surrounded him.

'Charlotte found a sprig of heather for you,' he said. 'In December too.'

I tried to turn my head, to speak, but my body punished me with a fit of coughing so violent that everyone fought to contain it. There was someone behind me, supporting my shoulders, a hand beneath my chin, another brought something soft to my mouth. Wet flesh and blood jammed my throat. I felt panic rise in my chest, an iron taste on my tongue then at last, air.

My words all folded away now, tucked beneath the earth forever. Shadows passed and then gathered round me.

The Lord is my light and my salvation; whom then shall I fear?

Papa's voice. I felt hands over mine—Anne's or Charlotte's? Cool skin against fire. Diamond-cold world and angels closing down on me with eyes like stone. A realm without sky or hills or horizons or the dear, fallible earth. Papa was summoning it. Or was it just sunlight on my face? I was pushing through the Fairy Cave and out into the awful glare. No Anne or Charlotte, no good smells coming from the range, no vegetable peelings, no chamber pots to be emptied, no mess and sprawl and noise of animals, no wind in my face, or cloud or sudden shower, touch of sun upon a newly spun spider's web, its maker suspended, fat-bodied, at the centre of a new world. No blackbird dropping from the sky, yellow beak, yellow-rimmed eye, the sharp green of the lawn. Where was Keeper? Dear, brutal boy; dark eyes that followed me always, monstrous paws, meaty breath. Here was another place, so dazzling that I could not see. No muddy boots, no peat-stained petticoat. Aunt would be happy about that. *Aunt, Mamma, Maria and Elizabeth.* Branwell too. All cold. Icy angels edged towards me, lips of blue. Branwell came, hair so red against the whiteness. Ice and fire. I felt a cold hand reaching for me. I could not catch my breath. My lips were moving now. Forgive me, Papa but I cannot—

Lead us not into temptation

Breath won't come. Lead on my chest. They must not shut me in a coffin, Anne. Who will bake the bread? Lay me in the peaty earth. A terrible light coming now, a tidal drag pulling me under, quicksand; thunder of wings; reaching hands, pulling, pushing, I do not—Eyelids burned to the rim, scourged to the bone. Turn away, resist with every last strength in my—

Quiet. The hush that descends when the earth stops exploding. Hands and knees, darkness. The sense of falling gone now. The End. Then a movement so familiar. Could it really be? It is the wind! The same wind that cuts across the moor tops in all weathers, in every season, and there, *there* is a glimmer of friendly light, a scrap of moon over the dark hump of the hills! The ground beneath my hands is solid and springy at the same time, as I have always known it. I stand and by some miracle, the strength has returned to my body. When I look down I see that I am wearing my winter cloak and my brown boots. The wind is butting at my face, drying my tears, though I do not remember crying. It is cold, but it is the chill of life not death. Curve of heather. The moon is over Keighley. It's no more than a sliver but my feet have known these pathways since childhood, and it is enough. I take a step and then another, testing my bones, my flesh. My breath is coming faster now but the pain in my side is gone, my cough quite healed. I stride out in the old way and when I reach the swell of Penistone Hill, I start to run, the friendly earth carrying me up, up. Up to the crest of the hill I climb, and then down again towards the village, my boots clattering on the lane. There are no lights to be seen. The cottage windows are all dark and not a living soul abroad. When I reach the parsonage, I let myself in through the front gate. It closes silently behind me.

It is late. Hours since Papa would have locked the front door for night. But look, there is the glow of a candle upstairs, coming from my bedroom window. The wind swirls around me, catching my cloak. The window is open, I see, just a crack. Someone is crying and it sounds like Charlotte. I hear a mournful howl. Hush now. The wind is howling too, carrying snow in its icy palms. Snow is already gathering around my boots. The branches of the cherry tree are pawing the starry heavens. I look for the spot where the branch broke beneath my weight all those years ago. It is there, above me, the wound now hardened by time. The trunk of the tree has thickened with age and the bark has lost some of its ruddy shine. Even in the dark I can see the striations that mark it, broken circles reaching towards the sky. The wind drives through the thorn bushes and turns my hands to stone, but Keeper is waiting for me, Charlotte is in need of comfort, and here is Papa's tree, strong and steady in the wildest of weather, no longer young.

The last of the six Brontë siblings, Charlotte remained at the parsonage for the rest of her life. Servants reported hearing her walking around the dining table in the evenings, as she and her sisters once did when reading aloud to one another. In 1854, and after much persuasion, she married Arthur Bell Nicholls, her father's curate. Their happy marriage ended the following year with her death in early pregnancy of hyperemesis gravidarum, an extreme form of morning sickness. She was a few weeks short of her 39th birthday. Following the literary sensation of *Jane Eyre*, with its early chapters based on her experiences at Cowan Bridge School for the Daughters of the Clergy, she went on to publish *Shirley* and *Villette*. Her first novel, *The Professor*, was not published until after her death.

Stung by the harsh criticism of her beloved sister's work, Charlotte wrote a now-famous foreword to the 1850 edition of *Wuthering Heights*. Making no mention of Emily's education or considerable intellect, she described her as a 'nursling of the moors,' a creature 'wrought with a rude chisel' who did not fully understand the terrible nature of what she had unleashed upon the literary world. This contrasts significantly with what Monsieur Constantin *Héger,* the girls' old tutor at the *Pensionnat Héger* in Brussels, had to say about Emily. Questioned in later years, he offered presumably the best compliment available to him at the time: 'She should have been a man—a great navigator. Her powerful reason would have deduced new spheres of discovery from the knowledge of the old; and her strong, imperious will would never have been daunted by opposition or difficulty; never have given way but with life.'

Charlotte also edited a later edition of *Poems*, by Currer, Ellis and Acton Bell, making numerous amendments to both Emily and Anne's work.

Charlotte's good friend Mary Taylor emigrated to New Zealand. She never married but lived an independent life as a shop-owner. In 1874, she led the first all-women's ascent of Mont Blanc.

In May 1849, five months after Emily, and eight months after the death of Branwell, Anne Brontë died of tuberculosis. She was 29 years old. Her second novel *The Tenant of Wildfell Hall* tells the story of Helen Graham, a woman in hiding from an abusive, alcoholic husband. She died in Scarborough, having begged Charlotte and Ellen Nussey to take her there when she was gravely ill. According to her wishes, she was buried in the graveyard of St. Mary's church which overlooks the sea. Before the trip, she had written to Ellen about the possibility of her own death: *if I thought it inevitable I think I could quietly resign myself to the prospect, in the hope that you, dear Miss Nussey, would give as much of your company as you possibly could to Charlotte and be a sister to her in my stead. But I wish it would please God to spare me not only for Papa's and Charlotte's sakes, but because I long to do some good in the world before I leave it.*

Patrick Brontë outlived all his children. After Charlotte's death, he was cared for by her husband, Arthur Bell Nicholls, the curate he'd once termed *an unmanly driveller*, an accolade Arthur earned during his first failed attempts to court Charlotte. Patrick died at the parsonage in 1861 at the age of 84.

During Emily's lifetime, *Wuthering Heights* was only ever attributed to Ellis Bell, as per her wishes. Though she corresponded with her publisher about the writing of a second novel, no papers relating to it have ever been discovered. Some speculate that Charlotte destroyed them, wanting to pre-empt further criticism of her beloved sister; I prefer to think that Emily disposed of her words in her own way.

Keeper, Emily's bull mastiff, followed her coffin as it was taken to the church of St. Michael's and All Saints in Haworth, and sat in the Brontë pew throughout the service. Emily was buried in the family vault, along with her mother, aunt, sisters Maria and Elizabeth, and her brother Branwell. She was 30 years old. Keeper is buried somewhere in the parsonage garden. His enormous brass collar can often be seen on display at the Brontë Parsonage Museum.

ACKNOWLEDGMENTS

Numerous sources informed the writing of this novel, but I found myself turning repeatedly to Juliet Barker's hugely comprehensive biography *The Brontës*, and also to *The Brontës: A Life in Letters* by the same author, which helped me capture the spirit of their correspondence. The pandemic put paid to a trip to Belgium to research the Brussels section of the book. I am, then, particularly indebted to Helen MacEwan, whose *The Brontës in Brussels* allowed me to visualise the city and the *Pensionnat Héger* as Charlotte and Emily would have known it. I am also lucky enough to live within travelling distance of the wonderful Parsonage Museum in Haworth. I have been a frequent visitor for years; long before the idea for this book started to form in my mind. Even now, I become breathless when I enter through that front door.

Like all writers, I was a reader first and this was entirely down to my mother. An exceptionally clever woman, she loved her time at the local grammar school and was devastated when her parents could not afford to support her through Sixth Form. It still pains me to think how she must have felt when I dropped out of that same Sixth Form some thirty years later. She became a librarian but soon grew disillusioned with helping old ladies find the latest Georgette Heyer. Against her parents' wishes, she joined the Air Force and was sent to Coltishall in Norfolk, where she met my father, who was completing his

National Service; outranking him, as he liked to point out, from the very beginning.

Throughout her life she read voraciously and was delighted when I followed in her footsteps. Long before I started school, she'd taught me to read and write, would walk for miles to take me to and from the library each week. I can still remember the joy of staggering up to my bedroom with a new mountain of books in my arms. When she returned to work, far too much of her salary was spent at the W H Smith in the Pentagon Centre in Chatham, feeding my insatiable appetite for literature. The stories I hold most dear from childhood: *Anne of Green Gables*, the *Little House on the Prairie* series, *Swallows and Amazons* and its sequels, Enid Blyton's adventure books and school stories, Noel Streatfield's many novels, the never-ending Chalet School series and, a little later, *The Greengage Summer* by Rumer Godden—all these were given to me by my mother and will forever remind me of her. And it was my mother, seeing me bored and looking for something to read one rainy day when I was around thirteen years old, who went to her precious set of collector's editions on the mantelpiece and handed me *Jane Eyre* and *Wuthering Heights*. Try these, she said.

This book is in memory of Joan Goddard, née Nicholson.

I was so excited about the publication of *The River Within* in 2020 that I forgot to write any acknowledgements at the time, so these are long overdue.

In 2017, an early version of *The River Within* won a prize in The Northern Writers Awards. It was the first time I'd entered any literary competition—the idea hadn't occurred to me until my daughter was awarded a prize in their junior category in 2016—and it was the start of everything good. The support, encouragement, and opportunities that New Writing North, the organisers of the awards, give to emerging writers is a gamechanger. An added bonus is that a number of the other winners I met at the prizegiving ceremony have now become friends. Thanks in particular go to Tawseef Khan, Laura Bui, and Sophie Parkes-Nield for your friendship and support. Meetings of *The* Writing Group at Chapter One Books in Manchester are a joy.

The New Writing North prize included a manuscript assessment by The Literary Consultancy. By that time, I'd begun to have doubts about the book. On the form I submitted with the manuscript, I had one question: is it salvageable? Imogen Robertson, the hugely experienced author assigned to help me, showed me all the ways in which that might be possible, all the opportunities I'd missed. I am so grateful for that early masterclass.

As a result of the New Writing North London Talent Party, I met my agent, Sam Hodder from the Blake Friedmann Agency. Throughout the writing of *The River Within*, and also *Fifteen Wild Decembers*, Sam has offered vast amounts of editorial advice as well as endless support. His extensive knowledge of the publishing world, cheerful encouragement, and ability to give incisive criticism with the gentlest of touches are exceptional.

When Europa Editions bid for *The River Within*, I could not resist the opportunity to work with an editor of Christopher Potter's calibre. Christopher has edited numerous world-class writers over the years, so it was thrilling to hear that he wanted to work with me. He pulls my sentences to pieces and puts them back together again, points out every inexact expression, sniffs out a lazy train of thought—in short, he teaches me with every edit how to be a better writer. I also want to thank the rest of brilliant team at Europa Editions for all their support for my writing and everything they do to bring world literature into our bookshops: Eva Ferri, Sandro and Sandra Ferri, Daniela Petracco, Carolina Parodi, Naman Chaudhary, Leonella Basiglini and Ginevra Rapisardi. Thanks as well to Helen Francis for her copy-editing of both books.

I would also like to thank my colleagues past and present at York Minster Fund—Diana Terry, Heidi Carberry, Neil Sanderson, Danny 2Sheds Knight, Ellie Davies and Michael Benson for being interested in what I get up to outside of work, for the steadiness that days in the office give me (the perfect counterbalance to the lunacy of writing) and most of all for the stupid fun. And, of course, to my dearest and closest friends, Becky and Lee Hopwood-Robinson, and Fran and Sarah Marwood, who are all I need in the world.

My husband Stephen was the first person to read my writing, over 20 years ago now. I'm forever grateful to him, and to my daughter Isabella, for their support and encouragement. They won't thank me for going on about it though.

My father Colin did not live to see the publication of *The River Within*. He was hugely excited that I'd won a prize though. Not much of a reader himself, this did not stop him pressing my early work into the hands of anyone who showed zero interest. He always maintained that the three women in his life—his wife, daughter, and grand-daughter—were extraordinary. He was at least right about two of them.

Lastly, I would like to thank everyone at Lucy Cavendish College, Cambridge. At the age of 25, when everything was a quiet mess of my own making, you gave me the chance to begin again.

Keeper, watercolor by Emily Brontë © The Brontë Society

About the Author

Karen Powell grew up in Rochester, Kent, but now lives with her family in North Yorkshire. She works at York Minster Fund, an independent charity which raises money for the conservation and restoration of York Minster. Her novel *The River Within* won a Northern Writers Award and was published by Europa Editions in 2020.